Nikos Kazantzakis

TODA
RABA

TRANSLATED BY AMY MIMS

SIMON AND SCHUSTER
NEW YORK   1964

FOR
MADAME HÉLÈNE STOECKER
A GENTLE, UNYIELDING SOUL

This confession in the form of a novel has but one hero. Azad, Geranos, Sou-ki, Rahel, Amita, Ananda and the Big-Jawed Man are merely different facets of a single consciousness that experienced and mirrored the complex, fluid, many-sided reality of the Soviet Union.

. . . Only the Negro is outside—and above—the hero.

A CRY CAME FROM MOSCOW.

Sou-ki, the consumptive old schoolteacher, was sitting on a stool. With a startled gesture, he hid the letter in his perspiring breast.

"Tchita!" he called.

Not a soul!

He turned his frail face toward his squalid house. It was pitch dark behind the wide-open door.

"Tchita!"

He got up. His cadaverous fingers were trembling as if they were about to break into a dance. Sou-ki took a step, straightened his wasted body with an effort, and stood erect on the threshold. One of the frightful big cities of California: heavy, sticky air, harsh grinding of machines, a sickening odor of sweat and rancid grease, howling of scrawny children squalling and wiggling like starving little monkeys. The yellow ghetto, Chinatown.

Sou-ki smiled; a sad, wan child was playing in the dark. His son Ni-nel. He had an orange in his right hand and the whole of his little body drooped over to the right as he tottered about.

"Tchita!"

A young yellow woman in a worn earth-colored kimono appeared, her narrow eyes very full of sorrow, her mouth set tight.

"Tchita, they are calling me. I must leave."

"Yes," said the little yellow woman, and she went back into the darkness.

A sob; then once again, no sound. Sou-ki strained his ears: still no sound.

7

"Stop trembling, Sou-ki," he said to himself, clutching his weak chest.

Amita, the graying poet, was bent over his manuscript, writing long verses down the page with a delicate hand. The shabby little room was almost empty: a few books, a jug of water and a yellow canary. On a black lacquered bric-a-brac stand in the background, a slender gilded statuette of a smiling Buddha, its long legs crossed, a faded blue lotus blossom on its knees.

Beyond the open window were the limitless expanses of the blue Japanese waters, from which a soft mist was rising under the autumn sun.

Amita was writing a verse drama about thirteen children singing and playing together on the lawn in the spring-time. Suddenly thirteen soldiers, rough, simple types, entered, out of breath. They'd been out hunting, hunting for men. They saw the children.

"Have we got our orders?" one of them asked.

"Yes, I think so. . . ." another answered.

"Then let's kill them!"

The soldiers bent over slightly, made a little flurry with their right arms, and mowed the children down. Then someone said:

"We haven't got the orders!"

The soldiers laid their thirteen shields over the little corpses to cover them up, and then they went away. Up the gentle flowery slope they climbed; they paused for a moment at the crest, took another step and vanished.

Then the little children lifted the shields and bowed to the public.

"Don't weep! It's not true! It's not true! It's only a play," they cried.

Amita's gaze turned far out to sea as he raised his head with its long gray hair. He gazed beyond the sea, and melancholy crept into his black eyes.

"Amita, have you no shame?" he cried. "To be writing

and arranging patterns of words, for your own amusement!"

His gaze turned toward the Buddha. A smile slit the Buddha's face from ear to ear, like a sharp blade, and the long, narrow, jet-black eyes exuded a look of mild depravity. Amita shuddered.

"I am ashamed," he murmured. "Enough!"

He took his big bamboo stick and started off toward the sea.

Iron foundries. The tremendous presses moved deliberately up and down like jaws. The mouths of the furnaces opened and closed, gulping down suns. The air crackled as it streamed in and played about the furnaces, the workmen, the machines.

Suddenly a bare arm emerged out of the semi-darkness and swung over to the filthy wall. As it rose and fell, it formed big letters. The workers stood erect, their stiff backs creaking as they did so. The arm leapt wildly from one letter to the next. With mouths gaping, the workers watched its motions.

"A-n-n-i-v-e-r-s-a-r-y," they spelled out.

The skinny bare arm moved on and on. Its meaning spurted from it like blood.

". . . Revolutionary . . ."

The workers felt a momentary thrill. Their hollow temples rang with the triumphant strains of the "International"; their hearts opened up and tossed like little red flags.

Azad, the old worker, raised his arm, and with tense, burning fingers added TO MOSCOW in huge letters.

In the ghastly Jewish ghetto of the city of Lodz, Rahel raced into the streets in the rain. A suffocating fog hovered among the houses. Running with the swiftness of flame, Rahel burst into the great courtyards of the factories, slipped down the dark corridors, and cried, "Comrades."

Flames were darting from her beautiful eyes.

9

"Comrades! Let's stop work! Let's choose our delegates for Moscow!" she kept shouting.

A Polish soldier dashed down the corridor in pursuit of Rahel. He caught her; she escaped from him and cowered in the mud in a corner of the factory. But Rahel's forehead, her curved nose and her eyes were glistening in the darkness. The soldier made another lunge, grabbed Rahel by the throat and bashed her head furiously against the wall. Once, twice, three times. Blood streamed through her black hair, choked her throat and poured down over her flimsy yellow blouse.

In the gleam of dawn the sacred Ganges flowed red, its waters thick with filth. In the basement of a textile factory the air was damp and stifling. Nothing could be seen. . . . Suddenly a ray came through one dim skylight; then one could see yellow mats and about thirty thin-armed, hungry-faced workingwomen squatting down, two thick bronze rings on their mud-colored ankles.

The Hindu workingwomen were bending over, each of them with a little white rice and some grains of red pepper in the palm of her hand. Holding their breath, they carefully placed the grains one by one in a square frame on the ground. Then they pulled back their hands and looked. . . .

This morning they were hastily putting the finishing touches on a little picture in a primitive mosaic. The outlines of the picture were bold, and the forehead, nose, goatee, savage eyes and sarcastic mouth were made of red pepper.

The Hindu women jumped up and down on their bare legs, clapping their hands with joy. At last the gift they were sending their brothers and sisters in Moscow had come to life before their eyes. Lenin! Lenin! Lenin! He looked at them all in turn, and he smiled, smiled like the terrible Shiva, the god with the innumerable hands and feet, the lord of destruction and love.

10

A young workingwoman with powerful hips and a wide sensual mouth held out her arms. They laughed and cried and wished her *bon voyage*. They wrapped her up in the ample folds of an orange woolen shawl.

"Bring us a handful of sod from over there!" cried one old workingwoman.

"Speak out over there, don't be afraid, Gandhara!" shrieked a young workingwoman through her tears. "Tell them we are suffering."

Ananda, the aged monk, crept out of the rotted hollow of a tree. He wore a tattered monk's frock, yellowish brown like the color of the tomb when it has just been opened. From his birdlike neck a mendicant's bronze basin was hanging, with the following inscription engraved on it in Pali:

Close thine eyes, thine ears, thy mouth, thy nostrils, thy fingers, close thy spirit, empty thy entrails; the world does not exist!

The old man walked a little way in the mud of the sacred river. He stopped and perked his ear toward the dark forest to the north. His ear caught the songs of the birds, the roaring of the lions, and the heartbeat of the trembling hares and wolves and gazelles. . . .

His ear bounded over the forest, strained toward the gigantic fat plains of the Punjab. It descended into the gorges of the Himalayas and arrived at the frontiers. Leaving India behind, it skirted Afghanistan, climbed up to the highland regions of the Pamir, penetrated into Tajikistan and Uzbekistan and into the deserts of Kara Kum and Kazakstan. It went on to Adai between the Aral Sea and the Caspian, crossed the deserts of Kirghiz and Kalmuck, and suddenly ended up, refreshed and contented on the surface of the water, making a delightful journey up the broad blue ripples of the Volga.

The old monk Ananda smiled. He had felt God within

11

him, deep in his vitals, enshrined there cross-legged, impassive and deaf. God didn't have any ears. And suddenly someone had shouted over there in the North. The human shout had struck God first on his right temple and then on his left temple and had forced God to create ears for himself.

The old monk Ananda smiled.

"Poor God!" he murmured. "Poor humanity! So I must bring you help. I have pity on you. I am coming!"

Taking his mendicant's basin in his right hand, he turned toward the North.

Moscow. Rain. Villages glistening in the murky air. All sorts of races. Yellow, black, white: the delegates. The sidewalk pavements flooded with red apples, smoked fish, salted cucumbers, little toys made of sulphur-yellow wood with green and red flowers. Muzhiks walking past clumsily in their large, well-greased leather boots. They were dressed in cowhide *shubas* and had tangled, sticky beards. The pungent smell of the stable filled the air.

The icon of Our Lady the Iviritissa wept beneath the archways at the entrance to Red Square. The little chapel in the middle of the mud was on fire, and smoke rose from it. By the chapel door two rows of beggars, majestic old men and monks with long shiny hair. Some of them were kneeling, others bending and rising like reeds, all of them softly murmuring one mysterious word: "Christ!"

Opposite the chapel, a young workman raised his arms in front of the wall. His leather shirt gleamed in the fine rain like an iron cuirass. His arm made sweeping jerky movements. He was sticking up placards for the great festival. All at once the dingy wall was covered with brightly colored placards. A white sickle intertwined with a black hammer was seen springing out of the rosy flames of dawn. Or Lenin with uplraised hand, standing in a flood of light. Or workers and peasants shooting out of the dark earth, stretching their earth-stained hands toward the light. Or a Red soldier with a star on his forehead, shading his serious, piercing eyes with his hand and scanning the desert far off in the distance. The Kremlin, heart of Moscow, rose menacingly in the dusk, the golden cupolas of her churches swarming with plump black crows. There were young women kissing big red satin stars. And in the brightly lit basements, children were sticking white letters on broad scarlet banners: PROLETARIANS OF ALL COUNTRIES, UNITE!

Some red soldiers passed by, and the earth shook. A ten-year-old Pioneer halted on the edge of the sidewalk, spread his arms, and let out an ecstatic "Ah!" An old bourgeois leaning against his door was seized by a mild fit of panic.

"That 'Ah' will swallow up the world!" he whispered in a choking voice.

In the Chigi Palace in Rome, Mussolini's mighty jaws were clamped shut. His ears were cocked apprehensively toward Moscow.

The Red Star was rising at the Pole.

Semi-barbaric races: Voguls, Yakuts, Ostyaks, Karagas, the Altaic peoples, Laplanders—coarse, warm bodies cleaving to the frozen steppes. Hypnotic Mongol eyes, glossy blue-black hair, elegantly simple hunting and fishing weapons, sealskin canoes, reindeer rugs and coats covered with primitive designs, the triangle and the swastika their main motifs, along with the great polar suzerain, the Bear.

Two big-jawed Lapp rogues were huddled together, sitting face to face, cross-legged, drinking away. Greed in their expressions, intense pleasure in their bibulous flesh, the blinking, dazed eyes of the eternal animal.

They were both talking animatedly about the spirits of the sayids. Evil spirits terrifying in their extreme capriciousness. The sayid that lives in the Rock of Estrovsky, in the middle of the River Niouda of Karelia, uses his long hands, so they said, to help with the fishing. But look

13

out for yourself, they added; and when you throw him bread crumbs, be sure to mutter: "As many fish as these crumbs!"

Another sayid, Tchom-tchitchit-tchi, nests in the rock; he gets angry when he sees a woman. If your wife is out fishing with you, cover up her face, for if the sayid sees her, he'll raise a violent wind and break the boat. There are other sayids that reign over the mountains, over reindeer and over children. Others over the Bear. And still others over love and death.

A young man in a leather blouse was sitting beside the two Lapps. When he turned abruptly toward them, the Lapps fell silent. The young man's smile had something mildly awe-inspiring about it. They stretched their thick necks and pricked up their ears.

"There's a new sayid," the young man said. "He has appeared just these past few years. He comes and goes over the earth, carrying a heavy hammer in his hand. He whacks the other sayids with it and smashes their skulls."

Terrified, the two Lapps eyed each other uneasily and rose to make their escape.

"A new sayid? What sayid?" they asked.

The young man's soft voice slowly let one simple, pleasant word fall onto the endless snows—the name of Lenin.

From the turquoise-colored minaret in Bokhara the green-turbaned old muezzin was staring at the train departing for the fabulously distant Tartar land of Khitan, for Moscow.

His son Hussein, a komsomol, had gotten a letter and was leaving. The old man stretched his two tremulous hands into the red twilight air.

"Curses be on you, Hussein," he said.

Noon in Shanghai. Swarms of men and women with crippled feet. Motor cars roared past, and behind their glass panes big white lords and great blond ladies leaned

14

forward, laughing and showing the glitter of gold teeth in the sun.

Sickly, unprepossessing students wearing big spectacles tore through the streets. Scattering in all directions, they slid into the packed cafés, posted themselves at the entrances to factories, schools, banks and barracks, and with quivering hands hurriedly passed out red handbills bearing this message:

"Workers, peasants, soldiers, exploited men, enslaved women, choose your delegates. Moscow has called! . . ."

Some cavalry came rushing out with short iron-headed clubs in their hands. Panic! Streets were emptied and iron shutters dropped with a crash. In front of the Hotel Astoria one cavalryman threw up his hand in fury and let it fall on a student's skull. The student's skull cracked and a jumbled mass of brains, hair and little pieces of spectacles spilled over the sidewalk.

Crete is a red rock on an indigo sea. On the map Crete looks like a long ship floating between Europe, Asia and Africa. Men exploit men on this rock too, but on this rock there are a few men who suffer and struggle and do not pardon: a few pale, resolute tobacco workers, some longshoremen, some sailors and some wretched war cripples.

Geranos was aware of all the suffering, and understood it. But he was making an effort to isolate it from the suffering individuals so that he could work out a metaphysical synthesis of man's struggles on earth.

Geranos was himself suffering and struggling in the old monastery of Apezanes that looked out over the sea toward Libya. He was trying to express and to save his soul through the medium of words, and at the same time to express and save the souls of the people around him. His frail body was being consumed by the spirit.

This evening, while his head was drooping over his chest, Geranos suddenly heard a great cry inside him. In his shock he began to walk excitedly along the seashore, breathing in the salt air in greedy gulps. His mind was

15

like a taut bow. Moscow! Moscow! Who had called? How he had been yearning to go there!

Since his childhood on this African island, he had always pictured Russia as a magical land, boundless, snow-covered, teeming with color and variety. Muzhiks in wide red belts, green-eyed women, wild dances, the sad, heart-breaking music of the balalaika.

Under Turkish rule, when the old Cretans got drunk they would turn their red fezzes around, parade into the Turkish cafés and start singing at the risk of their lives:

Liberty! Liberty!
The Muscovite is on his way down!

And now in his maturity, Geranos suddenly felt an old Cretan inside him, his grandfather, red fez turned around, singing this same refrain at the top of his lungs.

Sunset. Throughout its whole expanse, Africa was still seething in the boiling heat. Banana trees, coconut palms, and rubber trees had turned black. The boom of drums was rising on the hill, and the entire hill, dry and distended as it was, gave back the echo like a drum.

Flat feet, delicate legs, beautiful black bodies. Smell of musk and maize and sweat. As the dance erupted, women with hanging breasts lit fires and emitted strident yells.

The frenzied shaman, Toda Raba, distributed masks. He was arrayed in rags of different colors that floated about and kept parting and coming together. From time to time they revealed his big sturdy body in flashes of steel-blue light. Varieties of ironware—keys, nails, whistles, little bells, horseshoes—made a joyous, ominous clangor about his neck, his waist and his ankles.

An assemblage of wooden gods on a bloodstained stump. They were trembling, and over them, making one of the group but soaring above the others, hovered the God of Fear, huge, emaciated, black and sneering.

Toda Raba grasped the big drum and scrambled to the

16

top of the hill in front of the God of Fear. After throwing him a big piece of meat, Toda Raba fawningly offered him a calabash of Khourma wine.

"Fidi-Moukoulou! Fidi-Moukoulou! Fidi-Moukoulou!" cried Toda Raba, raising his arms. "All is well on earth: food, women, corn! All is well on earth! But why did you create the rich? Why did you create the English?"

Then lapsing into silence, Toda Raba put his ear close to the ground to listen. He heard nothing. He heard nothing, yet he laughed and sniggered. His teeth gleamed between his enormous lips, and the women whinnied like mares.

Toda Raba raised his arms again. He snatched the dreadful mask of Fidi-Moukoulou, hurled it to the ground and addressed himself to the men:

"Fidi-Moukoulou has ceased to hear, has ceased to kill and has ceased to eat! Fidi-Moukoulou is dead!"

His lips foaming, Toda Raba drew a big curved knife from his belt and began to change the shape of the mask. He made a new nose, chopped off the heavy jaw, cut the hair. The necklace of enemies' teeth around the stodgy neck he left intact. Toda Raba slashed and slashed and slashed. His brain, eyes and hands were concentrated on a different face.

Suddenly the new mask materialized before the howling men, its mouth huge, its skull bald, a threat in its eyes.

"Lenin!"

"Here's the one who hears, who kills, who eats!" cried Toda Raba. "He has called. I have heard him. 'Toda Raba, come!' is what he shouted. 'Toda Raba, come! Toda Raba, come!' And I am going."

He hung the mask around his neck, adjusted it over his broad chest, took a bundle of sugar cane to eat on the way and went off toward the North.

2

"OM MANI PADME HUM! . . . Om mani padme hum! . . ."

Midget gods, demons, dragons. Dancing, grinning monsters in blue silk parasols as tiny as mushrooms. Trumpets, big bells and little bells, and diminutive Buddhas in bronze, wood and ivory with a serpent's eyes and woman's breast and an utterly malign expression . . .

Bric-a-brac. A disgusting smell of tallow and sweat. To right and left, two big prayer-wheels, those Buddhist contraptions which they turn round and round, one hundred and eight times, with the petition of the believer attached to them.

"Om mani padme hum! . . . Om mani padme hum! . . ." The kneeling bonze kept repeating the ritual refrain in cadence while his body swayed from side to side.

Sou-ki bit his lips to keep from screaming. His sunken temples were burning as he circulated about this miserable hovel where gods and demons were lodged. Here the heroic, desperate faith that had aspired to find human salvation without the aid of prayers and gods had deteriorated into a polytheism congenial to the slack and stupid human heart.

"Who was Buddha?"

The bonze clasped his hands together and, lowering his eyes, muttered: "God."

Sou-ki gave an angry start. The being who had created the world in a flash and destroyed it, sitting motionless with arms and legs crossed; the being who had created and destroyed gods and cowardice in every guise: here he

18

was after his death, turned into the leader of the flock of gods and of cowards in every guise. His terrible naked word had been too much for people to bear.

"Who was Lenin?"

Again the bonze lowered his treacherous eyes, clasped his hands and muttered: "God."

In disgust Sou-ki gave him a push with his finger.

"Rascal," he murmured, "rascal, liar, coward!"

Sou-ki trotted around Vladivostok at his jerky pace. Night fell, and out of the stinking alleys and the humming port, out of the old ramparts and from underneath the earth, masses of Chinese began to flow into the main streets where they cowered on the pavements. Skinny bodies, the nimble movements of climbing deer, eyes watchful and searching, the short shrill squeaks of rodents. Longshoremen, conjurors, traders.

They were laughing, coughing, smoking. One old Chinese man, lying flat on the quay, was staring out to sea and singing. Sou-ki stopped for an instant. It was a wild, gay, jaunty song, like a hunting tune. This might have been a man lying in a forest to ambush some woman he was trailing—some woman or some juicy fleshed beast.

One Chinese man had decorated his shop front with a crude picture showing Lenin with thin, drooping moustaches, slanting eyes and yellow skin. The picture was encircled by Chinese verses interlaced with ears of corn and heavy poppy flowers. "Lenin is not dead," read the poem. "He lives among us eternally. Future generations will adore Lenin, for his great heart has suffered for China."

Big drops of rain fell and the air cooled off. Some young Mongol girls went by, their breasts precociously developed. They laughed, turned around, then hurried on their way. Heavy-bearded sailors followed them with panting breath. The air was saturated with the brief, bitter love of the ports.

Sou-ki nibbled some sunflower seeds and went quickly

on. *Pékinskaya Ulitza.* Red paper lanterns, strange letters shaped like swords, knots of ribbon, serpents and pagodas, an odor simultaneously flat and penetrating: the Chinese theater.

Sou-ki was late. He tiptoed as he entered the hall. They were playing "Rytchi Kitai," "Roar, O China!" Sou-ki watched with bated breath. All the horror, the humiliation and the danger of the suffering the Chinese proletariat had to endure were bursting into view on the stage.

"Why this suffering? Why?" sighed Sou-ki, digging his nails into his frail chest.

Heaps of human flesh, angry shouts, sobs. . . . A little Chinese woman was circling about the stage like a flame, exuding an atmosphere of undaunted courage. A cry of revolt gushed from her. She came and went in solitary despair. . . . She had a piece of thin rope, and with it rolled about her arm, she went up high and began to sing a song, sorrowful, monotonous, tremendous—like China. Then she tied the rope to the mast of the ship and hanged herself.

Sou-ki was shaking; his spectacles were dim. He clutched his throat; something like a scream or a sob kept rising there. An angry shudder passed through the frames of all the people in the hall. All the yellow bodies were soundlessly roaring. As they got up to leave, a very pale Chinese general in the first row was biting his lips. He had come from Shanghai and was on his way to Moscow. The whole crowd pressed excitedly around him, everybody bumping into everybody else; they gazed at him with somber expressions on their sallow faces. They moved toward the exit in compact masses, emitting guttural exclamations that sounded like the shrieks of big birds.

Sou-ki went home alone and disturbed. Who had cried out? That night, in the cruel little eyes of his race he had had a glimpse of long massacres, and he had been shocked at the sight.

"This is the first shock I have received from Soviet-land," he thought with terror. "I am trembling. You are too weak, Sou-ki; you will have to die."

The next day, Siberia. Interminable, hopeless tundras, giant rivers, marshes, crows. Sou-ki craned his neck out of the coach window and stared. Russet horses with blond manes, cows, buffaloes. A village came into sight. Some red-bearded, blue-eyed muzhiks bolted clumsily into the train like cattle. The whistle blew, and once more the endless tundra was silently sweeping past.

Sou-ki felt happy. His frail little body seemed to be swelling to an enormous size, it was becoming a sixth part of the earth, and in his cough-racked chest a star danced. He dozed against the window, with his crammed portfolio held fast to his knees. Everything he had been able to find that was good over there in America he was taking to Moscow. Perhaps it would be of a little help in the reconstruction of the U.S.S.R.: school programs, statistics, social insurance laws, plans for workers' houses. . . . In a handkerchief down at the bottom of his cheap valise, Sou-ki had also brought a handful of seeds of the best American corn.

A beggar came in who had the appearance of a worker, with his leather blouse and his honest, demanding glance. He got up in the middle of the coach, coughed, and then, with moving, oratorical gestures, he delivered a long speech. Sou-ki woke up and listened. "The conditions of post-war life . . . the economic situation . . . rising unemployment . . ." The beggar watched his auditors with a cold eye as he took off his cap and gathered the pennies in a grimly detached manner, without any bows.

The hours passed and the days. Villages steamed among the black fir trees where they were hidden. It was raining, and everything was tenderly submerged in the fine rain. Ah! How far away Moscow still was! Two muzhiks beside Sou-ki were chatting in low voices. "Soviets . . . collectives . . . Lenin . . ."

"Yes, yes, *batyushka*, we have to light a candle to the devil. He's the one who dwells on earth; he hears; the other one doesn't hear," said one of the muzhiks, shaking his head.

Two Samoyeds got on and sat down opposite Sou-ki. One was big, lean and toothless; the other thickset and swarthy, with a narrow forehead and frightened, affectionate gray eyes. Sou-ki, who happened to be eating, offered his distant brothers some tea and some butter and an apple. He urged them. They responded with smiling suspicion and ate cautiously and anxiously. When Sou-ki offered them a little vodka, they recoiled in fright. What did this stranger want of them, and why did he give them something to eat and to drink for nothing? "There's something questionable about it, let's be on our guard," they thought. How was it possible for these sons of a harsh climate, where the struggle for existence was ruthless, to imagine such unexpected generosity? As if they sniffed the odor of a bear, they came on slowly and circumspectly, refusing to take a drink. The vodka was there, the beloved princess who inhabits the palaces of the polar regions; they saw it and they approached it as if it were a trap.

"Do me a favor, will you?" said Sou-ki, touching them on the knees.

They straightened up, their ears twitching with alarm.

"Sing me something," Sou-ki went on, "a war song or some lament about love or death."

The two Samoyeds consulted each other with silent glances. They refused.

"We don't know any," they said.

Then, to awaken their courage, Sou-ki began to hum some Chinese melodies. The Samoyeds listened, pleasantly lulled by the sorrowful airs. Sou-ki smiled and grew silent. Suddenly the shrill voice of the younger one rose in a song as tuneful as the Chinese air, as melancholy and as monotonous. The theme came and went and then came scurrying back like a hungry sea gull. The two

Samoyeds had a slightly misty look all over them. There was silence again. Sou-ki was pale and tremulous. The other Samoyed, the toothless one, explained: "It's a song one sings when one is drinking. The dead old father is talking with his son who tries to console him.

"'Do you remember, father, when you came back in the evening, exhausted from bending over the water all day, and your nets were empty?' 'Yes, yes, but life was beautiful!' 'Do you remember, father, when you were groaning with pain, your body covered with ulcers on its pallet?' 'Yes, yes, but life was beautiful!' 'Do you remember, father, when you were starving to death, and you wept and beat your wife?' 'Yes, yes, but life was beautiful!'"

Sou-ki's teeth were chattering. He slumped down into the corner and had no more to say.

At some little village an old beggar got on, moaning, and dragged himself, dripping wet, into the coach. He propped himself against the doorway. Big drops of water were glistening in his long, unkempt beard; he smelt of dung and the damp forest. Slowly, with large, solemn gestures, he made the sign of the cross; then he folded his arms over his breast and began to chant a grave, melancholy old church song. He called upon the good God of the old days . . . and he had finished. Once more he crossed himself; then slowly he went up to each traveler, placed his hand on his breast, and bowed all the way down to the floor.

Sou-ki was tired and very sad. Ah! how far Moscow still was! He rose and went into the dining car. His throat felt parched. Workers and peasants, the smell of leather and of shoddy sheepskin coats . . . Alongside Sou-ki, an old worker was emptying big glasses of vodka at a gulp. He pulled a smoked fish from his pocket, cut it up and savored it in a leisurely way; he filled his glass again.

Sou-ki felt pity flooding his heart. He spoke to the old man and listened to him talk. The old man was contented;

23

he described the white nights and the pitch darkness of his polar village. Then he fell silent and stared ahead of him at nothing. Abruptly he lowered his voice, leaned against Sou-ki's shoulder and said:

"There were five of us. We saw him trip; he was pretending to be drunk. But he didn't fool us. I cried, 'Stoi stoi, dorogoi! (Stop, friend!)' He stopped. We went at him . . . and . . ." With his index finger he slit his own throat as a gesture.

"Why? Why?" cried Sou-ki in terror. "He had done nothing to you."

"Stoi, stoi, dorogoi! We rifled his pockets; we found plans, documents! He was a White!"

"What documents? What documents?"

"How should I know?"

The old man returned to his talk about white nights. He described the aurora borealis. His blue eyes shone and grew appealing and tender as the light suffused them. The whole aurora borealis appeared, spread over his wrinkled countenance. . . .

The rain had stopped. A flock of wild ducks passed, long necks craned. Far away, the blue Lake Baikal sparkled laughingly among the high mountains. At the little town of Sloubianka, a tattered young tramp climbed hurriedly aboard the train. He was clamoring vociferously and there was blood on his head. He dropped into a seat and the conductor asked him for a ticket. Fumbling feverishly in his pockets, the tramp pulled out a handful of black bread crumbs. He squeezed them with passion and began to knead them with his dirty, bloody hands. The bread was quickly reduced to a soft, greasy dough. The tramp began to model it at furious speed . . . And presently there was a bald head with a little nose, a wide sarcastic mouth, slanting eyes and a goatee. The tramp rose and proudly proffered Lenin's head to the conductor as a substitute for the ticket. Resting there on that horrible hand, the head smiled with an intense quivering vitality.

. . . The whole coach began to laugh. The conductor got annoyed, handled the poor sculptor roughly and turned him over to the militia man who had run to the scene. Then, seeing that Lenin didn't do him any good, the hoodlum demolished the work of his passionate hand, and the fine face of the prophet once more disintegrated into a filthy dough.

Sou-ki stopped at Irkutsk in a state of great weariness. The last night in the coach he had been spitting blood. But he didn't want to take to bed. He tramped around the big Siberian city at his jerky gait. "If only one could get a grip on one's own soul!" he murmured. "If only one could keep death away for a few years more! I have a great hope! I have a great hope! How could I die?"

Sou-ki visited the schools. There the air was all vibrant. He inhaled it avidly and felt better. Little blond Slavic heads with turned-up noses were gleaming on the benches and in the courts; or else the crudely shaped heads of little Buriats, Yakuts and Samoyeds, with their flattened noses, Mongol jaw-bones and glossy black hair. Sou-ki had an impulse to run his hand over these little Soviet heads, these tender shoulders. . . . "These shoulders," he thought, "are carrying the whole future of the world. If they are solid, then everything is safe. If they bend, then we are lost! Oh, if I could live to see them in ten or twenty years, in a generation."

Looking ghastly, supporting himself against the wall, and coughing with the palm of his hand over his mouth, Sou-ki listened to the teacher.

"What is the purpose of our schools? To hammer out good fighters. This generation has one definite mission: to fight. We are arming it. We are preparing it. First, physical culture, for the body has to be strong. Then scientific culture, for we must know how to use the forces of nature. Finally, social culture: these little citizens that you see playing in the courtyard have their own Soviets, their own committees for culture and

25

hygiene, their own newspaper. They are interested in the whole of our economic, political and social life. When they leave school, they are armed for the class struggle."

As the young schoolmaster concluded, Sou-ki thought for a moment that he saw a firebird on his forehead.

"You know the oath that each child has to swear? No?"

"No," answered Sou-ki in confusion.

" 'I want to toil with the worker and the peasant. I want to fight with them against the common enemy. I, too, want to help the Idea to conquer. I want to become a useful and loyal combatant helping my older comrades. That is why I have come to school.' "

After a long silence, Sou-ki seized the young teacher's hand and laid it on his own breast.

Sou-ki joined in the children's games, jumping and laughing with them. His poor sick body became vibrant and young again. He grasped a little Pioneer by the arm.

"*Tovarishch*, how does a Pioneer differ from all other children?" Sou-ki asked him.

The child became suddenly serious.

"A Pioneer never tells a lie and is never afraid. He does not smoke or drink, he does not eat sunflower seeds; he brushes his teeth and bears cold, fatigue and hunger without complaining; he obeys his leader. He goes to the village, brings help to the peasants and tells them about Lenin. All of us who wear the red tie, you know, are children of Lenin."

"Who was Lenin?"

The child cast a severe look at Sou-ki and went on:

"We Pioneers write to other children in Germany, France, China, all over; these comrades wear the red tie too, but hidden inside their shirts. For their homelands are not yet free. We all make a pact with each other and swear that when we are grown up, we shall unite and all together we shall make a great revolution and deliver the human race."

"Deliver it from whom?"

"From whom? From the capitalists, the kings, the priests!"

He flushed.

With his big childish eyes he gazed far away into the distance beyond the leafless trees. Then, throbbing with excitement, he suddenly turned toward Sou-ki and asked him a question:

"Are there men among you too who exploit other men? What are you doing to deliver them?"

Evening had fallen. A flock of crows flew over the school and perched on the trees. Sou-ki tremulously bowed his head, while a blush of shame illuminated his purple cheeks. The child waited a few moments but seeing that no answer was forthcoming, he turned on his heels and disappeared.

Sou-ki was exhausted. Again that evening he spat blood. He had a fever. He was unable to sleep. Finally toward dawn his eyes closed and a dream inundated his delirious brain. The whole earth was like one immense plateau, the whole earth was swarming with countless throngs of silkworms. Buddha was standing erect in the middle like a giant. He smiled. He turned to the East and to the West, to the North and to the South, and with both hands he threw big batches of green mulberry leaves. Sou-ki listened joyfully to the deep, infinite murmur made by the countless little mouths as they fed. Buddha stood and smiled and kept throwing, throwing. . . . And then! Big glittering wings sprouted on the worms; they turned to butterflies and soared into the air. Sou-ki watched them, marveling. . . . All of a sudden something stirred in his brain, and Buddha was imperceptibly metamorphosed into Lenin. Then the air became full of airplanes.

Vera Ivanovna, the innkeeper's daughter, was sitting at Sou-ki's bedside. For three days she had been taking care of the little Chinese man in his fever. Vera Ivanovna was twenty, blond, athletic, fresh and blooming but without beauty. Under the Czars her father, Ivan

Petrovich, had been employed by the police. He was intelligent and industrious, and the Soviets had made use of him. He ran the hotel with taciturn conscientiousness. Although his heart refused to accept the new state of things, necessity forced him to adapt himself and to serve in a trustworthy way. He was being used, but he was not given the right to vote, for he belonged to the dislocated, ambiguous class known as the "*lichentsi*": ex-bourgeoisie, suspect intellectuals, traders, priests, kulaks. His daughter Vera, who was a fanatical Communist, felt almost physically humiliated at having to bear her *lichentsi* father's name. Several members of the *komsomol* refused to shake hands with her. The University closed its doors to her. Vera Ivanovna could not endure her father; they hardly ever spoke to each other. Her mother, who was religious, she looked upon with shame and contempt.

When Sou-ki opened his eyes, he saw the young girl and smiled. He was frightfully pale, his cheeks were hollow, and his sunken eyes had shadows around them.

"Are you reading, Vera Ivanovna?"

"Yes, Comrade Sou-ki; I am preparing my lesson for this evening."

"Do you give lessons, Vera Ivanovna?"

"I am enrolled in the '*Koult-Pakhod*,' " the young girl smiled.

"The *Koult-Pakhod*?"

"Yes, Comrade Sou-ki, the campaign against illiteracy. Two thousand of us, men and women, have sworn to rid the district of Irkutsk of illiteracy in one year's time. We have elected a general staff, and have worked out a plan, and each of us has taken his position in the battle. As for me, I have charge of a sector of thirty illiterates. I want to give all my time to it and all my soul."

She was silent for a moment, then she added, flushing:

"You see, Comrade Sou-ki, I have to work for two, for my father as well as myself."

28

Sou-ki had closed his eyes; he was listening in happy excitement.

"Ah! Comrade Sou-ki, I am tiring you," exclaimed the young girl.

Sou-ki opened his eyes and stretched out his cadaverous bluish-yellow hand. "Ah! go on talking; talk, Vera Ivanovna! I feel better."

"I must leave. It's late, Comrade Sou-ki."

"Tell me about your parents."

"No," answered Vera brusquely. "Leave them out of it!"

"Tell me about your little brother. He came to see me last night. He opened his shirt and showed me the red tie he had concealed."

Vera's eyes sparkled. There was something proud and ominous in her voice as she started to talk about her brother.

"Every Sunday he would secretly remove the cross that Mother had hung about his neck and he would slip away to the camp of the Pioneers. One day Mother found out that Ivanushka was taking his cross off and absconding. She flew into a rage, ran after him, and caught him. 'Either the cross or you don't go,' she said. The child got very upset and wept. Mother was adamant. For several Sundays the house vibrated with the sound of screams and weeping. But one Sunday I didn't hear them. I went in and found Ivanushka standing at the window and gazing into the street with clenched fists and an air of intense concentration. 'What are you doing, Ivanushka?' 'I'm waiting.' 'What are you waiting for?' 'To grow up. To be able to earn my own living. Then I shall throw the cross away and leave home!' "

Stirred by the story, Sou-ki raised himself on the pillows. A question was blazing on his bloodless lips. But at that moment the door swung open and Lyuba Nikolayevna, the mother, appeared on the threshold, a cup of tea in her hand. When she saw her daughter, she stepped back. The tea spilled and her hand got burned. Vera Ivanovna glanced away, and got up and left. Lyuba Nikolayevna set the half-empty cup down on a little table near Sou-ki.

"Ah! What a hell, dear friend!" she said with a sigh. "What a hell!"

Sou-ki made no reply. He recognized the roots of this heartbreaking situation. He understood the girl and was on her side. But he also understood the mother and pitied her. The war! The war! The terrible idea which is forever appearing on this earth, sword in hand. Why? Why?

Sou-ki closed his eyes; he felt exhausted. He heard the poor woman lamenting and whimpering as though from a great distance.

"I can't live any more in my own house. I love my daughter, but I can't bear to have her around. I go to church, I have my icons, I light the night-candle. My daughter follows every movement I make, and says nothing, but she looks at me with such an air of scorn that I feel unable to breathe. Often I rove around the house for hours and hours trying to get away from her gaze. . . ."

Sou-ki smiled. He saw the children, he saw the parents, he saw old houses crumbling and hearts being torn apart. . . . He was glad.

"I want nothing more," he murmured. "I want nothing more. I am content."

"Tchita, the Russian child is the world's only hope," Sou-ki wrote to his wife. "Tchita, I am sending you a little red tie. I am leaving today for Moscow, and Ivanushka, the innkeeper's son at Irkutsk, made me a present of it. I beg you, Tchita, open our son's dear little shirt, and put it around his neck. When I come, I shall tell you why."

3

It was nighttime and raining. Someone said: "Here's the frontier." Rahel quivered.

She rushed out, but could see nothing. A light went on, then another and another. . . . She got off into the dark and walked a little way. Suddenly she halted. A sweet, sad melody on the balalaika. An old man was struggling toward the train through the storm.

"*Dyadya!*" cried Rahel. "*Dyadya! Rossiya?*"

The balalaika stopped a moment, and in the silence the old man answered: "*Rossiya . . .*"

A cramped room with young Jews and Jewesses on the miserable bed and the hard sofa, gesticulating, discussing, drinking tea. There in Kiev, all of Rahel's acquaintances had gathered to celebrate her arrival. Sitting knee to knee, they were letting their hearts and minds destroy the world and build a new one out of thin air.

The pale and headstrong Dina, demonically possessed by painting and poetry, was curled up in a corner, looking on with animation. In all her work she was making a desperate attempt to express the naïve, heroic, suffering soul of the proletarian. She was exhausting herself without money, without genius and without love. The beautiful Rosa with the long reddish hair and the slender, fragrant body smoked, poured tea and stretched out on the bed. "By day I work for the Party," she said. "I do my share of the common work: I fulfil my duty as a citizen. But the nights I keep for myself, for my young body which is doomed to die; I fulfil my duty as a woman."

Itka, with the lioness' head and the lucid, balanced

brain, worked for the Cheka. She was sensitive but pitiless. Supplied with neat answers to all questions, her mind saw clearly within a limited range. Her heart was tranquil and glowing with health. She had no anxiety, physical or metaphysical, to harass her, for Karl Marx had answered all questions, metaphysical, economic and moral, and Lenin, by a series of impeccable actions, had transmuted these answers into reality. All the Communist had to do was to understand and obey.

Talking and drinking tea with these three ardent Jewesses were Sasha Kuzmich, the sensitive, ironical art critic; Mark Avramovich, secretary in the Commissariat of Finance; and the thin and intense Efrem Mikhaïlovich, who had tubercular rings around his fiery eyes. Rahel was darting back and forth in the dark little room like a flame. She was small and delicate, and had big eyes like a gazelle's. The deep wound on her forehead was still fresh; a red scar extended all the way down to the eyebrows. Although she was a militant, intransigent Communist, her sensual mouth was brimming with questions that transcended Communism, and she had a restless heart.

The overheated atmosphere rang with shouts. Sasha Kuzmich had gotten up in a state of excitement.

"The proletarian art is the art that expresses the deep consciousness of the proletariat," he yelled shrilly. "It cannot—and I would even say it should not—be understood as yet, or loved, by the proletarians. Why? Because there are too few proletarians who have attained the consciousness of the proletarian class with adequate clarity."

Dina looked up in her corner. She was pale.

"Yes, yes, Sasha Kuzmich, proletarian art expresses the deep consciousness of the proletariat. But that's precisely the great problem that is agonizing us: to find the new form of beauty. For example, the symbol of our industrial, materialistic age is the Factory. That's our new cathedral. Ah! But how shall we paint the Factory in a way that expresses the deep meaning, the invisible spirit, the whole mechanized, suffering, courageous soul of our time? What did the medieval cathedral make of its spire that soared away from earth until the sharp point of it was lost in the heavens? It expressed the mystical tension of the Christian soul. How shall we express the spire or the curve or the horizontal line of our own soul today?"

A gentle sneer appeared on Efrem Mikhaïlovich's face.

"Poor artists!" he said in a sad, sarcastic tone. "But don't you understand? We are going through a period of transition; it's very interesting but very unproductive. We have almost no present; our mind understands only the past; our hearts aspire to nothing but the future. My friends, we are an intermediate species, transitory pithecanthropusi destined to die without a trace. That's why some of our artists have failed to understand anything, and believe they can express the new soul with old symbols. The others have understood but so far have not discovered the new form. What is our duty? To prepare the way for the new species, to help it by our own agony and our own experiments to achieve a stabilization. Our destiny is to labor and to disappear."

"You're too optimistic," retorted Sasha Kuzmich angrily; "you don't understand, Efrem Mikhaïlovich. Our age is not a time of transition, it's the beginning of a new culture!"

"On the contrary, on the contrary, Sasha Kuzmich," exclaimed Efrem Mikhaïlovich, "our time is nothing but the exaggeration of the preceding culture that we call bourgeois. Communism merely brings to their most extreme and most logical consequences certain essential elements of Western civilization. Two especially: the materialistic conception of life and the cult of the machine. That's why I call our time an end and not a beginning. That's why real art, great art, cannot exist."

The two antagonists were seething as they confronted each other. But Dina got up, deeply stirred.

"An artist paints an autumn tree," she said, as if she

33

were merely going on with her secret thoughts. "If this artist is really modern, if he is racked by the terrible problems of our time, that tree must express the whole soul of today, with all its suffering and all its revolt. If that same tree was painted by an artist of the decadent period, it would have something aesthetic and refined and morbid about it. In the eyes of a real artist every leaf of a tree reflects his whole age.

"I once read a sublime story in an old book about the lives of the saints. An ascetic was standing at the door of his cell holding the leaf of a tree up to the light, and the tears were streaming from his eyes. 'But why are you weeping, father?' someone asked him. 'What do you see in this leaf?' 'I see Jesus Christ crucified,' the ascetic answered. 'I see all of suffering humanity.' That's how a real artist has to see each leaf today."

Dina collapsed onto the sofa, exhausted. Mark Avramovich began to laugh.

"You remind me of the poor philosopher in the boat," he said. "The philosopher said to his boatman, 'Do you know philosophy?' 'No.' 'No? Then half your life has been lost.' A little while afterward, a violent storm came up. 'Oh, philosopher,' called the boatman, 'do you know how to swim?' 'No.' 'No? Then your whole life is lost.'

"I hear you talking about art and beauty and autumn leaves," he went on. "Poor philosophers! But in the U.S.S.R. at present there is only one problem: to live. Are you blind? We are walking on the edge of an abyss. The NEP has produced the two poisoned fruits that Lenin foresaw: the Nepman and the kulak. We've got to beat them to death. But that's dangerous. The whole boat might capsize: our co-operatives are still in no condition to replace the Nepmen; nor our collectives, the kulak. Abandon your philosophies, comrades, and help us! Proletarian art! That will not be born from your discussions, but from the final triumph of the proletariat. Push a little, comrades, hustle the future on! The storm has come up, let's abandon philosophy; let's swim!"

The shrill voice of Sasha Kuzmich was heard again:

"What a lovely society men of action will bring into being! Ants. Machines. Barren hearts. Hell!"

Rahel opened her beautiful, hungry, restless eyes. Russia, Our Mother Russia! She was treading its sacred soil at last, she was hearing the melody and passion of its voice! She drank in every word. As she lifted her eyes, she saw Itka, the girl with the lioness' head, preparing to pounce.

"Mark Avramovich is right," Itka began. Fierce, clipped overtones rang through her hushed voice. "Mark Avramovich is right! Buddies, we've entered the pitiless zone of immediate action! In the old days, poets and writers and visionaries were in the vanguard and sowed seeds in the form of phrases, phrases packed with explosives—bombshells. One day the phrases burst; then came revolution, war, massacre, famine, and the day-to-day struggle with reality. The poor bloodless intellectuals fled in terror. They had believed that liberty would arrive some fine day without violence—like spring. The imbeciles! But liberty always comes in blood—like war. Yes, yes, don't scream, Dina! Some intellectuals, I know, have remained with us, and others have cropped up. But when I run into one of these intellectuals on my way to work in the morning, my brief case under my arm, my shoes down at the heels, shivering, I feel sick at heart. So what do these deluded bystanders want now? Don't they seem a bit like parasites? Once it was the Idea that they were shouting for and summoning. The Idea came. Now we no longer need to sing its praises, but in the most prosaic fashion to feed it, to clothe it and to lodge it. Don't fret, Sasha Kuzmich; I'm going to tell you one more little example: catch it now! In summer when I have four weeks' vacation, I wander through the fields and I come upon male beetles that have fallen over on their backs and split open and are lying there with their insides spilled out. They have done their duty and passed on the seed; and now they have crawled aside, turned over on their

35

backs, and died. When I see these poor beetles, yes, yes, don't laugh, I think of our intellectuals. They too must resign themselves to dying quietly, like beetles!"

The four Jewesses burst out laughing.

"I love these male beetles," said Rosa, "these Tolstoys, these Dostoevskis, these Gorkys, with their legs up in the air!"

Sasha Kuzmich, whose mouth made one think of a goat's, bit his lips.

"And afterward?" he exclaimed. "Afterward? Yes, the sublime moment of amorous intoxication has passed. The male beetles have to die; they are dead. You alone are left, you men and women of action. What are the results?"

"Here they are!" shouted Efrem Mikhaïlovich, scarcely restraining his fury, his bloodless lips edged with foam. "Here they are." He pulled a little Russian review, the *Ogoniok* (*the Leaflet*), out of his pocket, found a page with a photograph and passed it around under the noses of all present. "Here they are! Look! So read! A *komsomol* has just killed a schoolmate with an axe while the other boy was sleeping. 'Why?' they ask him. And this young-ster, this *komsomol*, this hope of Communism, answers: '*Potomu chto on Yevrei, ya Russki!* (Because he is a Jew and I'm a Russian).'"

Mark Avramovich frowned.

"Efrem Mikhaïlovich, you are a romantic," he said. "You are incapable of understanding reality and of collaborating with it. There are one hundred and fifty million of us and we're not angels, just poor human beings brutalized by the Czarist tyranny and brutalized by economic slavery. A mysterious, hard, recalcitrant mass. How many men and women are sweating, rising up and exhausting themselves to budge this heavy mass a little, to wake it up a little? Don't you see? Don't you under-stand? How do you dare be so unjust?"

Itka, who had turned pale, held out her arms in a gesture of warning.

"And yet, and yet, if you want me to please you, Efrem Mikhaïlovich," she said, "I will! I want to make every concession to you, for we are facing all our weaknesses and we're not afraid. Yes, even among those who are pushing at the wheel, how many have remained pure? Some are worried about nothing but getting there; others are opportunists who have already arrived, and they won't stir any more or take any more risks for fear of losing their position; others—and they include many of the best—have withdrawn and are scraping along in bitterness. Yes, yes, Efrem Mikhaïlovich, we also know that most Communists have a materialistic conception of the world that is infantile and crude. To the destroyers it was indispensable; to the builders it is becoming a menace. We need to cleanse the party and to broaden our minds. We don't need you, Efrem Mikhaïlovich, or people like you—romantics, mystics, émigrés—to point out these defects to us. We are working night and day, and yet our impatient hearts are still dissatisfied with the progress we are making, alas! But come then, dig into the job yourself and you'll see!"

Rahel's big eyes were filled with tears. How she loved Itka, that clear, positive brain, that vigorous body and those eloquent lips! Suddenly, as she noticed the beads of perspiration on her friend's broad forehead, she became aware of all the pain and effort involved in Russia's effort to move a step forward. She turned toward Efrem Mikhaïlovich, and told him in her sibilant voice:

"Efrem Mikhaïlovich, Itka has beaten you; you have nothing to say in reply!"

The poor consumptive felt himself crimson under Rahel's mocking gaze. In Poland earlier he had been in love with this dangerous young Jewess. She had been exciting to his body and his mind, and in her greedy, pitiless way she had consumed him. When she found a foreigner, an Arab, stronger than he, she had left him. Efrem Mikhaïlovich took a moment to collect himself before answering.

"I am not a man of action," he said sadly and scornfully. "That's why I have the strength as well as the right to see things a little more broadly than you men and women of action. You are confined in your trench, which is necessarily narrow, and you are fighting: you see only one sector of the battle. 'Shoot in this direction!' you've been told. And you shoot. If you saw the whole, perhaps you would have no further desire to shoot; or at least you would be somewhat distracted by the beauty or the horror of the spectacle. Thus you would have wasted time and energy. The good fighters are the ones who wear blinders. You wear blinders, my friends. I would not care to rob you of them."

"Oh! Oh!" they all shouted in chorus, bursting into laughter. "He spares us!"

"You are slinking away from the battle," said Rahel, turning toward the sick man. "Since when did Efrem Mikhaïlovich begin to have pity on people? He's getting old!"

Efrem Mikhaïlovich smiled as he looked at Rahel. "That beautiful body," he thought. "I had it once; those beautiful eyes that are jeering at me now were once fixed on me in rapture; that insatiable mouth said to me, 'The two of us together can annihilate and re-create the world!' " He braced himself for a mental effort that made his temples snap, so intense was it. When he spoke, it was in a voice so gravely sorrowful that everyone was moved and listened in silence:

"One spring day a few years ago, I was wandering in the ruins of Pompeii. The sky was a little overcast; weeds had pushed up to the doorways and into the abandoned courtyards; the streets were the way I like them, deserted. I was wandering all alone in the empty city. I would tap the stones with my stick, and then go on, whistling to myself. Suddenly a voice broke into words inside me. 'Terrible God of Abraham and of Lenin,' it said, 'grant that I may someday stroll like this through Paris and

London, and that I may ask my comrades questions in Russian!' After the voice had ceased, a gentle misgiving invaded my heart. The cellars of Pompeii were overflowing with provisions; the women were shameless, fragrant and sterile; the men, rascally little tradesmen, sardonic and weary. All the gods—Greek, African and Asiatic—were there en masse, horded together in democratic misery: cowards and gluttons, bereft of faith. The whole city, overturned there at the foot of Vesuvius, was laughing without fear and without God. I squatted down on a stone; and in a flash everything became clear to me. I saw!"

Tired out, Efrem Mikhaïlovich interrupted his story to cough. Perspiration was trickling down his forehead. He sipped a mouthful of tea and regained a bit of strength, then continued:

"The whole earth from that instant seemed to me like Pompeii a few minutes before the eruption." Abruptly Efrem Mikhaïlovich got carried away, and his voice rose almost to a scream:

"What good is such a civilization with its street-corner women, its mechanical men, its syphilitic god? Let the barbarians come to cleanse the earth of this ordure! In this tubercular chest of mine I feel a pitiless vulture that is hungry and has no love for human beings. I have a clear image of the world at this moment of history in which it has pleased fate to give me life: the suffering, hungry masses are moving toward the groaning table where the great lords sit enthroned, paralyzed, lethargic and insolent. The great lords suddenly hear the commotion and turn around. First they start laughing, then they get pale and subside into anxiety as they see their slaves and their machines rising for the attack! This is a sublime moment and I savor it with relish!

"I also know what you Communists do not know and do not dare to know; that as soon as the attackers get the power—the table—they too will start to get fat and paralyzed. And other hungry, suffering masses will rise on earth again. So will waves of human beings rise and fall in an unceasing rhythm until the end of time. That's what I know, oh, you little practical souls!"

Efrem Mikhaïlovich gasped and stopped talking. Seized by a fit of coughing, he hastily pulled out his handkerchief and went over near the window. Rahel, lights flickering in her eyes, was resting her chin on her hands and with a faraway look was staring out the window into the bluish atmosphere.

Suddenly Dina got up. "Efrem Mikhaïlovich, I am with you!" she exclaimed. "Now I see."

But Mark mumbled "Mystic," and his lips writhed in scorn.

"It's you who are the mystic!" shouted Efrem Mikhaïlovich, who had caught the word. "You're the mystic and you, Itka, and all of you Communists! You believe in the golden age which you think will come when your idea triumphs, you believe in the disappearance of classes, in the end of wars! Poor complacent optimists! Poor mystical simpletons! You believe in happiness!"

The corners of his mouth were foaming. Only Rosa had pity for him. She got up, put her arms tenderly around his waist, and made him sit down. Caressed by a woman's hand, the sick man was calmed and began to smile.

"Pour me a little tea, Rosa. I'm thirsty."

After drinking it, he lightly touched Rahel on the knee and said to her:

"Rahel, pardon me; I have wronged you."

Rahel left, feeling troubled. She roved rapidly around the streets of Kiev. The reddish chestnut trees of autumn were ablaze in the damp air. Some big drops of rain fell. Rahel felt a sensual delight in the coolness on the nape of her neck and on her feverish face.

"Itka, you're right. We must fight! Fight!" she murmured to herself.

A large church courtyard. A beggar and a few ragged

old priests skulked away like rats, scraping against the wall. The doorway had been pushed awry and out of shape by a growth of young ivy. With sudden horror Rahel saw a picture rising out of the weeds. A picture of her sister Lia, the traitor, killed by a revolver in a Kiev courtyard. It was Lia's Communist husband who had killed her: she was the mistress of the bishop.

"Strike! Strike!" cried Rahel again with hatred.

Rahel entered the church; she wanted to enjoy its miserable, neglected condition. A fat archimandrite in the golden cope was chanting in a low, warm voice; a few old women were on their knees; a verger, young and green, with the placid face of a eunuch, was lighting the night-candles. The elderly porter came up to Rahel. In the shadows he failed to discern the curved nose of the Jewess and her triumphant eyes. He looked at Rahel with a beseeching air: saints were being maltreated; churches were closed; priests were hungry; priests and saints and little angels and Jesus Christ were suffering. Bending over and peering into this believer's blue eyes, Rahel could see the saints in them running in droves, barefoot, starving exiles with ex-votos hanging all over their chests.

"What is your name?" she asked in the old man's ear, her voice making a hissing sound.

"Vasiliĭ Dmitriyevich."

"Vasiliĭ Dmitriyevich, there aren't any more saints. Look down to earth; there are Soviets, komsomols, and a Red army. Lift your eyes to heaven: there are airplanes!"

A soldier with a muzhik's heavy face approached, holding a lighted candle.

"I want to see your holy relics," he said.

The porter hurried to him and guided him down into the crypt. Perched to the right and to the left were skeletons and mummies. The soldier demanded precise data.

"Who's this tovarishch? Why doesn't he have any fingernails?" he asked.

"A martyr prince."

The soldier made a gesture of impatience.

"*Dalshe! Dalshe!* (Go on!) This one? Where's his head?"

"A decapitated monk. Smell that odor!"

"If you pour benzine on bones, the bones will absorb the smell of benzine. *Dalshe!*"

The porter talked and talked, perspiring with the effort of explaining. The soldier sank into deep reflection.

"There's one thing I can't understand," he suddenly said. "Why are there animals? Do you know, *batyushka?*"

When the old porter emerged from the crypt, out of breath, he caught sight of Rahel striding out of the doorway.

"The devil take you," he muttered, crossing himself, and he spat on the floor three times.

In the vestibule, which was ornamented with discolored frescoes, Rahel came to an abrupt halt. A thickset man was coming in with a wild, arrogant air, his lips compressed. A look of fixed exaltation burned through his big shell-rimmed glasses. There was something both sublime and ridiculous about this man. The force of madness or of genius issued from his ravaged, brutal head. Rahel felt a tremor of fear.

When the Big-Jawed Man came into the church, the Vesper service had ended. Vasiliǐ Dmitriyevich ran up to him, but the stranger put him off with a summary gesture. The archimandrite, sensing the presence of a V.I.P., invited him to his home for tea.

"A few old friends," he said, "will be there. You're a journalist? An American? Statesman?"

The stranger looked about the archimandrite's room with a glum, predaceous expression. He stared at the unctuous, pot-bellied priest in the old greenish frock with the big stains of butter. The fat splendor of former good cheer was still evident on the priest's cheeks. Languorous-eyed Russian Christs with meticulously combed hair and painted cheeks were all over the room. The big bronze samovar was boiling, and for a moment the archimandrite Joachim's jovial face was veiled by the steam.

"Write," suddenly shouted the archimandrite, "raise your voice, protect the Church!"

The big jaws snapped open. "One day when Jehovah, Jesus Christ, Mohammed and Buddha were stretching out their hands to ask alms of someone, that someone said to them: 'I have no more bread for you, I have no more prayers, I have no more pity.' And these gods answered, 'If you have no more bread, or prayers, or pity, we shall die.' But this someone shrugged his shoulders and said, 'Die!' "

The archimandrite Joachim uttered a muffled growl: "Who said that?"

"I did."

The archimandrite moved his short chubby hands in the direction of the samovar.

"Yes, but the Church is not afraid."

"What are you doing to win?"

"We have founded a club. I explain the Gospel. We find work—embroidery, linen, lace—for ladies in adversity. Every Sunday we take tea together."

"I'm talking about the kind of inner effort that gives man the strength to move mountains!"

The archimandrite Joachim took a deep breath, making a noise as he inhaled. He grasped the teapot, put two spoonfuls of tea in it and poured out boiling water. From a big cupboard over his bed he drew out sugar, caviar, butter and salted cucumbers. He smiled, made the sign of the cross, and slowly turned his wild boar's neck.

"Anyutka, my daughter," he said in his melodious bass voice, "bring the cups."

By now the Big-Jawed Man was mutely listening to Joachim's two friends as they expounded their grievances amidst explosions of abuse and invocations to God, the old traditions, honor and the law. Finally the stranger got up, unable to restrain himself any longer. "Absurd

43

people!" he thought, and an ogreish laugh distorted his face.

When he got back home, he pulled out a little note-book and slowly wrote:

"I hate the Bolsheviks. But above all I hate and scorn their contemptible enemies. War! War! War against our enemies and our contemptible friends."

4

THE SOUTHWEST WIND from the Kara Kum Desert was blowing at Bokhara, and the mud-houses were baked and crumbling. Strong smells of rotten melons, cinnamon and urine saturated the air. Wide divans were lined up along the sidewalks with red rugs and yellow mats thrown over them. Cross-legged and silent, the Mussulmen drank *kotchaï*, green tea, and refreshing sherbets. Their heads glittered with the *tubeteikas*, skullcaps embroidered with gold and brilliant flowers, that they were all wearing. Lazy camels were striding with long rhythmic gait along the shadow-filled bazaars.

A little girl of seven went by. Her hair, rubbed with bay oil and glistening in the sun, fell in innumerable slender braids over her frail shoulders and bobbed over her precociously swaying hips. Each braid was tipped with a big piece of silver or a shell dug from the poisonous waters of the River Zeravshan or with a tiny bronze crescent. The little girl tinkled as she passed. Like a young animal in heat she exuded a disconcerting odor of musk. Her black eyes made up with *courma* had a sullen, perverse expression.

The burning dust rose in gusts, seeping into body and brain, making everyone feel thirsty and choked. But of a sudden there appeared Kok-Goumbas, the "green cupola" of the great Mosque, the slanting Chir-Arab and the Magak-i-Altara Mosque! Heart and eyes became refreshed. Above these mud terraces and this stinking mass of humanity, God burst forth like a colossal cactus flower— young, sensual and merciless—scornfully sucking from his mud roots, men and terraces both. Man athirst and exhausted, groveling in the dust, lifted his eyes and, perceiving him, smiled. It was not God, it was himself, the worm metamorphosed into a butterfly.

Amita, too, lifted his eyes and smiled. Bokhara! Bokhara! How he had longed for this moment! He felt as if this escapade of the senses were a sin against the austerity of Moscow. Had he not sworn to renounce art and beauty and to devote himself wholly to the harsh duty of the present hour? Yes, yes, but now he was tasting this sweet, forbidden fruit of Bokhara with delight! He walked rapidly across the dark bazaar roofed with painted beams and matting. He wandered into the narrow, dirty lanes: in one place they were making turned-up slippers for women and red and green harnesses for donkeys and horses; somewhere else they were hammering out delicate, red copper vases in the shape of birds. . . . Amita was in haste to reach the beautiful turquoise mosque in the background. Through the melodious hum of the bazaar, he had caught the clear, imperious voice of the muezzin soaring into the air like a naked sword. It was desperately summoning the faithful to the noonday prayer. "*Lailah, il Allah . . .*"

Dogs were panting in the shade; fat agas paraded past, lording it on donkeys; Moslem women, their faces concealed by heavy black cloth, shuffled past in Turkish slippers worn down in back. Suddenly the gigantic cupola of the mosque reared itself. All of Saxon-blue faïence, it gleamed in the sun like the tent of some fabulous sultan, flaunting its silk and emeralds in the very center of the mire where it had been pitched. The god who dwelt in such a cupola, one felt, loved this earthly life and the warm colors and the shrouded women.

Amita leaned on the majolica wall in rapture. The green-turbaned old muezzin bending down from the minaret to call and summon was slowly moving about on the narrow balcony of the tower with his hands glued over his ears. He looked to the East and called, he turned to the North, then to the West, then to the South, and with his head facing the other way called ecstatically. He paused for a moment as if he intended to scan the distant horizons and watch the pilgrims surging up above the Mongol walls and the flat desert and the rose-colored mountains. But no pilgrims surged up, for they were all buried in the sand, or else had fled as far away as possible into the desert. The crescent in the heavens had been transformed into a matter-of-fact sickle, and God no longer lived in people's hearts. Yet the muezzin, aloft on his high turquoise tower, called out and did not despair. What is the highest duty of man? To cry into the desert! A few urchins gathered around and began to bellow and to miaow in order to drown the muezzin's voice. . . . But with his head immersed in his solitary God and his hands glued over his ears he went on with his frenzied chant, not even hearing the voices on earth.

Amita smiled sorrowfully. Once this vast Registan Square had been overflowing with delirious pilgrims. In the months of April and May, when Bokhara was in blossom, central Asia had flocked here to mourn for the two assassinated sons of Ali-Hussein and Hassan. Throngs of wailing pilgrims and rich caravans of merchants and the holy prostitutes . . . Young boys mounted on white horses, each with a pigeon in his hand and straw on his shaven head, led the terrible procession. Behind them in white vestments the fanatical followers of Mohammed shot out, brandishing their yataghans. They were beating their breasts as they howled, they were slitting their skulls and blood was running over their curved moustaches and their white mantles. For forty days and forty nights they beat their breasts and rhythmically chanted the terrible refrain, "Hassan! Hussein!" So the sacred orgy of the springtime ran its bellowing course under the blossoming trees!

Amita felt a sudden shock. Out of all this hurricane of human souls, out of all these bodies scattered in the dust of Kara Kum, what was left? Only one green cupola! If only one could live far away from the world of passion and ephemeral ideas, if only one could rise above action and create a work of art! Did not one perfect verse outweigh the conquest of an empire?

The green-turbaned muezzin appeared at the door of the mosque. He scrutinized Amita with a sad and hostile air, and sighing with weariness came down the broken steps. Old women selling coarse woollen stockings and green and yellow handkerchiefs were ranged on the bottom step, enveloped in their ragged *feredjes*. A white stork left the slanting Chir-Arab, rowed its way through the blue air and lodged its long red foot in its nest on the summit of the cupola of Magak-i-Altara. White-bearded old Moslems slipped into the courtyard and squatted silently in the shade.

Leaning against the wall, Amita savored the passing moment like a taste of honey. He closed his eyes. In the remote distance he heard the cooing of a pigeon. . . . A woman on a terrace laughed a hearty laugh and brought freshness into the desert. . . . A tree shed some leaves. . . . A raven passed and its wings rustled like tearing silk. . . . Suddenly the sound of someone chanting in a sorrowful voice made Amita open his eyes: a blind man crouched in the shade, his body swaying, was beginning to recite some melodious verses from the Koran. His beggar's hand, painted with henna, was flapping up and down, pointing toward the desert. Once more Amita closed his eyes and smiled. "Ah! What a simple thing life was and how good!"

An abrupt fanfare of trumpets and hurried steps. The old men at the foot of the ruins raised their heads and then lowered them, muttering; the women closed their *feredjes* in haste; the old muezzin spat and vanished. Men and women were getting a jolt, for their sons and daughters, the *komsomols*, were marching behind the Red flag. Amita opened his eyes with a start. Here were new violent processions, new passionate refrains, a new kind of young

Moslem face in a state of exaltation. Hard and scornful, they were passing in front of their fathers and mothers with metallic glints in their eyes. They crossed the great courtyard and marched along the creviced wall of the beautiful mosque, the thud of their footsteps echoing in the dust as they disappeared. The pigeon returned and the woman's refreshing laugh. . . .

A sturdy young boy passed, balancing a big basket of grapes and melons on his head. Amita bought some, filling his hands, and fled into the blue shade. The hours went by. . . . Gradually he forgot Communism and the purpose of his pilgrimage and the struggles tearing his heart. His heart was no longer torn; it was merely a simple living thing, a little animal curled up in the shade. His legs crossed, his hands filled with melons and grapes, Amita felt suddenly happy.

The hours went by like flashes of lightning. . . . A bronze basin was slowly thrust under Amita's heavy eyes. As he looked up, he saw an old monk in an earth-colored frock stooping down in front of him and smilingly asking for alms. Amita placed some bunches of grapes and a slice of melon in the basin, filling it up. But the beggar continued to hold his hand out. Amita cast a troubled look at him. Where had he seen these clear disturbing eyes and this bitter mouth? Like a long thin blade, the smile cleft the old ivory face from ear to ear. Suddenly the gilt statuette in his little room in Japan loomed up in the sun.

"What do you want now, father?" murmured Amita.

"There are three steps in alms," said the old *bhikku*, still holding his hand out. "The first and lowest is the act; you have performed that. The second, a higher one, is the word; I'm waiting for it."

"Father," answered Amita, "I am happy. Sit down beside me and let us share my happiness. That is all I can give you."

The monk smiled.

"What is your name?" he asked.

49

"Amita."

"Poor Amita! That's all that you can give? A little melon? A little happiness?"

Amita put out his own hand.

"I know who you are," he said. "Have pity on me. Give me the highest alms!"

"Close your eyes, your ears, your mouth, your nostrils, your fingers; close your spirit, empty your entrails. The world does not exist!"

But with a violent movement Amita drew back his hand as if a burning coal had been dropped upon it.

"Nothing exists," he exclaimed; "nothing exists. Everything is a phantom of our hungry spirit, of our fearsome soul. Nothing exists save the cry of my own heart. That is enough for me."

"Everything exists!"

A dry little laugh. The vertical rays of the noonday light flickered for an instant. When Amita lifted his head, the air was empty.

Amita bounded up, flushing with shame. "Amita," he mumbled, "aesthete, bourgeois, traitor!" He ran to the Soviets of the city. "I am a stranger," he told them. "Help me. I want to know the Soviet life of Bokhara!" They assigned him a guide: Giulsum Khatizade, a Moslem woman *komsomol*, sunburned, full-lipped, with bold, laughing eyes.

She stared at little Amita in fascination. "Let's go," she said with a laugh. "I'm going to show you a sight you're not expecting. Let's get going right away!"

A spacious hall packed with men and women workers. Men and women jammed together on long benches were munching sunflower seeds and nibbling apples while keeping their eyes riveted on a stage in the rear. At last the curtain rose, revealing a tribunal, a table covered with a sparkling cloth, high seats draped in red satin, and on the walls Lenin, Karl Marx and Rosa Luxemburg.

Giulsum Khatizade explained that this was propaganda

for hygiene. A play. The judges were doctors and the audience was the jury. You will see, she said. The *dramatis personae* made their entrance: judges, public prosecutor, lawyers. The president rang a little bell and the trial began. The accused was a worker who got married when he was sick and infected his wife so that she died in childbirth. The mother-in-law entered—an indignant virago who pronounced a fiery declamation against her daughter's murderer. Witnesses made their depositions. The prosecutor made a speech, the lawyers made speeches. The audience was in a state of feverish excitement. This drama had ceased to be make-believe and had become a fact, a horrible everyday fact. They argued and discussed, unwilling to pardon the accused. "Yes, yes," exclaimed men and women both, "the accused is guilty of taking a woman before he was cured." "There are extenuating circumstances," said the men! "No!" shrieked the women. An aged woman worker raised her hand to say: "I should have acquitted him if his repentance could bring the dead woman back to life!" And this outburst from the old woman decided the case. The accused was condemned. The workers got up and left, still passionately arguing the issues in the street.

Giulsum Khatizade took Amita's arm. She too was moved. Every aspect of the struggle to awaken her country intoxicated her soul. She had completed her studies at the University of Moscow and had wanted to come back home to work in this desert. To work, to fight, to make a little contribution to the awakening of people's souls, to produce a spark of light with her own blood and brain . . . Giulsum turned and scrutinized this delicate, taciturn, yellow man who had come from the other end of the world to witness their efforts. A feeling of tenderness seized her and she squeezed his arm.

"The U.S.S.R. is immense," she said in a voice charged with pride and awe. "How benighted it is! What an effort is required! When muzhiks travel, they take a precise number of lice along with them as a talisman, for they regard the lice as the spirits of their ancestors. That's how benighted we are! We're driving ahead. Did you ever see a cart being drawn by snails? That's the cart that's hauling the Idea in this land of Russia."

Amita was moved as he listened to his companion. That mysterious shaft, the Light, come no one knows whence and going no one knows where! The cost in agony and blood as it pierces the darkness! Eternally, without beginning or end, and perhaps even without a purpose. As Amita turned around, the glare of the electric lamp caught his face, and the girl saw his beautiful black eyes watching like a pair of deer.

"Comrade and stranger," he said, "what good is this struggle man makes?"

And she gave the arm of this stranger who was her guest a light, serene squeeze.

"Let's forget the questions, comrade!" she responded in a gentle voice. "Let's fight! There is no other answer."

With a laugh she took a cigarette, tapped it on her nail and lit it.

"The young Idea," she said, the laughter sparkling in her eyes once more, "is like a betrothed young girl. Though it hides itself, its voice shatters mountains."

"Where are we going?"

Amita felt weary and would have liked to be left alone.

"I'm hungry; let's go eat," cried the sturdy komsomol, as she dragged her companion off.

Pilaf with red pimientos, little pieces of skewered meat, cakes dripping with honey, sweet wine. Amita observed his companion as she ate with joyful, ravenous gusto, completely occupied with this high physical need. What a strong, free animal! Amita sat motionless and silent, savoring this moment of solemn sensuality. The young girl lit another cigarette. Satiated now, she started laughing and chattering. She was twenty, she worked ten or twelve hours a day, and she was happy. She lived alone.

Her father had died over on the banks of the Volga during the famine; he had been an itinerant blacksmith. Her mother had married a man from Turkmenistan and had thrown her out of the house. *"Komsomol!* Whore!" she had shouted after her.

They talked about marriage.

"If I love someone, I shall marry him and live with him," she said. "Naturally I'll be faithful to him since I love him. But if love passes? Then I'll leave him or he'll leave me. No time for sentimentality or for making a fuss. We have other fish to fry."

A little vagabond boy crawled among the tables, and quickly swept up the remains, bread, meat, cigarette butts, and disappeared.

"All these children," said Amita, "are born of your easy marriages. Have you no pity on them?"

"Most of these children will be picked up by the State. The best will become good Communists. Others will die of cold and hunger. But Russia is big. . . ."

Amita suddenly realized that Russia is really big, fertile, incessantly fecund, incessantly renewed, like the earth. Five millions mowed down by famine, five millions and more fallen in the wars; and then new millions of children springing out of this land. . . . In the U.S.S.R., men teem in millions like ants, rise out of the earth and are swallowed up in the earth, in compact masses.

Amita and Giulsum got up and left.

"We'll spend the evening together," Amita found the courage to say. "When you talk, I have the feeling that I am traveling and discovering Russia in you."

She laughed. Then, looking at the slender, delicate Japanese with a touch of scorn, she said: "You seem like a poet to me." But she quickly shrugged her shoulders and added: "Nichevo! What's your name?"

"Amita. And yours?"

"Giulsum Khatizade."

"Where are we going?"

Amita suggested the theater to her, for the players had just arrived from Moscow. Giulsum agreed with delight.

The play had already begun. The scene was stark and extremely simple: sharp shadows, tattered costumes, eyes and lips—the whole mask in fact—merely a crude daub, like the costumes, dances and death masks of African savages. The actors shot up and leapt like springs; the contemporary soul in all the violence of its revolt was deploying itself in action and contorting the human body. One was immediately knocked by it into a state of vertigo. With quivering sensitivity Amita grasped the essence of the art: it was an act of holy intoxication, of heroic and despairing escape beyond space and time and beyond logic. The role of words was secondary, for the intoxication came entirely from the rhythm that took possession of these frenzied actors with their floating rags, their shrieks and grimaces. Amita had been only vaguely aware of what piece was being played. He remembered merely that there was a medieval market with pointed houses, narrow alleys and visionary monsters gnawing at street lamps, and that the time was midnight. Rabbis, thieves, merchants, prostitutes, priests and kings congregated and dispersed, calling upon their God—some upon Jehovah, others on Christ or Mohammed or Mammon. They arranged their little affairs in the name of their God, and in his name they satisfied their shameless passions. Suddenly a gigantic broom appeared, and in a flash all of them, men and Gods alike, were swept up and vanished. Giulsum had understood one thing only, but she had understood it better than Amita: that the old God who protected all the rabbis, priests, thieves, prostitutes and kings had been swept up and was no more.

"Do you know who was holding the broom? Do you know?" With palpitating impatience she answered her own question: "Lenin!"

With a jolt Amita realized that Lenin had already acquired the force of the legendary knight who killed the horrible monster and delivered the princess—the human soul.

At midnight Amita stammered out a timid entreaty to accompany her to her room. Giulsum stopped him with a burst of laughter.

"And you still dare to claim that you are not a bourgeois! One would think that you were asking for the moon! Let's go!"

Amita's eyes wandered voraciously around the young Soviet girl's room. Lenin's delicate-featured face, sharp as a sword; a little table, a sofa covered in red cotton cloth, some books of Lenin and Bukharin, and Karl Marx's massive head on a stand. Giulsum lit her little samovar, opened a cupboard, and pulled out bread, nuts and dried figs. They ate and drank and talked about Lenin.

"Oh, when will the Red flag cover the world?" cried Giulsum with tears in her eyes.

She questioned Amita about the proletariat in his own country, about his friends and about their effort to awaken their people. Over this tea in this icy room he suddenly felt the awesome presence of the Idea in a way he had never before experienced it. They had forgotten that they were man and woman on this red sofa, and they talked until dawn about hard-working, suffering humanity—and about their duty to improve the level of life on this earth a little, as much as they could, before they died.

"Comrade Giulsum Khatizade," said Amita, pulling the flimsy window-curtains a little way apart, "look: the dawn is breaking already."

"Rahel the Jewess greets Amita the poet, wishing him strength, happiness and a good and a merciless heart. Rahel offers her right hand and says: 'Good day, Comrade Amita. I'd like to see you today.'"

As soon as she had gotten off the train, Rahel had laughingly left this Oriental greeting for Amita, and gone off around the city. She felt worried.

"On the success of this mission," the leader of the Cheka at Kiev had told her, accenting the syllables as if he were scanning some lines of verse, "your fate in the Party will depend."

Rahel could still see the pale young man wearing the sober uniform and behaving so curtly. She had trembled a bit as she stood before him and received his instructions.

"Bokhara ... Baku ... Astrakhan ..." he had enumerated. "Visitors—four especially. Take careful note of their names: Amita, Geranos, Azad and another mysterious personage who has been traveling around the Ukraine and is leaving for the Caucasus. Send brief, fair reports. Be on your guard, Comrade Rahel!"

On the outskirts of Bokhara, the sand smoked under the torrid sun. There the beautiful ripples began and the whole desert became a wild beast stirring in the sun. A hand lifted the door-curtain of a *kibitka*—a sheepskin tent. Within, a man and a woman with protruding cheekbones were visible crouching in front of the fire; the kettle was boiling. In one corner were a curved sword and a revolver. In the other corner the cradle of the newborn baby had been hollowed out of a tree trunk. War, hunger, love, all of human life had taken refuge under this poor tent in the desert. Amita lowered the curtain under an impulse of shame in the presence of something sacred, as if he had come upon his own mother in her nakedness.

He went on alone and troubled. The mysterious, playful letter was torturing him. Rahel ... Rahel ... Who was she?

He ventured into a little village full of dirty huts made of mud, cow dung and straw. Not a tree, not a leaf! The women were grinding corn on the terraces, or delousing their youngsters. The men in wide, brightly colored cloaks were thronging toward a big, low house. They entered and started talking in hushed voices . . . . Amita followed the crowd and found an agricultural exhibit in the middle of the desert! Agricultural machines, samples of choice wheat and cotton, books and newspapers in the Uzbek tongue. A beautiful series of colored plates on the wall, and under them in big letters: HOW TO CARE FOR THE BODY, HOW TO AVOID MALARIA AND TUBERCULOSIS, WHAT ARE THE DANGERS OF ALCOHOLISM AND PROSTITUTION? Two young boys and a young girl in the *komsomol* explained each of the pictures to the stupefied, half-savage onlookers. They kept starting the machines and turning them off; they opened the books and read aloud. On the red cover of a reading book Amita saw a silhouette of Lenin smilingly leading a little Uzbek boy by the hand.

Amita approached the young *komsomol* girl. Apparently about sixteen years old, she had a yellow face with planes so sharply modeled it seemed as if it were a block of hard wood sculpted by some bold expressionist hand. She came from far-away Siam and was studying in Moscow.

"I love Russia," she said, "but I long to go back home to Siam. There is much work to be done there."

"Your country must be beautiful," Amita said, "its mountains, its flowers, its songs."

With her slanting serpent's eyes the young *komsomol* cast a scornful smile at Amita. After a moment's silence she suddenly exploded:

"All the beauty on earth is a luxury, good for those who have eaten and have the time to see and enjoy it." She was almost screaming and her thin lips were making a vehement hissing sound. "But people who go home from the factory every night or from the master's fields have neither the time nor the eyes to see; and their hearts are all tight! Let us find deliverance first, let us first have a little chance to breathe. Later on we shall enjoy your sunrises and your sunsets!"

Amita reeled under the outburst.

"Yes, yes," he murmured as he went off in confusion.

"Let us be delivered first, let us first have a little chance to breathe. This young girl has gone straight to the appalling truth that I am looking for. She is naïve, ignorant and young. But the pitiless moment that we are passing through she is experiencing in an immediate way. No, she isn't experiencing it . . . she is in this pitiless moment."

Right in the middle of the village Amita was treated to the spectacle of a ruddyfaced, gold-toothed Englishman in a colonial helmet. They walked a little way together.

"What do you think of Soviet Russia?" Amita asked.

"Very inconvenient."

"Inconvenient? Too big, too poor, too dangerous?"

"No, one can't find what one wants. I wanted some clothes. . . ."

"Perhaps they don't have clothes or good toothpaste; but they have one very rare article."

"What's that?"

"Faith."

His hand on his belly, the Englishman started to laugh. Amita felt irritated.

"Don't you realize the danger?"

"What danger?"

"That threatens Great Britain. She is sitting on something that is moving under her."

"What's that?"

"On Egypt, on the Indies, on Africa. On the human heart."

The Englishman controlled his mirth.

"Perhaps in a thousand years," he said, "in two thousand years . . ."

"Twenty centuries ago the Romans who held the earth in their claws," Amita retorted in a dry, bantering voice, "talked with the same confidence as you. They were tough and arrogant, lords of the earth. They had a formidable army and a formidable fleet, an organization and discipline of iron; all other peoples worked for their aggrandizement and comfort. Suddenly the human heart stirred and all powerful as it was, the structure toppled to earth."

The Englishman faced Amita and looked at him brusquely. Was he crazy? After a little hesitation, he remarked as he stepped away: "You seem like an apostle—or a humorist. I like you; come to take tea with me someday at my place."

Left alone, Amita flushed.

"I got carried away," he mumbled. "Why?"

It was already late. Women were squatting in the dust suckling babies covered all over with flies. Smoke was floating peacefully in the evening breeze over all the cabin roofs. That is man's real flag, Amita thought with emotion. As he left the village, a young girl with erect, rounded breasts was whispering with a bearded man. The word Rahel rose to Amita's lips, and he hastened his steps. The air had cooled off somewhat and a light, fragrant breeze was blowing. The canary-colored apricot trees and the blood-red pomegranate trees were gradually shedding their leaves. Autumn was murmuring its way down the gentle slope to the River Zeravshan. . . . Amita had once seen a Persian miniature on an old parchment: a young girl with almond eyes and a black beauty spot between her eyebrows was nonchalantly stretched out on the banks of a blue stream. In her right hand she was holding a canary and in her left a scarlet apple. . . . Amita felt as if he were quietly dissolving into this Persian miniature. As yesterday, in front of the turquoise cupola, he was again overcome by a delightful feeling of utter languor. For the second time he felt his poor heart turning into a small animal: a squirrel giving out little squeals of joy among the autumn leaves.

During the days that came later, Amita struggled to remember where he had been when he had seen Rahel for the first time, the marvelous Rahel who disappeared so suddenly! He thought he had seen her under a blood-red autumn tree at the entrance to Bokhara. Her long blue hair clung to her forehead and temples. She was wearing a beautiful saffron-colored shawl. The whole of her being exuded a vaporous glow in the twilight—like a burning coal.

"Comrade Amita," she cried as she saw him pass. "I am Rahel."

Amita forgot what their first words were. A gentle vertigo had possessed him as if he were taking a spring-time walk in the forest with the cherry trees in blossom. A low humming of bees, the tang of bitter almonds. He remembered only that a few minutes afterward when he saw the turquoise-colored cupola of Magak-i-Altara in the evening shadows in the distance, it had seemed to him round and proud and pointed like a woman's breast. Everything was effaced. . . . Only a few verses in Japanese were found later by the Cheka in the dead woman's notebooks:

Cast your gaze, O God of terror, on this superb young girl who walks the earth—Rahel. Her forehead is Fujiyama at dawn, her eyes are gentle and pitiless like the eyes of a young lioness at play. Her heart is a marvelous cactus flower surrounded by big thorns. And over the abyss, her little outstretched hands are clasping you, O God of terror.

On another sheet of parchment the following was written in Chinese ink:

O Rahel, O radiant head floating above the black waters of the abyss. Birds and serpents, children, flowers, wheat and women, all the seeds of the earth have taken shelter in your sweet warmth, while divine forces howl and strike blindly at everything in their way. O God of death, this little ivory ark is all that shines, calm and undaunted, above your wrath. O Rahel, my hands, my poor hands of clay are passing lingering caresses over this radiant head in the darkness of the night.

In Amita's mind Bokhara underwent a change. Gone were mosques, Persian miniatures and autumn graces.

From that time on, when he walked with Rahel, Bokhara presented itself to his eyes as a war tent. He heard ominous Asiatic voices in the air: the voices of Uzbeks, Sarts, Kirghiz, and of the people of Turkmenistan, staring in the direction of Europe as they curled their delicate moustaches.

"Why did we meet?" asked Amita, sinking his gaze into Rahel's long almond-shaped eyes.

"To destroy us both and to re-create the world!" she answered, and the image of Efrem Mikhaïlovich rose before her. She saw him sitting beside Amita, livid and with his little racking cough. She smiled.

"Why do you smile?"

"I'm thinking of that sticky molasses Tagore. He dreams of an idyllic union between Europe and Asia. He chases around the world with his white robe and his big vegetarian belly, preaching love. The fool!"

"What's that wound on your forehead, Rahel?"

"It's nothing," the Jewess answered, crimsoning. "I fell in a factory at Lodz."

That evening, on the eve of their departure for Baku, Amita continued his journal:

This world will be destroyed; it will be destroyed by violence. We are entering into a new Middle Ages. The old world is still powerful; the young world is not yet ripe. A zone of transition, of groping, of action and reaction, of wars.

What is your duty, Amita? Abandon beauty, gods and verses. Abandon happiness. Put on your iron shoes! Tighten your belt. Be a man of your time, a warrior!

Don't forget the Englishman! Don't forget Giulsum Khatizade. Don't forget the young komsomol girl from Siam! Let us be delivered first! Let's first have a little chance to breathe!

Rahel, over a jet-black abyss I saw the red line which is life rising, rising, rising—like a fever.

61

5

"MOSCOW! MOSCOW! Tchita, my wife, and
you, Ni-nel, my son, I feel you with me day and night in
this great happiness that has come over me. At my feet
I can detect three shadows: the shadow of a puny sick
man named Sou-ki, that of a small, sad woman and that
of a child playing with an orange. And so my flickering
eyes see this Red Benares with you and they are happy.

"Tartars with hypnotic serpents' eyes, Jews with
piercing, uneasy glances; thin, wild Cossacks with eyes
haunted by the desert; handsome, devil-may-care
Georgians who love wine, women and war; dull traders
from Azerbaijan, from Turkmenistan, from Kirghiz;
the Yakuts, the Uzbeks, the Bahkirs, the Kalmucks—
distant and mysterious brethren smelling strongly of
buffaloes and horses . . . Compatriots of ours, tan-colored,
sickly Chinese selling leather belts and diabolical little
toys on every street corner. On the sidewalks, men and
women muttering long guttural sounds display fruits,
books, babies' bibs, plucked chickens and statuettes of
Lenin. Workingwomen go by with scarlet kerchiefs on
their sturdy, alert heads. Bands of vagabond children hug
the stoves at the doors of the big restaurants, or rummage
painstakingly through the trash bins. . . .

"A tall handsome old man with a well-groomed beard
and a look of unbending firmness about him—a nobleman
in the good old days—had posted himself at the entrance
to a big hotel and was selling an amber pipe. Another
old man caught sight of him from the sidewalk across
the way and hurried over to him, sloshing through the

mud. He seized both his hands, pressed them affectionately, and asked question after question. But the other one, the ex-nobleman, smiled tranquilly, impenetrably, sweetly, resting his hand on his friend's shoulder and patting it pleasantly, while he kept repeating that word so redolent of the Oriental and Russian soul: '*Nichevo! Nichevo!*'

"Churches all splendid with gold and cupolas in the shape of gigantic figs, flattened turnips and pointed Tartar helmets; Chinese walls and medieval turrets in the very heart of Moscow alongside skyscrapers built out of iron, reinforced concrete and glass in a bare, severe style of architecture. Written in big letters in the streets, on the façades of churches and on the trolley cars: PROLETARIANS OF ALL COUNTRIES, UNITE! Red stars on the soldiers' foreheads. Then suddenly toward evening, above all this mighty, disorderly hullabaloo, the harmonious tolling of the deep Russian bells, plaintive and insistent, completely patient in their despair, still summoning the faithful.

"The Russian reality, Tchita, does not exist; it is in a state of becoming. It is a river flowing on, and as it flows, it opens up and creates its own bed. Don't look for rigorously logical connections. The Russian reality is replete with contradictions, facts that are logically inexplicable and remnants of old realities. Other elements in the reality are survivals of things that have miscarried and still go on in some monstrous form. Things are just beginning to live and still have all the awkwardness, the complexity and the charm of a newborn baby. Moscow today is the center of the earth, the holy crossroads where East and West, North and South meet. Moscow is the rose of the winds. Her body and her soul are mosaics composed of all races and all desires. Chaos—that's the first great impression, dear Tchita!

"Moscow is the perfect incarnation of the Slavic soul. Without any logical plan Moscow has grown like a forest

63

around its red seed-bed—the Kremlin. On this hallowed hill rise the gloomy castles of the Czar and the golden cupolas of his neighbor and confederate, God. The city flooded over, winding along the sandy banks of the Neglinka and the Moskva rivers. A new and bigger Tartar wall was built to contain it. But the city ramified like the forest, and once more it was encircled by new walls, the 'white walls.' Again it overflowed, spilling out over the plain. The three hundred peoples and tribes of all the Russias flock to Moscow, and their souls leave an imprint in the colorful, barbarous mosaic that is the city: carpets, embroideries, songs, customs; virgin, chaotic intellects; mystical or brutal passions. Moscow is a melting-pot of all the semi-barbarous peoples of the East. A few days ago an Armenian comrade recited to me three sorrowful lines of verse by one of their poets, Toumanian. These verses obsess me. They made me shudder:

> Man, the bloodstained mouth, raw cannibal,
> Hands streaming with blood, advances inch by inch,
> But he is still far from the path of Man.

"Here as I study Moscow—her schools and institutions, her campaign against illiteracy, her army barracks, her prisons and clubs—I see this fierce beast, shoved and hustled by cajolery or force, taking the path of Man.

"From the other side of the earth, the West provides Moscow with books and ideas, theories and machines; and the result is an imperious need to bring the fine Asiatic madness under the control of the rigorous logic of the West. In the streets, on the trolley cars, in the offices you are confronted by rough, stern men, men consumed by a fixed idea, all system, action and logic, as different as possible from those weary dreamers and mystics who used to abound in Russian literature before the Revolution. I stopped at a corner of Sverdlova Square, and standing on my tiptoes I peered through a window. A school. The walls were covered with Red flags, and on the flags they had pinned photographs, postal cards, sketches and newspaper clippings representing Lenin. I could see Lenin as a tiny child, chubby, laughing and curly-headed; then as a young boy looking fresh and hard in a student's uniform. Then as my eye went up the wall, scanning the succession of likenesses, I could see the violent, sarcastic mask of the great warrior gradually emerging. I could not see the pupils, only the head of the schoolmistress who was standing up and talking in a low, warm voice. She was about fifteen years old, and her face was hard, obsessed, without charm.

"The rhythm of Soviet Russia is masculine. Men and women are dedicated to hard work. The U.S.S.R. is perhaps the only country today where the men are superior to the women. Before the Revolution it was the women of Russia who were going ahead; the atmosphere was saturated with intuitions, premonitions and yearnings, and woman with her intuitive qualities, her passion and her propensity for yielding to the impulse of the heart, with her capacity for sacrifice, inevitably took the lead. But now men have gotten the upper hand: the vague desires have turned into concrete realities; the idea has to be adapted to necessity, and passion has to be subordinated to a rigorous, exact discipline. That's why Russia's rhythm today is masculine. Russia has a tendency to become Americanized—that is, to envisage reality in the most practical way and to use the most modern methods for the reconstruction of individual and collective life. The danger threatening the whole edifice is so serious that unconsciously all strong souls in Russia race in the direction that spells safety—that is, into the realm of action. And so in this arduous drive the men get worn out very early; they spend themselves completely in a few years, and others come in masses from the remote reaches of the steppes and the Russian forests to replace them. The idea is very young still and it is greedy. It wants men. In no country of the world do men use up their energies with such frenzy, gusto and speed.

"Traveling around Moscow as I have been doing, you

65

find a second basic impression crystallizing in you: you have entered a fortress of partisans. Yes, poor Sou-ki, you have come to a city at war, bristling with towers and battlements. The enemies are approaching and the knights make haste to don their coats of mail behind the great bolted gates. In Moscow the air you breathe is fraught with preparation for war. Walk in the parks or streets, go into schools, factories or commissariats, attend their games or festivals, everywhere you smell the sharp tang of powder. A great threat and a great hope hang suspended over all their heads.

"One morning as I was walking through Red Square, I suddenly heard the tramp of marching feet. Soon Red soldiers were coming on in close ranks: pointed Mongol helmets, gray cloaks trailing the ground, and faces wearing a look of sober exaltation. Red Square echoed like a drum. Passers-by got out of the way, and a little old woman crossing the square with her basket of apples let out a shrill scream as her beautiful red apples were strewn over the big stones. The close ranks were advancing at a rapid, savage gait. The officer went in front and began a wild song. When he passed in front of me, I saw that his mouth was twisted, the veins of his temples were frightfully swollen, and though the morning air was icy cold, sweat poured down his forehead. He sang alone for a few seconds, and as he walked along, you thought he was leading some mad, delirious dance. Then suddenly the song burst like a storm from all the soldiers' breasts, and Red Square shook like a battlefield.

"The crowd had queued up expectantly in front of Lenin's mausoleum, which was dripping wet and all aglitter. In the misty air I could make out the faces vaguely: big muzhiks, lean workers, sad little Chinese men, handsome German boys. . . . For long hours they waited in the mud, shivering, their eyes fixed on the Holy Sepulcher of the Red Christ. Suddenly a big block in front of the door moved: the guardian was opening the entrance. The crowd slowly filtered into the black hole and disappeared. There was a descent; it was warm and I could hear people's hearts beating. When the dull, heavy countenances of the muzhiks in front of me suddenly lit up, I craned my neck and saw the bald skull of Lenin! There he lay in his worker's blouse, his right fist clenched tight, his left hand open on his breast. An atmosphere of quiet serenity and fulfilment hovered over his sleeping head. In this bald skull, Tchita, and behind these closed eyelids all of Russia was crying out, asking for help. Lenin was the strongest soul in Russia, and consequently had the greatest responsibility. He began the march alone, poor, without arms or friends. He invaded the endless spaces of Czarist Russia. What did this little traveler in the worker's cap want? To overthrow the empire, to expel the Czar, the generals, the noblemen, the priests and the bourgeoisie. To create a new world. This simple man, stretched out in front of me after the terrible weariness of the day, was sleeping the sleep of the just. He had come into this world and had fulfilled his duty.

"When I returned to the surface, I scrutinized the men and women eagerly. I saw their eyes flashing, I observed the play of light on their faces and the nervous gestures they made with their hands. Worn coats, leather blouses, big boots, shaven heads. And little by little I discovered that all these disparate masses are bound together in a deep unity. Individuality is subject to a superindividual rhythm. This is the third great impression which has gripped me in Moscow. Here there is faith. Faith has always and necessarily had this consequence: it unites effort and establishes order. It gives man a strength deeper than his intellect. It makes him yield to a rhythm higher than his own desires and interests. The fire that burns in the great Communists of the U.S.S.R. proceeds from a source greater than their own petty egos. It is the fire of a demon.

"A demon is breathing over our time. 'I am coming. I

67

have no pity!' it cries. 'I am the future!' I hear this cry, Tchita, and I think of you, I think of Ni-nel, and I am disturbed. Yes, yes, Tchita, do not weep! I am a weak man and I must die. Make a strong man out of our Ni-nel, Tchita."

After writing this letter to his wife, Sou-ki crumpled into the corner of the sofa, exhausted. His frightfully wasted face was radiant. His cheeks were flaming. His eyes with their heavy violet lids stared into a corner of the room where a photograph of Lenin as a child was hanging. He gazed and gazed and felt happy. Sou-ki saw countless armies of white children . . . in red ties. He heard shouts of joy far off. . . . Countless armies of yellow children . . . in red ties. He heard more shouts of joy. . . . Countless armies of Negro children . . . in red ties.

6

WHEN AZAD SET FOOT on Russian soil, his big worn-out body trembled in agitation. Batum. Magnolias, banana trees, luxuriantly beautiful mandarin orange trees, leafless Japanese *khourmas*, lacquered and laden with red fruit. He hurried along the clinking pebble path of the tropical garden. His simple, ardent heart leapt. He gazed at the warm blue sea. Far away on the edge of the horizon, he could see the inaccessible peaks of the Caucasus shining clearly.

Ten years before, Azad had traveled these same areas mounted on a thin, nervous horse. He would make sudden forays into villages, revolver in hand, hunting for bandits, kulaks, speculators and Whites. On his breast Azad could feel the tiny hard identity mark of the Chekist. What suffering he had endured! What suffering he had inflicted! Always faithful to the Idea, this fiery Armenian had never been able to surrender to the rigorous discipline of the Party. He had always fought as an independent. As soon as the moment of exaltation passed, his activity came to an end.

Azad was a stormbird and could not resign himself to the everyday tasks of patient construction. He went to Italy, to Spain, to America, a tireless agitator. He was cast into prison and liberated. Everywhere he created around him the tumultuous atmosphere he required in order to breathe. Now he had returned to his own vast land. In his ebullient joy he laughed and wept as he strolled along the seashore all alone. Wasn't he at last treading the soil of Paradise? The air was pure: the

Czars were gone, as well as the grand dukes, White generals, prostitutes and speculators! The great dream he had conceived in the time of hunger and blood now loomed before him as a reality. If he could only linger a little while in these Caucasus Mountains where he had struggled so hard, and see and touch this marvelous soviet reality here, before going on to Moscow! A sudden fit of impatience came over Azad. He walked faster, no longer wishing to be alone.

The Soviets. The simple, coarse faces of sailors and workers; and a single intellectual countenance belonging to a thin, red-bearded monkish fellow who was attractive and talkative. A little Jew with a black goatee opened a brief case crammed with papers and spread the contents on his knees. Bending toward Azad, he arrayed figures, drew lines, twisted this way and that, and jumped up on his chair. As he expatiated, a border of white foam appeared around his lips.

"Everything's going well, production is rising . . . rising . . . wheat, coal, oil, electric stations, co-operatives, collectives . . ."

Azad listened enthralled. He hugged the Jew, then turned and hugged the stocky, bull-necked president.

"Long live the world revolution!" he shouted.

The president got up and talked emotionally, while a taciturn young worker alongside him, with a shaven head, bit his lips and thought: "The president babbles; the president is sentimental; we'll have to get a new president." A gleam suffused his gloomy eyes.

The little man drew more documents out of his brief case: statistics on colored diagrams. Before Azad's eyes he spread the red, blue and green columns that got bigger and bigger with every year until they gaily wrested themselves away from the white glazed-paper background and vanished in the air. The little man wet the tips of his fingers with saliva and leafed through the sheets. Black arrows flew back and forth like swallows. Circles and

70

triangles in violet, Saxon blue or orange . . . Azad's eyes were dazzled: out of the statistics, butterflies and birds of paradise were taking wing and filling the morning air with splashes of bright color. There was a silence. With his hands and knees buried in the gay statistics, Azad lapsed into meditation for a moment. His whole hard life of roving and fighting and starving passed before his feverish eyes. Then the terrible years of the revolution—years of blood, famine, fear . . . He had sown in blood and mire, and now the harvest was piled up in his hands and on his lap! With a smile of exhilaration he bowed his head and suddenly burst into tears. "What a driveling idiot!" thought the young worker to himself with a frown, and he got up, tightened his belt and went out.

Noontime. On the outskirts of Batum, where two years before a huge orchard of mandarin orange trees had flourished. Today an Armenian engineer, fiery-eyed and extremely thin, got up on a towering oil pipe and made a sweeping gesture around him. He was showing Azad the magical transformation of the soil. All the mandarin trees pulled out by the roots, hundreds of workers at their jobs, immense oil depots, the new naphtha distillery that was going up . . . The pale features of the Communist engineer glowed as he orated with arms outstretched.

"Everything in reinforced concrete . . . everything in iron . . . speed . . . economy . . . exportation . . ."

Azad listened in rapture to the sweet melody of the figures and the plans.

"The three stages already behind us . . . War Communism . . . Renovation of existing machinery . . . Modernization of the old factories . . . Now we're creating . . . Vast plans . . . Giant electrical centers . . . A railroad linking the cotton of Turkestan with the wheat of Siberia . . . A colossal canal from the Volga to the Don . . . Tractor factories . . . Agricultural machines . . . Indus-

71

trialization to the limit! . . . The peasant surrounded by electric wires. Lenin's great dream of iron!"

His fluttering eyes wet with tears, Azad clasped the engineer's hands.

A ruined building: the prison where the English tortured the Reds. The ex-blacksmith Savinkof, who had risen to a top managerial post under the Soviets, pushed Azad into a suffocating cell.

"It was here," he said, "that I stayed for long months, awaiting death."

With his hand, which still bore the blacksmith's calluses, he pointed out bloodstains on the damp walls. Here and there one could still make out the crudely scratched names of companions of his who had starved to death, or been strangled, or gone mad. A smile played about Savinkof's brutal, childish mouth as he told the old stories about the events of ten years before. His shaven head, tight leather belt and high Russian boots gave him a look of fierce latent strength.

"The Latin peoples are a vanishing race," commented Savinkof, summing up his experiences in his own way. "They go into the enemy's territory, make contact with a new idea and soon get contaminated by it. Then they go to pieces and fraternize with the enemy. The Anglo-Saxons are the dominant race of the present; their race is still unexhausted and cruel. They invade their enemy's territory and kill him without remorse. The Russians are the race of the future: chaotic, barbarous, full of contradictions. They approach their enemy, kiss him on the mouth, ask his pardon and kill him. A scene quite incomprehensible to a Latin soul or an Anglo-Saxon was often repeated among us during the civil wars: before killing his enemy, the conqueror, whether Red or White, kissed him on the mouth, as on Easter day, saying to him: 'Batyushka, little brother, forgive me; I have to kill you!' "

Azad was nervously chewing on his moustache. With a

sudden movement he put his hand over Savinkof's mouth.

"I know," he said. "I know. Keep quiet, Comrade Savinkof!"

Prisons, clinics, clubs, schools . . . Azad was tired out. On the way home he ran into a humble Communist funeral. A cart . . . the red-draped coffin . . . the young woman seated beside the coffin leaning on it and watching the passers-by . . . the horse with garlands of red paper flowers. The driver whipped the horse and they sped away as if they were in a hurry.

Azad arrived back home. He was lodging with his old friend, Nikolai Darian, a worker. They had known each other in the factories of Milan, and had fought side by side in the civil wars. Now Darian was unemployed and isolated, suspected of oppositionism and of being an anarchist. Azad found his friend in the act of quarreling with his wife—a robust, jolly Georgian woman. She was demanding that her last-born child, a two-year-old boy, be baptized in the church. The father was pounding the table with his fists and hurling insults at church, priests and God.

"Azad," he cried, "you're the one who will have to baptize him now, this very minute, in the name of Lenin."

"Well," retorted his wife, "then tomorrow I'll baptize him in the church in the name of Christ."

The old worker flew into a rage. Snatching the child from his mother's arms, he wrapped him up in the red tablecloth, put a postal card with Lenin's picture on it into the child's hands, and lit an oil lamp for candles. The child started to whimper, while the woman eyed her husband merrily.

"All right, old man! All right, old man! Have your whim," she said. "Tomorrow you'll see. You may name him Lenin, or Marx, or Devil; but I'll baptize him tomorrow and give him my father's name, Mitrofane!"

73

Azad laughed. "All right, Katinka Mitrofanovna, here goes," he told her. I'm baptizing him. Come on! One, two, three!"

He lifted the child into his arms with a laugh; but as soon as he began to pronounce the ritual formula, Soviet-style, Azad felt something stir within him, and a slight quaver came into his voice.

"I baptize thee not in the name of the Cross, that sign of ignorance and slavery, but in the name of the Red flag, symbol of labor and of life. With one same love, love the workers of every country, every race and every color. With one same hatred, hate the kings, the speculators and the priests of the whole world. Be a loyal companion to Lenin; hold ever high and steady the flag of science; and fight to the death for the Third International. Thy name is Profsoïous!"

The mother, who had taken refuge in the kitchen, came back. She seized the child, lit a big fire, heated some water and put in some bay leaves blessed in church on Easter Day. Then she began furiously rubbing the little body that had just been baptized in air. All the while the protesting child was emitting frantic shrieks.

Satisfied, Nikolai Darian poured some tea and brought out bread, fruit and a bit of cheese. Azad talked about the marvelous things he had seen during the day; his eyes and ears were still bursting with them. Darian responded with amused sarcasm.

"Poor Azad, so you're still innocent!" he gibed. "Words, words, factories in the air . . . Don Quixotes!"

"Shut up!" Azad shouted, and started to deliver a speech.

But Darian got carried away and kept on:

"The workers are masters! Poor Azad! Some of them, yes . . . They spend their time in noisy arguments in the party cell, the *yacheika*. . . . The others, the great mass—slaves! Yes, yes, don't laugh, old man, slaves! What Soviets? What suffrage? Election? How stupid you are,

74

Azad! Someone comes to the factory with a big brief case under his arm. He says: 'Elections!' Right away, music—drums, trumpets, flutes. 'The International.' The workers follow in a queue-leu-leu. Everybody arrives. The party secretary proposes his candidates. Who are they? No one knows them—and no one wants them. Who's against? The secretary stretches out his neck and glares at us in rage . . . he gnashes his teeth . . . he glares at us . . . Who's against? Against? Oh, nobody! Who dares, when he's left unemployed! A few people, the bravest ones, vote with their feet by discreetly departing. The rest of us raise our hands, every last one of us, and shout, 'Da zdravstvuyet!' Then at once, the drums and the flute. 'The International.' The masquerade is over."

Azad rose with fire in his eyes and laid a rough hand on Darian's shoulders.

"Stop mocking, you animal," he bade him. "Shut up! You're lying! You're an anarchist, you've been unemployed, and you're vengeful! No! No! Shut up!"

Just then Darian's eldest son came in. Boots, blue blouse pulled in at the waist, a strong body and a hard eye. He had overheard, and he cast a severe glance at his father.

"Nikolai Darian," he said dryly, "you must look out for yourself. You get worked up too much. Take care!"

"Is this the Chekist speaking?" asked Darian ironically.

"Yes, Nikolai Darian, it's your son, the Chekist."

After a moment's silence he turned to Azad and addressed him in a firm, sad tone.

"Comrade Azad," he said, "if you have come to us here looking for Paradise, go away, go away quickly! Neither paradise nor hell; just this Earth! We are working and groping and building. Comrade Azad, excuse us. That is all we can do."

"You're too restrained, Comrade Alexeï Nikolayevich," answered Azad with irritation. "In our time, we wanted to turn the world upside down."

"And you did turn it upside down, Comrade Azad. And now we have the very serious task of building on the ruins you left. Stubborn patience and silence: quite different virtues . . . We want to be left in peace, Comrade Azad."

Then Alexeï Nikolayevich poured some tea, cut a slice of bread, spread out *Pravda*, and began to eat and read without paying any more attention to the two old men.

Azad turned livid. Was this boy going to call him to order? We want to be left in peace! Well, my little fellow, I'm not going to leave you in peace!

Azad took a step forward. But Darian pulled him back.

"Let's get out of here!" Darian muttered to him. "Let's go out!"

Out of the corner of his eye Alexeï Nikolayevich saw them go.

"Old riffraff!" he said and frowned.

Azad did not stay with his friend long; he wanted to be alone.

"Run along," Azad cried, "don't say any more to me. I want to be left alone. I'm going off to a desert island and raise pigs. I hate man. If he has ceased to be hungry, if he's eating, he gets fat and becomes an animal. If he's hungry, he snarls, and gets blind like you! I like pigs!"

Darian went off laughing. Behind him Azad heard a gay voice saying, "I like pigs too!"

Turning around, Azad saw a woman with big blue eyes and a pale, emaciated, almost starving face. She was smiling at him. Her shoes were out of shape and run down at the heels. After a moment's hesitation, Azad flung his arms wide and dashed toward her.

"Anna Georgiyevna!" he exclaimed.

How she had aged! What proud sadness in her laughing eyes! Azad gazed at her, unable to control his grief. Memories flashed through his brain: the beautiful Anna Georgiyevna, in her humble, ragged *shuba*, on horseback at the battle of Perekop . . . Anna Georgiyevna, exhausted, her eyes red from insomnia, presiding over the revolutionary tribunal. Without a tremor this little hand was signing the death warrants of all the infamous ones; this little hand was bent on purging the earth. Another flash: a city in the Ukraine . . . With the Whites approaching, the comrades had abandoned hope and were preparing to flee. Anna Georgiyevna took off her leather cap and laid it on the table. "I'm going to stay," she said simply.

"Anna Georgiyevna!" Azad embraced his old comrade, caressing her thin shoulders and her emaciated hands. They talked . . . and talked . . . Recollections of joys and sorrows came crowding back. Azad asked eager questions about their old companions. Mad . . . dead . . . in exile. That one in power, and grown a little stout . . .

"And you, Anna Georgiyevna?"

Anna smiled.

"I give English lessons. Sometimes I'm hungry; sometimes I'm not hungry. . . ."

"I can't bear any more of this," Azad exclaimed.

"What are you going to do, then?" said Anna in her sweet voice as she took Azad's feverish hand.

"What?" said Azad in reply. "But are you blind? Don't you see? There's something not right in our Russia! What it is I don't know. . . . There's a stream of mire . . . of red mire. . . . Let's get together, we old fighters, we honest ones, the ones with fire. Let's create a different stream, even if we have to make it out of blood. Let's climb the hill again. Let's purge the earth once more! Can't this little hand sign the death warrant any more, Anna?"

Anna shook her head sadly. With maternal pity she gazed upon this elderly child who was unwilling and unable to understand.

"Don't you understand, Azad?" she said gently, trying to quiet him. "Our role is finished. We are ghosts. We had a job to do and we have done it. We are drained out. Our mission is at an end. Don't you realize it, Azad? Let's step aside, that's the more dignified way. Let's step aside without complaining. Did we work in order to get recompensed?"

"We worked in order to create a juster world! Where is it?"

"It's coming, I'm sure, Azad; but it's coming very slowly. We have to have patience. We old fighters, as you call us, have no patience. That's why we fought well; it's also why we must step aside now. We are in the way and a detriment. Don't you understand, Azad?"

"No, I don't understand," Azad answered.

"That doesn't matter," said Anna with a laugh. "You will understand."

The next day Azad wandered alone on the outskirts of Batum. He was feeling sad. Yes, yes, now he could see. The eyes he met were a little dull . . . The faces downcast . . . The fire—where was the fire? "I no longer feel at home," he said to himself, "I'm roaming around a strange U.S.S.R. Red tape . . . shopwindows with furs and jewelry . . . yacheika . . . vodka . . . I'm stifling!" He suppressed his cries of grief and anger. His spirit was floundering. Azad walked fast. Down in the valley the tropical trees were darkening and the sky was suddenly full of clouds. Flashes of lightning silently came and went in the distance. Copper glints showed in the far-off sea. Azad hurried on. He came upon a cluster of little white-washed houses and a tavern among some eucalyptus trees. Some stools were brought and little cups of Turkish coffee prepared. Villagers drew near, curious and suspicious.

"Where do you come from? Why are you traveling? Where are you going?" they asked.

They talked and argued and complained: taxes . . . bread . . . in the old days . . .

Azad got impatient.

"Come, fellows," he said, "let's be frank! You!" he shouted to a plumpish peasant who looked like a rogue, "come here. How is life today? Look me in the face!"

"Very good, comrade, very good. There's only this:

before the Revolution each of us had two changes of clothing and now, ten years after the Revolution, we have only one."

"Don't complain, friends!" said Azad. "In some places people don't have even one change of clothing."

"Then do they go around stark naked, comrade?" an old man asked.

And since he got no reply, he shook his head, and added: "They must have had the Revolution twenty years ago!"

Some of the bystanders laughed, while others stole discreetly away.

One old muzhik came up to Azad, doffed his skullcap, made the sign of the cross, and started to talk to him.

"Christ has sent you here, *batyushka*," he said. "Help us. What are we to do? Give us some advice! They tell us: 'This is how you must cultivate your field; here are ploughs that are the last word, machines, fertilizers. Work! Here are pamphlets, read them, and open your eyes!' The most intelligent people read, *batyushka*, and open their eyes. They cultivate better and produce more. They begin to satisfy their hunger and to breathe. When they sit down to the table in the evening, they are grateful to God. Suddenly the village Soviet comes snooping around, and asking questions. Then they shout: 'Kulak! Kulak!' Right away, crushing taxes, the cow is sold, the horse is sold, and they sink into misery once more. What are we to do, *batyushka*? Cultivate just enough land to keep from starving. Then they'll leave us alone. That's the way!"

"But the total production in the Union will go down," exclaimed Azad furiously. "That's a catastrophe!"

"How will it be a catastrophe? I'll have something to eat."

"But how about the others?"

"Every man for himself."

Azad got up, waving his long arms.

79

"The devil take you, you dirty bourgeois beasts!" he screamed at them.

A broad-shouldered man of about forty, with a bony, pock-marked face, arrived at that moment. With a laugh he extended his hand to Azad, exclaiming in a warm, rather husky voice:

"Comrade Azad, don't you recognize me? I am Ibrahim —Ibrahim Chabanof!"

Yes, yes, Azad remembered! The story was coming back to him.

His native city, Astrakhan. A White general engaged in espionage. He kept a tavern opposite the workers' club. "We got orders, Ibrahim and I, to kill him. I went in and asked him for some wine. As he bent down to the tap, I pulled out my revolver; he noticed it, leapt up and screamed. Ibrahim, who was waiting at the door, rushed in, knife in hand, and ripped his belly open. He screamed again. The police flocked into the tavern; I got away. They arrested Ibrahim and threw him into prison."

Now they were sitting in the tavern, and Ibrahim was telling his story.

"I left Astrakhan and fled to Kalmuck. When they asked me who I was, I started to whine and said: 'A Persian. I had a shop, but the Reds have ruined me.' 'Do you know how to teach?' they asked me. 'Sure I do,' I said. So I became a schoolmaster. Among the Kalmucks I found other comrades. We worked and the Red circle expanded. One day we got big news: the Reds were on their way down to the Caucasus! At the head of eleven Kalmucks, I left to look for the Red army. On our way we picked up Armenian comrades, Moslems, Greeks, Russians. We were all brothers. We suffered from hunger and cold. Our hair got long as manes, and icicles hung from our moustaches. One night we burned some railroad coaches to get warm.

" 'Why burn the coaches?' someone said. 'They might be good for something.'

" 'Yes, to get warm,' I answered. 'When we come into power, we'll make twice as many with our own hands, three times as many. Now let's get warm, comrades.'

"We arrived at Vladikavkas. Gingiskori was there with his Red soldiers.

" 'Comrades, today it's the city or death!' he cried to us. 'Forward!'

"We dashed into the streets, some with rifles, some with cans of oil and others with machine guns. Tsik! Tsik! Tsik! We shot with machine guns mounted on our heads, yelling 'Hurrah! Hurrah!' all the time. We advanced and within two hours we had taken the city. We were in rags and starving to death. So we forced our way into the bourgeois houses, barged into the kitchens and ate. We opened the wardrobes, and put on the clothes. It was war!"

After finishing this story, Ibrahim Chabanof sat in silence, still shaking and perspiring. He lit a cigarette, then straightway crushed it out on the table. He poured wine, filling the two glasses. His eye roved about the peaceful, commonplace tavern, where the proprietor, napkin in hand, was carelessly chasing the flies away. He scowled.

"Oh, the war!" he finally muttered. "Now we are ruined!"

Azad gave him a startled look.

"You too, Ibrahim? Shut up!"

Ibrahim spat on the ground.

"Lice!" he said. "Lice!"

"Who are lice?"

"The kulak, the Nepman, the bureaucrat! They're sucking our blood."

Azad silenced his friend.

"Say no more," he commanded. "The Idea has just been born, Ibrahim. It's hungry and it eats. Let it eat."

"No, no!" exclaimed Ibrahim in a choking voice. "It eats and gets fat and stops moving. In order to act, man has to feel hunger, Comrade Azad. Hunger! Hunger!" He struck the table with his big fist clenched, as he repeated the word. "Our Communists today, what do they look for? Comfort! Do you hear that, Azad? Comfort! Bah!" Once more Ibrahim spat disgustedly on the ground. "Do you hear, Azad? Comfort!"

Azad got up and stood for a moment at the door, contemplating the tilled fields and the plump crows hopping in the furrows. Then he turned back toward the table and grabbed Ibrahim by the shoulder.

"What are we going to do?" he asked.

"Wait."

"Wait for what?"

"For the new revolution. It's coming," said Ibrahim with a laugh, while Azad watched him in silence.

"It's coming," Ibrahim went on. "Get ready, old Chekist. I'm putting myself under your orders once again. I love you because you have no pity."

Azad made no reply, but a noiseless sob constricted his throat.

"Is it true, Comrade Azad, that you have never felt repentance for your actions?"

"Why repent?" Azad responded. "I have never acted in my own interest. I was hungry, cold, exhausted, and I wanted to sleep. But a hand clutched my throat and threw me out of my bed into the street. You know that very well, Ibrahim."

"Azad, didn't you feel pity just once, just one time only?"

Azad straightened himself up and knit his thick eyebrows. "Why do you ask me? I don't want you to."

Ibrahim placed his hand on his friend's knees, and a caressing tone came into his husky voice. "Don't be offended, comrade! Don't talk. Let's drink!"

But Azad left his glass untouched.

"Once, one time only . . ." he said.

82

Azad fell into meditation. He had become very pale. When he suddenly started talking, he was gasping.

"Nine years ago," he began, "I was working in the Polish Cheka at Kiev. They notified me that a Polish spy, a Jewess, had been arrested. 'Hurry to the prison right away,' the chief commanded me, 'and open the inquiry. This Jewess holds the strands of a vast conspiracy in her hands. She is the bishop's mistress, she knows everything. Make her talk.'

"It was the month of January. I threw my miserable sheepskin *shuba* around my shoulders and ran to the prison. They had isolated the Jewess in a little cell. 'She doesn't want to eat or drink or sleep, but she is calm,' the guard told me.

"I opened the cell door. In the dim reddish light I saw a woman standing against the wall. She stared at me with a mocking expression. For a moment I felt my knees folding under me. I had never seen so beautiful a woman: blue-eyed, black-browed, as lithe as a serpent. I controlled myself, for I knew about all the temptations and I had no fear. Gruffly I began to question her. She laughed and smiled, calmly shifted her position against the wall and arranged the curls on her forehead. But she did not answer.

"I departed without having gotten a word out of her. Feeling extremely unhappy and tired, I went to see the chief. 'I beg you to excuse me from this duty,' I pleaded. 'I like this woman more than I should. I can't be impartial. Tell someone else to do it.'

"The chief was irritated. 'You're the one I'm sending,' he said. 'In this affair we're not judging the woman only. We're judging you as well, Comrade Azad!'

"I obeyed. The next day I went to the prison again. The Jewess got up and kept her arms quietly folded over her breast as she listened to me. I swore to her that she would be permitted to live if she would expose the plot. After a moment's silence, she said with a laugh, 'I want to die!'

83

"I told her my whole life-story about all my sufferings: how I had become a Communist; about our dreams of humanity and justice. I grew eloquent, for I loved this woman and I shuddered at the thought of her death. When I had finished my sad confession, she shook her long black hair and said, 'I want to die!' 'No, no,' I said, 'you will not die! Don't meddle with politics any more, and your life will be safe!'

" 'If you let me go free,' she replied, 'I shall put myself at the head of the conspiracy again. I shall go to Poland and lead the Poles. I hate you!'

"I went home in grief. My colleagues were intrigued by the situation. When I implored them to intercede with the chief, they laughed. 'But if you don't want to see her any more, sign her death warrant,' they suggested.

"Sign her death warrant! Suddenly an idea flashed into my mind, and I hurried to the chief. 'I want to marry this woman!' I told him. 'You assume full responsibility,' he answered. 'Marry her!'

I ran to the prison happily. The woman burst into laughter and eyed my worker's hands, my sheepskin *shuba*, my uncouth face with a look of disgust. She said no. I entreated her. Then suddenly springing up, she took her fur down from the wall where it hung. While the whole cell was filled with the lovely fragrance of a woman of the aristocracy, she wrapped herself in her fur with a faint shiver, and said dryly, 'I accept. Let's go!' "

Azad paused. He had a parched, inflamed feeling in his throat. He drained a glass of wine, then another and another. . . . His poor fingers were unsteady. Ibrahim, who knew very well the terrible end of this love story, felt compassion for his friend.

"Let's be off, Comrade Azad," he said. "It's late. Look, it's stopped raining."

He rose, pulling Azad by the arm. But Azad jerked himself away.

"Are you afraid?" he asked with a sneer.

Ibrahim sat down again, beads of sweat trickling down his forehead.

Azad went on. He was ghastly pale, talking very rapidly, mangling the words. "The next day we were married. One night six months later I killed her. I caught her rummaging through my papers . . . I followed her into the street . . . She was running, she had not seen me. She went into the home of a White. I overtook her in the courtyard underneath a staircase. I emptied my revolver into her head. That's the whole story."

Azad gritted his teeth; they were chattering.

"Are you cold?" asked Ibrahim.

Azad smiled sadly. "Since then," he said, "I've never had pity."

7

TIFLIS. A GEORGIAN BANQUET. Bottles of marvelous wine: Tjinandali, Napareuli, Teliani; tiny pieces of skewered meat, *shashlik*. More bottles of wine gurgling as they were passed from hand to hand, joyous and bubbling, remaining on the table a split second, then quickly staggering away and disappearing. Levan Menchvili, a great patriot and a poet who appealed to the emotions, was chosen *Tamadan*, or "dictator" of the banquet. Four musicians arrived. Popular songs rent the air with the sweet heroic sounds of the national instruments: the *sandsavari*, the *tchianouri*, the *tari*, and the *dhaïra*. Little by little their hearts were warmed and thawed out: the mystic lucidity of wine helps men recognize their brothers. They recited verses, kissed each other, banished the misunderstandings that intrude in the cursed moments when Reason prevails.

Geranos, tanned by the sun, was drinking away, his dark head full of the Caucasus. Just tonight he had returned from his long wanderings in the mountains and villages of Georgia. His eyes were still dazed. Elegant silver-plated belts; long, finely wrought daggers; curled moustaches; monumental headgears of sheepskin; music; wine; frenzied dances; a blazing sun caressing and ripening these fair human products. The autumn dragged along in the forests, blood-red. The barberry bushes glistened like gorgeous spots of blood among the russet chestnut trees and the golden birches. In the bottom of the wild valleys, the great Kura River unwound like a snake for days and days on end: greenish, brilliant. Geranos felt as if his head were flooded. He tasted the velvety wine of Kakhetie and for a while permitted the arrow of his soul to soar away in a voluptuous arc. Wasn't he a free man? Wasn't he the master of his own impulses and his own will? The unfamiliar woman next to him seemed to have a shining halo that absorbed her face. She had turned toward him. Geranos heard only her caressing voice softly reciting a song of Our Lady of Georgia, Queen Tamara:

She passed through a village and this village turned into a city. She arrived in a city and this city became Tiflis. The Georgian princes followed her. The Tartar beys followed her; the Turkish pashas and the Persian emirs. . . . All the long-horned stags ran before her arrows. . . .

Once again Geranos saw the tops of the Georgian mountains crowned with their ruined castles, haunted by the bloody or sensual legends of the great Amazon:

On her head Tamara wears a warrior's helmet. Long earrings dangle on both sides of her head. Her eyes are of sapphire, her teeth of pearl, her neck of jasper. She wears a coat of mail. Her steed is sable-colored. Beneath the coat of mail, a soft, soft satin . . . The princes, beys, pashas, emirs do not spare their steeds, hoping that Tamara will cast a glance their way. But Tamara is not thinking of them. For her favorite falcon has flown away beyond the Kura, perched itself upon a cliff and no longer wants to return. . . .

The caressing voice of the strange woman at his side fell silent.

All of a sudden Geranos' spirit was overwhelmed with sadness. Above it floated the pale white body of Tamara. Geranos relived the surcharged day when he had ventured on horseback into the steep gorge leading to the city of the caverns, to Vardzia, the "Fortress of the Roses." There, inside the caves carved in the flanks of the mountain, the beautiful queen had spent her broiling summers with her legendary lovers. A long, voluptuous, painful cavalcade beneath the blazing sun.

At certain moments, Geranos had had the sensation of holding in his arms the beautiful body of a woman who had fainted. And tonight he could still feel, as though written on his own warm bosom, the epitaph inscribed by popular imagination on her royal tomb: "I was once Queen Tamara. I filled the sea and land with my name. I made the fish pass from the Black Sea to the Caspian Sea. My horses entered Isfahan and I sank my sword into the Square of Istanbul. Then, having finished all these deeds, I carried off to the other world nine meters of linen."

Suddenly Geranos had shuddered there among the shadows rising up from the valley of the Kura. It was no longer Tamara speaking, but the whole earth—as voluptuous, as powerful and beautiful as Tamara, and as ephemeral.

Abruptly the *Tamadan's* imperious voice broke in:

"Let us sing: *Horovela!*"

The first tones sounded with solemn passion. Little by little the melody grew sweet, then terribly sad. With a leap it thundered out, full of anger and hate. Toward the end it became restrained again, like a great heart resigning itself. . . . The *Tamadan* spoke to Geranos to explain it:

"This song should be our national anthem, the national anthem of the whole world. First the farmer is talking with his God, and then with his children who are working at his side. He is giving them courage. Then suddenly he gets furious. He speaks to his cruel master who is away now. He leans over his oxen, beats them, then caresses them, calls them his brothers, and exhorts them all—oxen, children and God—to get into harness and work."

Geranos raised his glass of Tjinandali. While traveling around the Caucasus, he had seen this dark, calculating creature nestled in the earth, the Peasant: his small eyes lying in wait behind his bristly eyebrows, like two noxious beasts at bay; his hairy arms hanging down to his knees like gorilla's paws, and his nails packed with black earth. Geranos had no love for the Peasant. He raised his glass:

"I drink not to suffering humanity, but to those who suffer for humanity!"

The woman next to Geranos was shocked. Geranos felt his vulture's soul liberated by the wine:

"I do not love man," he cried. "I love the someone inside him who is struggling for liberty."

"But this someone *is* man," his friend, the fanatical Communist Achod, interrupted angrily. Geranos turned around to look at his friend. Ah! How this new idea stirred the young people, till they were possessed and consumed by it! All at once Geranos loved this fierce brother at his side. He put his hand on his shoulder and said:

"How do you know?"

A spark of lightning flashed through Geranos' eyes. When he spoke, the words came from deep inside him:

"We must love not human beings, but the inhuman flame that devours them. We must fight not for humanity, but for this flame which makes fire out of the damp, crawling, nauseating straw that goes by the name of Humanity."

The *Tamadan* got up again:

"Let us dance!" he commanded.

All the revelers sprang to their feet. Chairs were dragged off to the side. Space was cleared. The demon of the dance seized the bodies and souls of the Caucasus. These refined intellectuals shed all their foreign artificial culture. Beneath their black garments appeared their ancestral *cherkeska* and the *bullet-sakile;* beneath their polished shoes the soft leather *chermes.* And on their belts invisible *handzals* sparkled.

Geranos remained calm and motionless in the midst of the frenzied dancing. He was storing up the surplus energy the wine gave him. He thought blissfully of certain ancient vases with shiny black silhouettes set against a red background. And in the center, holding himself motionless like a column crowned with vine leaves, his eyes sad, his mouth clamped tight, stood Dionysus: the source of the dance, of the joy, of the sacred orgy. All around him the fauns and satyrs and maenads, intoxicated by the wine and lustfulness, had lost their balance. For they could not get their fill of pleasure. They could not drink enough wine. Only the source of the intoxication remained limpid.

"You aren't dancing? Dionysus, I believe, also used to stand motionless."

Geranos turned around. Who was the person who had guessed his joy? He saw a man dressed very soberly and elegantly, who moved with short, fiery movements. His eyes were exalted and cold. Only his smile, broad and controlled and showing beautiful carnivorous teeth, betrayed the hungry sensuality in this disciplined man.

"Grigol Robakidse," said the stranger.

Geranos recognized a brother: a man with mad yearnings who put cruel restraints upon his sacred mania. They went off and sat down by themselves. Suddenly, as if Death kept vigil there, the confession spurted out. Robakidse started talking:

"Yes, yes, we shan't see each other again and that's all right. . . . But we have the time till dawn. I'm a writer; but my art has a mystical Idea. Every man is an ephemeral Son who contains the eternal Father within himself. The purpose of art is to discover the invisible spirit of the Father and to express it through the visible body of the Son. If man can grasp and express nothing but the Son, he creates a merely superficial work of art; if he expresses nothing but abstract ideas, nothing but the Father, he produces not art but metaphysics. The Effort to find the Word able to capture the immortal essence alive in us: this is magic. That's why art is a mysterious science, a veritable theurgy. Words attract and imprison the invisible spirit, force it to become incarnated and to exhibit itself

90

to man. *Sitka*, meaning Utterance, the Word, in Georgian means also seizure and sexual intercourse. The Word must seize, subjugate and fecundate matter. Just as Adam knew woman, so must the Word know Matter."

A smile appeared on Robakidse's sensual lips as he savored a few remaining drops of wine. His eye was still hard and cold.

"The consciousness of the West," he went on, "is dominated by appreciation of the individual; that of the East by a profound sense of union with the Universe. The Westerner has been liberated from the great Whole; the umbilical cord binding him to the Universe has been cut. Forces that have impoverished him and swelled his pride have turned him into a monad that reasons—in other words, that digs moats around itself and dwells in isolation. The Oriental on the other hand is a hybrid; he lives his life of trouble without losing his bonds with the Whole. The Father predominates in the Oriental, the Son in the Westerner. But holy wedlock has already been announced between Asia with her abandonment to the Whole and Europe with its individualistic logicality. We've all received notification of it in red letters. The social revolution in Russia is the visible manifestation of the cosmic revolution which is being worked out in our hearts. A new world is going to be born. A new Myth will arise, and all our relations with things, beings and ideas will be renewed."

Robakidse finished. With his lips closed, his eyes had the gleaming fixity of eyes scanning the desert.

Dawn had already penetrated into the room.

"Rosy-fingered dawn uncovers the East," said Geranos to this brother of his. "At our banquet of poets and *shashliks* tonight, you were the Socrates. Your demon tossed maliciously and voluptuously in the nets of the Word. For a moment I thought I saw Ares entwined with Aphrodite."

"The demon saw the trap too late," answered Robakidse with a laugh. "All the same the cunning fellow got a bit of pleasure in the arms of the Word. Now that day has dawned, it's a good idea to stop the talk. So let's give our conversation the ending that is traditional for Georgian tales: 'From heaven there fell three apples: one for the person who told the tale, another for the person who listened, and the most beautiful one fell into the abyss.'"

Geranos could not sleep. Early in the morning he took a car and went off by himself to a Greek village far away. Elated children crowded around him; the schoolmaster arrived; doors swung open, men and women came running out and mobbed him.

"A Hellene! A Hellene!" they cried.

They offered him honey, nuts, bread.

"Are you happy?" Geranos asked.

Prudent and crafty, the men held their tongues. But one old woman exclaimed: "No! We want to return to our own country."

"Why? Here you have land, cattle, houses, as well as your fathers' graves."

"Yes, but they don't let us lift our heads!"

"What do you mean, 'lift your heads'?"

"Get rich!"

Geranos turned toward an old man listening with his head down, and shook him by the shoulder.

"Which is more precious, in your opinion," Geranos asked, "individual interest or the interest of the community?"

"Individual interest is very sweet," the old man murmured. "You must excuse me, I'm old, I can't feel otherwise. . . ."

"But your son?"

"My son says the opposite. I look backward; he looks ahead. He despises me, but he doesn't tell me so. I love him, but I don't understand him. That's life."

In a corner of the little village square another old man was staring at Geranos. Never had Geranos seen eyes so beautiful and so sad.

"Geronta," he said to him in Greek. "Oh, old man, you seem very much distressed."

"Yes."

"Is someone dead?"

"I have sons; when they pass before my door, they hiss."

As Geranos left the village, he heard a quick step behind him. Turning, he saw a young boy making a sign to him.

"I want to speak to you," the boy called.

About fifteen years old, he had thick black hair and innocent fiery eyes. Beads of perspiration clung to the light down on his cheeks and around his lips. He spoke with great agitation, keeping his eyes on the ground.

"I want to ask you for some advice. Help me!"

"Tell me!"

"I'm a Pioneer, and now I want to become a komsomol, but my parents refuse to let me. Every day my father insults and beats me, and my mother weeps. What am I to do?"

Geranos remained silent. He shuddered. Fathers curse sons; sons despise fathers. Families are torn apart; hearts are torn apart. Geranos put his hand mutely on the boy's shoulder. The boy lifted his eyes and looked at him.

"I want to leave home," he said. "I can't live with my father any longer. Tell me, shall I be doing right? What would you have done in my place?"

For a few anguished moments Geranos thought it over. All at once he seized the young man's hand and pressed it.

"Yes, you must leave home. I hope that someday my own son will leave home as well, like you!"

Geranos went back home with the memory of his son Panteli, in Crete, obsessing his soul. His one friend: he had trained him to follow him and to go beyond him.

"Don't spare me," he whispered, addressing Panteli.

"I'm the monkey, you're the man. I'm the man, you're the man's son."

As soon as he got back to Tiflis, Geranos felt a need to talk to his son.

"Panteli, dear comrade and son," he wrote, "more and more as I travel around the U.S.S.R., I have the inhuman feeling that devoured me even earlier in Greece. What interests me is not man, nor the earth, nor the heavens, but the flame that consumes man and earth and heavens. It isn't Russia that interests me, but the flame consuming Russia. Amelioration of the fate of the masses or of the elite, happiness, justice, virtue: these things that lure so many people do not catch me. Only one thing thrills me: I look for it everywhere, and my eyes follow it with joy and fear. The red line that pierces and passes through men like a rosary of skulls. All I love is this red line, and my sole happiness is to feel it piercing and passing through my own skull, breaking it as it goes. Everything else seems to me ephemeral, smugly philanthropic and vegetarian, unworthy of a soul now emancipated from all hope.

"As you know, Panteli, my own guide is none of the three great guides of the human soul: neither Faust nor Hamlet nor Don Quixote, but Don Ulysses! It is in his ship that I came to the U.S.S.R. I don't have the unquenched thirst of the Western intellectual, nor do I oscillate between yes and no, only to end in total inaction; and I no longer have the ridiculous and sublime impulse of the noble tilter against windmills. I am one of Ulysses' sailors, with heart on fire and mind pitiless and clear. Not the Ulysses who returned to Ithaca, but the other one, who went home and killed off his enemies but one day fled away from his native land because he had suffocated there. In the arctic mist of the North, he has heard a new Siren. The Slavic Siren. And here we stand before her without stopping our ears or tying ourselves to the masts, coming and going in our ship like free men.

We listen to the marvelous song and keep our souls intact. Captain Ulysses, motionless on the prow, is shouting: 'Eh, companions! Open your eyes, your ears, your nostrils, your mouths, your hands; open your minds, fill your entrails!' "

8

WITH HIS FRIEND, Levan Menchvili, the
Tamadan of yesterday, Geranos rambled around the lovely
and voluptuous and somnolent city of Tiflis. It spread
nonchalantly over both banks of the Kura, attractive,
naked and mysterious like a woman. Over the centuries,
impassioned suitors have come to her from every horizon,
bearing in one hand the cross, the crescent or the Red star,
and in the other the sword. Byzantines, Persians, Saracens,
Czarist Russians, Bolsheviks. Genghis Khan pulled her
from her alcove so violently that her crown, the crenelated
"Kala," rolled into the dust. They all enjoyed her body;
no one knew how to win her heart. Even today she
repulses the embraces of the Red soldier.

"In our museum," said Levan Menchvili, "there is a
very beautiful Oriental picture. Seated on a black horse
is a half-nude woman with long, languishing gazelle-like
eyes. A kneeling emir is holding out his trembling hand
and placing it with a gesture of entreaty on the horse's
breast. The woman is happy and pays no attention. She is
Tiflis.

"If Karl Marx had been born at Tiflis," he added, "and
every morning had plunged his ponderous body and
bandit's beard into the warm sulphur water of the
hammam and then strolled, pleasantly weary, under our
flowering trees, I am sure he would have had a different
conception of life, a more human one. The destiny of the
world would have taken a different course."

They stood on the high hill at the foot of the ruined
fortress, the famous Kala. Geranos gazed at the lovely,
bare, reddish trees in the distance, and at the golden-

leaved trees in the narrow valley down below. How autumn dragged along this year through the Caucasus, as if reluctant to die! One afternoon in the gardens of Batum, Geranos had witnessed its birth; he had followed it to Borzhomi, then across the plains and mountains of Imeretia and Mingrelia and into the warm valley of Alazan. And now he found it again, bent over the waters of the great Kura and admiring itself like some royal peacock feathered in tones of gold.

Levan took Geranos' arm and said, with a quaver in his husky voice:

"We want our liberty, we are neither Communists nor reactionaries. We are Georgians!"

He seized a stone from the ancient ruins and showered frenzied kisses upon it.

"Georgia! Georgia!" he exclaimed.

A feeling of indescribable uneasiness came over Geranos. He felt indignant at seeing the fire of this intelligent man consuming itself uselessly, for objectives not only fragmentary but impossible to attain. He lashed out at poor Levan in a biting voice:

"This idyllic dream of an independent Georgia is a chimera unworthy of a thinking brain. In our time Georgia occupies a decisive position geographically and psychologically. It lies between the youthful strength of the soaring Soviet power, with its aspirations to inundate all Asia, and the aged capitalistic power, which tries doggedly to prevent it. Georgia is a mere grain of wheat between the two giant millstones."

"You're a fatalist!"

"I am a realist. I see clearly. I do not belong to the Communist Party. I'm no longer a man of action like you. That enables me to view the bloody tragedy we are living through—the tragedy of our time—with a more disinterested eye, and therefore from a slightly less limited perspective. I see further than you and I am not afraid of consequences.

"Every youthful idea, dear Menchvili, is imperialistic.

It hopes to save the world, as its own apologists claim, or, as its enemies claim, to conquer it. Naturally the world resists. The old ways the world pursues mean comfort for feeble hearts and crafty minds. The new idea takes the offensive. It is young and consequently full of strength and cruelty. What wild beast is more bloody than the tiger? The new idea, poor Menchvili! Well, look how the gentlest of new ideas descended to earth: 'Love one another.' When a particular individual or people would not, or could not, be made to understand this love by peaceful means, it was injected into their brains by splitting their heads open. This barbarous method of proceeding horrifies us; but don't you know that the entire history of the mind is steeped in blood? God, one might say, if you will excuse my using this old-fashioned word, hasn't anything of the socialist or the democrat or the Menshevik about him."

"I lost my only son in the Georgian revolt of 1924," murmured Levan Menchvili. "He was among two hundred young intellectuals whom the Reds piled into railway carriages and shot at."

Geranos got a jolt. Here he was playing with words in perfect freedom; nothing interfered with his ability to contemplate and grasp the abstract ideas from on high. But for the grieving friend beside him, the abstract idea had his son's blood spattered on it. Geranos' voice took on a slightly gentler tone:

"Your grief ought not to disturb your vision, dear Levan. Our individual joys and sorrows do not count, for at every moment and in every detail the destiny of the entire world is at stake. The demon of our time crushes without pity. Why? Because it aims, in the face of all resistance, whether from good or from evil, to drive a little bit forward. You, Levan Menchvili, and all of Georgia, and the U.S.S.R., and England, and the Communist idea, and the capitalistic idea are nothing but instruments, more or less blind instruments, in the hands of this demon."

Geranos and Levan had already come down to the street. Old churches with cone-shaped cupolas, reliefs of Persian lions, Byzantine crosses festooned with pine cones and heavy bunches of grapes. Narrow, shady streets, henna-tinted beards, the open-air bazaar, apples, pomegranates, red pimientos, grapes. The shashlik sputtered on the glowing embers.

"*Gamartchueba!* Victory!"

Levan greeted his friends with a withdrawn expression on his emaciated face. Spying on him out of the corner of his eye, Geranos felt compassion for him. "I walk beside a corpse," he thought.

On a little square in front of the barracks a thin, ugly officer with his mouth contorted was talking to thirty or so conscripts:

"You are not the soldiers of the U.S.S.R., you do not belong to any country! Open your ears, open your eyes, try to understand! Our country has no frontiers. You are the soldiers of the proletarian class in the whole world. The Red flag is not the flag of the U.S.S.R.; it is the international flag of all those who work and suffer. Try to understand!"

The loutish young peasants, enveloped in their long gray cloaks and with the Red star on their foreheads, opened their mouths, craned their necks and tried to understand.

Levan Menchvili walked faster; he had no wish to see or understand. His gray goatee quivered a little.

"What is this odor?" said Geranos to himself. "I walk beside a corpse," he repeated, going on with his thoughts. "This man at my side was once alive and full of good intentions. He denounced injustice and hated violence; he was one of the leading Mensheviks and advocated a just and peaceful understanding between exploiters and exploited. Poor Levan! He too, like his country, is a grain of wheat between two millstones, the bourgeoisie and proletariat. Like a good grain of wheat he occupies a position between those two powers that fight each other and collaborate with each other. He preaches peace, but the big millstones tirelessly proceed with their mission, and as soon as they make a slight movement, they grind him to bits. Levan Menchvili fought against the Czars and was condemned to twenty years' imprisonment. 'I fought for freedom,' he said. When the Bolsheviks came, Levan fought the Bolsheviks because they employed violence. 'I fight for freedom,' he said again.

"One day an Armenian Chekist arrested him and threw him into prison. For three and a half months, Levan awaited his death sentence. Many a time he fell asleep standing up against the window waiting for his turn. Three times he was condemned to death and three times acquitted. They tossed him back and forth between life and death, finding him neither dangerous enough nor innocuous enough. Finally one of his judges, who happened to be a friend of his still, made fun of him in front of the other judges. He mimicked Levan's voice and read some cloyingly sentimental passages from his books. The court rocked with laughter and Levan was saved. When he emerged into the light, he saw that his hair had turned white. He felt no joy, he was too tired. And now he roves around the U.S.S.R. writing books that no one dares publish, seeking employment, and getting shoved aside. Levan does not understand."

In his emotion Geranos brusquely grasped Levan's arm.

"What?" exclaimed Levan, turning with a start.

"Nothing."

Then a few moments afterward: "Did you suffer very much, Levan, in your prison?"

"Yes, in the beginning . . . Later on, I was too tired, and I ceased to suffer. Months of standing by the window . . . about thirty of us crowded into the same cell. The first few days I made several attempts to commit suicide: I couldn't stand the smell. Afterward I got used to it. From time to time, a Red soldier would appear and bark out a few names; we would kiss the companions whose names had been called and give them tobacco; almost always it was their last wish to have something to smoke while they waited for death. Most of them didn't come back any more. Others came back mad. A guard would stick a long needle into their arms, and they would no longer feel the pain. Each time that happened, the guard would say, 'He's crazy.' "

After a little hesitation, Levan added in a low voice: "One general, a few moments before he was shot, wrote a dozen lines of verse. . . ."

"What were the lines? Tell me."

"I can't," murmured Levan. "We still sing them under our breath, in secret."

Anger gripped Geranos. "Such men," he suddenly felt, "form a massive obstruction that keeps life from marching on. . . ."

He controlled himself and remarked: "The Cheka ought to be killing still."

They had arrived at the Georgian movie studio that Geranos had an invitation to visit. A new film was being shot. Levan realized he had talked too much, and felt cowed.

"Let's go in," said Geranos and, lowering his voice, added: "Calm yourself, Levan, I shall be discreet."

The star, a young blonde of easy virtue, leaned back on a chair, smoking. She was flirting. While two elegant young men moved in her direction, a glum worker standing in the corner spied on her: a wild beast he was, hunting for prey, and about to spring. . . . The director strode back and forth yelling, correcting, panting for breath. The scene began over again, the young star felt fatigued. Levan, crumpled up in an armchair, watched the elegant, shameless woman, and his eyes narrowed with distaste. He saw the hard man waiting to spring, and he winced with fear.

"Let's get out; I'm tired," he said, turning toward Geranos.

The evening air cooled his temples a little. He clung to Geranos' arm, and whispered plaintively:

"I don't understand. I sense the feverish activity in this new Soviet life, I admit that. I hate it, but I no longer want to oppose it. I have abandoned all hope; I am ready to collaborate. Bolshevism, you see, has lasted too long. I have often placed my talents and knowledge at the disposal of the regime; I have cried: 'Pity! I am with you, give me work.' Always they have spurned me. Why? I was starving to death."

A cold sweat stood out on his poor brow. As he raised his hands toward the heavens, his cuffs glistened for a moment in the twilight, very clean and terribly frayed.

Another wave of pity surged over Geranos, but he quickly recovered himself.

"Levan Menchvili, step a little bit away from your own bloody adventure," he counseled, "if you are capable of it. Gain some perspective, and look: you belong to the bourgeois class; you were rich and cultivated, one of the people who enjoyed life. A different class, that knew hunger, that had neither wealth nor cultivation, and did not enjoy life, has managed to get the power. It wants to keep it; that's its most elementary duty. You go to it and say, 'Give me work'; that is, 'Give me a position to hold, snatch the piece of bread from a Communist who has suffered and remained loyal and give it to me.' The new class replies: 'I don't want you. I have no confidence in you. So long as you still had your strength, you fought against me; if you get strong once more, you will fight me again. There's a bitterness in your heart which will not die until your heart dies.' 'But I'm starving to death,' you shriek, and the new class answers you: 'That's what I want! But I don't kill you; you're not that dangerous. Simply die and the sooner the better; clear the road. I don't grant you a living, so little by little you will lose your strength, malnutrition will undermine your body and mind, and you will die. You yourself will die, and all your class, and that's what I want!' "

Levan listened in terror. It was the first time, perhaps, that he had been made aware, in terms so straightforward and so fierce, that the life was being crushed out of him.

"But that's inhuman!" he stammered.

"Of course it's inhuman. Such cruelty does not agree with the conception of justice and liberty we have built up so painfully; and by 'we' I mean a few sensitive people, whose outlook is perhaps limited. But if that conception of ours were to win the day, this whole earth would deteriorate into a huge sanatorium swarming with weak people who excited the sympathies of others. And life would not dare to take another forward step for fear of trampling on these appealing parasites."

"That kind of stagnation I prefer to violence," Levan answered.

"Yes, yes, you prefer it to violence, that's why you are being eliminated. Life, you see, doesn't ask for your opinion. And if it sometimes deigns to hear the cry of a human voice and to be guided by it, that is not and never has been the voice of the conservatives. You remember the witty remark made by Paul-Louis Courier de Méré? 'When God wanted to create the world, the conservative angels, with tears in their eyes, shouted to him, "Lord, do not destroy chaos!" ' But God has never heard the angels on the right. That's why he is a creator and is forever driving ardently ahead."

"Let's go to Ahmed's, the Persian's and drink a glass of tea. I'm thirsty," said Levan, wishing to put an end to the painful conversation.

He no longer dared to face his destiny, for he began to understand.

Geranos made no answer. At the moment he was pondering an historical law no longer in abstract terms but in a completely concrete way; he saw it in its pitiless application to this touching man. It was crushing Levan; Geranos heard the bones creak. The whole thrust of Russian and human history condemned him to death. Like one of El Greco's portraits. Suddenly in the dusk there Levan appeared to Geranos like some green and yellow apparition, eaten away and drained of blood: a specter risen out of vast swamps.

9

"THERE WAS, THERE WAS, there was, there was not, and yet once there was a king . . ."

Azad listened openmouthed. In the little *chainaya* belonging to the handsome Persian, green-eyed Ahmed, he listened to Souleiman, a gentle, smiling old blind man. For a moment Azad forgot the bitterness his travels through the U.S.S.R. had produced in him. He had looked forward to encountering a lofty reality: disciplined, exalted citizens, women with the look of seasoned apostles. He had found men who had forgotten and women who were flirts!

And that abandoned child, that *bezprizornyĭ*, of the day before! Desolation! Shame! What a clamor he had raised among the powerful people of the day! He had carried the child away in his arms, stinking, starving, rotten with disease as it was, and set it on the big red table, where the bigwigs were assembled. . . . Ah, how he had fumed and raged!

"Have you no shame? Did we shed our blood to end with that child? I am Azad the Chekist and I suppose I have the right to speak. Idlers, climbers, brigands!"

What a scandal! They tried to shut him up.

"No, no, I intend to cry out against it! This abscess has burst under my nose!"

Azad sent long articles to the newspapers, urgent dispatches to Moscow:

"I ask that all the abandoned children be gathered up. And without delay."

Toward evening, exhausted and dispirited after having

scanned the evening papers looking in vain for his manifestoes, Azad had slumped into the green-eyed Ahmed's little chainaya. He had drunk cups of tea and smoked two hookahs. A pleasant listlessness had permeated his long limbs. Then Souleiman had come in, wearing his tatters with a proud air, groping his way with his long stick. . . . Azad allowed himself to be lulled by the seductive, monotonous voice. Though he understood nothing, he could easily catch the essence by following the entrancing rhythm of the words and the rippling, pearly light of the face.

"There was, there was, there was, there was not, and yet once there was a king who could not sleep. . . ."

Geranos appeared at the door of the chainaya. Azad looked up and fastened his burning, myopic eyes upon the tall, slender stranger with the piercing black eyes, the bushy brows, the aquiline nose and the expression of mingled eagerness and pride. . . .

"Who is this starving bird of prey?" thought Azad in perplexity.

Levan, behind Geranos, turned pale and drew back. Geranos felt his friend's tremulous hand grip his arm.

"This man . . . the fierce Cheka man who arrested me . . ." muttered Levan.

Levan was stammering, seized anew with terror. Hopping like a wounded bird, he slipped away fast and vanished into the dark alleys. Geranos sat in front of his cup of tea, watching Azad in fascination. He liked this lean, ungainly body, the furrowed face, the fiery eyes and all the passionate intensity of the simple-minded combatant. A red handkerchief knotted around Azad's neck in the form of a flowing tie made him look like a broken-down Pioneer.

"I like this red Don Quixote," thought Geranos. "He looks as if he were returning to his old manor, vanquished and happy."

Souleiman had fallen silent; Azad filled his hands with

106

pennies and sent him away. Azad felt abashed at being caught—he, the ruthless Chekist—in the act of letting himself be rocked to sleep by euphonious nonsense.

"Who are you?" he asked impatiently of the neighbor who was eying him in such a disturbing way.

"A pilgrim to the U.S.S.R.," answered Geranos.

"I too," said Azad, offering Geranos his hand with a sweeping gesture. "Why did your companion run away?"

"You caused him too much suffering ten years ago. Didn't you recognize him?"

Azad shook his head while a queer dry laugh contorted his lips.

"So many sheep passed through our hands. Loaded trucks, a flag on top, and the soldiers who were about to finish them off, sat on their heads. The heads gave a bit and swayed from side to side. Nobody had time to look at the faces."

All of a sudden Azad felt sad.

"Do you agree?" he asked, drawing close to Geranos. "Was it necessary to kill?"

"Yes, it was necessary," answered Geranos dryly.

"And suppose that the results are less than we hoped for. We have sown blood, we reap mire. Have you seen the abandoned children wandering in the streets like dogs?"

"Yes, I've seen the starving *bezprizornyĭ* and brutish peasants and tipsy workers and little young prostitutes and pushing Communists. I've seen this vermin on the big body of the U.S.S.R."

"Well, haven't you raised your voice in protest? Haven't you felt your heart waver?"

Geranos laughed.

"My heart stayed in place, for it knows. It knows how an Idea descends upon the earth or, if you prefer, rises out of the earth, and fights, and gets splashed with mud, and goes ahead. . . ."

"You are a man without sensitivity," exclaimed Azad

107

with a laugh. "I like you; you complement me. Together the two of us comprise one perfect man. Do you like Russia?"

"I like the fire burning Russia," Geranos replied with a smile.

But Azad did not understand.

"We like the same thing," he declared with delight. "We are brothers; give me your hand."

This misunderstanding became the foundation of their brief friendship. Three or four times in his life Geranos had yielded to the sublime, quixotic fever of friendship. Mad dreams; austere joys. Woman seemed like a degrading pleasure, and the whole world cheerfully shrank in the presence of these two male hearts that loved each other. Then little by little the fatal arc would take shape; and violently or mutely, the break would come with all its humiliations.

His eyes brimming with tears, Azad held his new friend's hands.

"We'll travel around the Soviet Union together. Muzhiks, workers, *komsomols*, the old carcasses of reactionaries, we'll see them all with our own eyes, and touch everything with our own hands. Then we'll take our pilgrim's staff and go around the world preaching the truth!"

Geranos, too, felt lifted above reality as he listened, but his head remained clear. Aware of the ever-present arc, he kept on the alert.

"Anyhow," he reflected, "let's enjoy the rise that comes before the fall. Let's give ourselves once again to the ephemeral but sublime experience."

Evening fell. Women with their heads carefully done up in colored scarves passed by on their way from bathing, swinging their wanton hips. Wishing to leave by himself, Geranos turned around and looked at Azad in wonderment. Who was this man? Azad smiled at him.

"I realize that you are educated, and you have delicate

108

hands; while I'm an ignorant blockhead—and look at my hands!"

As Geranos bent forward to look, he felt a thrill pass through him. Never had he seen hands so cracked and wretched, so chapped and pitted with scars, and at the same time so vibrantly expressive. Geranos felt all at once that he loved this man. But he repressed his emotion, and remarked:

"Look at this old fellow!"

The rhapsodist Sakhol was entering the Persian Ahmed's *chainaya*: a very artful old man who had his hand on the shoulder of a plump, dandified young boy. Old Sakhol sat down and took a sort of elongated mandolin called the *tzaz* from the boy's hands. He uncovered it in a leisurely, sensual way, as if it were a woman. Then the toothless old rhapsodist began to sing an erotic song:

"Your throat is like the morning: every time I lay it bare, it is day. . . ."

The word *bulbul*, meaning nightingale, kept recurring all through the song. A tender nostalgia pervaded the evening air. Old Sakhol, smiling his professional smile, came up to Azad and Geranos, improvising a tune:

"I am a hundred and ten years old, I've been married twelve times, and I've known the world. Known the world, but this is the first time I've found myself face-to-face with such a noble pair of friends."

Then, bowing to the floor, he added: "*Oskeldi! Oskeldi!* (We welcome you!)"

"Let's leave," said Geranos. "This Oriental music nauseates me. It's sensual and fake. Let's get some air. We're two men, let's talk!"

Dawn overtook them still roaming around, pale and happy, in the streets of Tiflis. They were destroying and re-creating the world. Drawing up plans, sketching a manifesto, drafting resolutions. They felt exultant.

"Geranos, help me, don't leave me alone. This evening I shall speak to the workers. Your words have cheered my heart, and I'm no longer afraid. I've decided. I shall shout the truth at the top of my lungs. My arrival in the U.S.S.R. will set off important events. Souls are ripe."

"Ripe?"

"Yes, yes, don't smile! Ripe for a new revolution against the red mire!"

Azad made his speech. His big body stood vibrantly erect. Proletariat, class struggle, liberty, justice, hammer and sickle: he floundered and mixed them all up. But, sparked by Azad's fire, all these ideas that had been threshed out so often they had quite lost all their shape exploded like bombshells. When the orator paused for a moment, one could see hundreds of heaving breasts. Azad stood as though transfixed, sternly appraising his audience. Lethargic, well-dressed bigwigs smiled in the front rows. A note of color was introduced by a number of powdered, silk-stockinged ladies scattered among them. Off in the back of the big hall, Azad could distinguish the lean ardent faces of the young workers. In this proletarian hall he thought he could already discern a class cleavage between those who lived in comfort and those who starved, between exploiters and exploited. Raising his fist, he shouted: "A new revolution!"

What? Was he crazy? The bigwigs squirmed restlessly, the workmen cocked their heads. Azad could no longer make out their faces; vertigo flooded his brain. He lost control over what he was saying and began to shout:

"I am uttering a cry of alarm! Old combatants, young workers, honest men and women! We are lost! Production, industrialization, wheat, coal, oil: these are nothing but means. The end is something different, something loftier—the soul! The revolution will be saved not by co-operatives, collectives, machines and offices, but by the soul! 'The basis of all society, the regulator of all our thoughts and feelings is the economic factor': so you tell the peasant. Then you are simple-minded enough to require the peasant to make sacrifices!

"But the peasant answers: 'No God, no devil, only the economic factor! Well then, let me cultivate my wheat in freedom and get rich; or else I'll cultivate only one single patch of land, the very minimum, just to keep my family from starving to death. As for the others? Let them die! Ideas, sentiments? Come now! There's nothing but the economic factor!'

"Lenin said: 'The peasant will become a Communist the day he is surrounded by electric wires.'

"And I say: 'The peasant will become a Communist the day he is surrounded by ideological wires.' Only a faith superior to economic forecasts can drive the peasant to make sacrifices; that is, can bring about the triumph of Communism in our land of muzhiks!

"Comrades," concluded Azad, raising his right hand, "I'm telling the truth; I'm not afraid! I shall go around the whole Soviet Union, appealing to every living soul. I'll go to Moscow, I'll enter the Kremlin, and I'll cry out the truth. What truth? This truth, comrades: if Bolshevism goes on being merely materialistic, it will founder in the mud!"

Still on fire, Azad brought his speech to an end. No one dared applaud.

A young worker got up with a threatening air. "Priest! You want to bring the old God, the big Kulak, in through the window!"

Azad turned toward him and in a sad voice replied: "My child, I believe neither in God nor in the devil. I believe in man. Only I appeal to man's deepest energies, to his soul. My child, you haven't understood anything!"

Geranos' friend, Achod, rose, looking livid and very upset. He spoke, however, in carefully considered words:

"Comrade Azad was a great revolutionist. He isn't any more. He has been left behind. He no longer understands our reality. Comrade Azad has ceased to be a revolutionist; he has become one of the people the revolution is aimed against. A romantic. We still listen to his opinions with respect, but I believe, comrades, that out of respect also, we don't need to discuss them."

These cold, biting words fell on Azad like a mortal blow. He looked at Geranos, beseeching his aid with his eyes. Geranos clasped the rostrum. He had a calm expression on his bird-of-prey face, but a diabolical sparkle flashed in his little eyes.

"Comrade Achod is in too much of a hurry to bury the living," he began. "Comrade Achod is persuasive and frank; he sees very clearly, but he doesn't see very far. Comrade Achod plows the furrow in front of him and he plows it well; it would be cruel to ask more than that of him. But Azad is a man with a great heart, a suffering heart. Ten years ago, Azad lived through a sublime drama. A handful of hungry, half-naked men, persecuted, besieged, without money or machines or electric wires; and these vagabonds fought and defeated a world armed with foodstuffs, machines and money. Why? Because Azad and his companions felt a terrible spirit in their breasts, the soul! Don't smile, Comrade Achod! I am neither a priest nor a fool. What I call 'soul' is that completely human and completely ephemeral spirit that impels you, too, Achod, to make daily sacrifice of your individuality without regard for your economic interests. You Bolsheviks are today the most idealistic people on earth, though you proudly proclaim yourselves materialists. For is it not the essence of idealism to sacrifice one's self joyously for a task that transcends the interests of our little individuality?

"Azad, I repeat, has seen this completely natural miracle: the soul, the little spirit that rises out of the depths of man's abdomen, conquering the materialistic universe. Ten years later Azad returned to the scene of this miracle. This man with the simple, profound heart encountered different standards, found matter exalted and deified and converted into the ideal of the new generation. Azad exaggerates because he is suffering. 'We are lost!'

112

he cries. 'We are lost, and for the same reasons that our enemies were lost ten years ago!'

"Comrades, hear this cry. Let us leave off discussing and probe in silence into our inmost souls: during these ten years has nothing changed in us? Hasn't the flame flickered out a little? Hasn't the momentum slowed up a bit? When Azad's heart cries out, it is the whole of the U.S.S.R., it is the Idea, it is the whole of suffering humanity!"

A murmur of anxious indignation ran through the ranks of the workers. The officials got up. This discussion struck them as inappropriate. They surrounded Azad, offering explanations and reassuring words. Yes, yes, there was something . . . but he exaggerated . . . all would be well. Achod, casting a look of hatred at Geranos, discreetly left the hall and went to his office at the Cheka. He drafted his report: Geranos had clarity as well as sense, he might become dangerous; Azad was a nuisance, talked too much, and did not understand. His mouth needed a bit of rubbing with red pimiento.

Geranos avoided leaving in company with Azad. Already he felt remote from this ardent, superficial man. He wanted to be alone. He had just received a letter from his son, and it troubled him. The boy had made some cutting observations.

"What do you really think, father? You withdraw from everybody, and you passionately defend ideas that you despise. You trifle, and at the same time you are bloody. A ferocious tiger is in your heart. Are you just a tightrope dancer? I don't like that trade, father!"

When he arrived home, Geranos got a shock. It was as if someone had grazed his shoulder. He felt the shadow of a hand there. A bitter, ironic voice rose out of his heart: a voice from deep inside, which Geranos recognized.

"It's a long time since I've heard from you, O leader of the flock of gods and animals and men!" said Geranos.

The voice answered:

"When you are alone, you can see the shadow of an old monk, basin in hand, at your side. I am there, going before you, and when you are cowardly, I tell you so. Geranos, you are a coward!"

Geranos trembled. The voice went on shrilly:

"Geranos, you are letting yourself down; you are beginning to get involved in the conflict of the shadows. Your mind is troubled. Your heart is shrinking. Are you no longer able to look with equal pity upon good and evil?"

Geranos said nothing. Again the voice began to whistle through the air like a whip:

"You have been going all the way down, taking the steps one by one. You saw the red line. Then you abased yourself to the step of feeling pity toward everything that lives and moves on earth. Now you're getting ready to descend to the lowest step of all: you're getting involved, you're taking sides, you're saying, 'I love this shadow and hate that one. I love this army of shadows on the right. I'm a Red!' "

Geranos was stung and exasperated. "You forget that I'm not your slave. Yes, we're both looking unflinchingly at the point where the journey ends: at the abyss. You're not afraid and I'm not afraid. But during this funeral procession that we call life, you renounce everything, you empty your entrails, and cry, 'No! No!' while I—I see, I hear, I listen, I feel and I touch everything avidly. I say 'Yes' to life and to death."

A tone of deep sorrow suddenly came into the voice as it said: "O fellow wayfarer!"

Geranos felt a pang in his heart; he pitied the faltering voice. "Why did you come?" he asked. "I thought you didn't want to enter the U.S.S.R.?"

"O fellow wayfarer, a cry impels me toward the North."

"Toward Moscow?"

"Yes," said the voice in a very low whisper.

"Are you getting involved? Are you getting involved?"

Geranos waited in agony, as if his whole life hung upon the answer. He asked again: "Are you getting involved?"

But the voice had vanished.

Geranos had a hard time restraining his tears. He threw himself on his bed, and began slowly tracing letters and sentences in the air with his finger:

"A Hindu struggled for a long time against the current that was bearing his boat toward the cataract; when the great fighter understood that all effort was vain, he crossed his oars and began to sing.

"Ah! let my own life become this song: 'I have ceased to hope, I have ceased to fear, I am free!' "

IO

"TWO MEN WITH HEARTS ripened by suffering
are getting ready to travel around the U.S.S.R. Their souls
have been gripped by a deep agony. The world they lived
in seemed to them empty and faithless, abandoned to the
dark, brutalizing forces of matter. One day these two
fellow wayfarers had the sensation they were standing on
the edge of an abyss; with a shudder of anguish they
thought they saw the world plunging headlong toward
this abyss. Their tortured hearts suddenly grasped the
painful, inexorable meaning of our time: that we are faced
with the end of a civilization and the symptoms that
always manifest themselves in times of decadence.
Materialistic explanations, which are solid enough as far
as they go, are used to integrate all human experience,
although they are utterly limited in scope. Shameless,
fearless thirst for gold and pleasure, organized injustice
and violence, individualism, selfishness and falsehood, the
outrageous overestimation of commonplace know-how,
subjection of the soul to the machine: this is our life.
No higher rhythm exists capable of bridling the brute
instincts of the individual and society. This means
decomposition. When the vile war came, it brought one
great good: it intensified the process of decomposition.
In a single year we live through more than a whole
generation could live through in former times. We are
plunging very rapidly toward the abyss.

"All of a sudden on the black horizon these two men
saw a new star rising like a drop of blood: the Red star.
It struggled, pierced through the clouds and cast a ray of
wan light on the face of the earth. We girded our belts

and set out on our way, with this Red star as our guide. A cry had come from Moscow: friends and enemies all heard this cry and their hearts veered, in love or hate, toward Moscow. Magnetized as they were, our two hearts turned toward the North in anxiety and hope. In that immense, beleaguered, bloodstained cradle of the U.S.S.R., who was the newborn baby claiming to save the world? The old man Simeon wanted to hold the Messiah in his arms before he died. One day he did clasp a newborn baby in his trembling but experienced hands. He scrutinized it breathlessly and relentlessly, his heart pounding in the raptures of hope. But his eyes remained pensive and wise. Who was this forty-day-old child, already steeped in the blood of thousands of slaughtered innocents? Was this shrill little cry the voice of the Messiah? This is the terrible moment we are passing through now, with its questioning, its stammering responses, its distant hopes. Though our hearts overflow with faith, our eyes stay clear. Our trip through the U.S.S.R. will be no more than a long, painful pilgrimage. We live in unrest, injustice and crime, and in the fervent hope of desperate men. In this dangerous time in which we chance to live and desire and suffer, what road will take us to a less horrible and less ugly world, to a world a little more just and human?

"We are not party Communists, who are blinded by the complacency of their faith; nor are we members of the bourgeoisie, who are blind because their rotten hearts lack all faith. Beyond our love for the country of our flesh, we love Russia; today she is the country of all people who are struggling in behalf of the light. Beyond Russia we love suffering humanity; and beyond humanity we serve a mysterious force which appears sometimes as flame and sometimes as light, which the mind calls truth and the heart love.

"What will be the results of our pilgrimage? We do not know. We are going to discover the truth for ourselves, with no biases except our own, and these are ruthlessly disinterested ones. If we were Communists, our task would be easy and the conclusions known in advance: consciously or unconsciously we would have distorted all the facts in order to subject them to the discipline of Marxism and to the simple, effective faith of men of action. Cannot everything, alas, be explained by the economic factor? We are living through the end of a civilization, and, as has always happened, materialism is hailed as the key to all mysteries. The world becomes a machine, and the explanation of everything a tour de force of ingenious dialectics. If we were anti-Communists, it would be equally easy to discredit the entire Soviet effort by accenting its comic side; by playing up the childish and often sanguinary muddles that any idea gets into during its lumbering, remorseless struggles to transform itself into reality.

"Ours is a more arduous task, and a more thankless one. We are not simple people who believe in happiness; nor weaklings who crumple to the ground in distress at the first reverse; nor skeptics observing the bloody effort of marching humanity from the lofty heights of a mocking, sterile wit. Believing in the fight, though we entertain no illusions about it, we are armed against every disappointment. We leave it to the slipshod romantics to discover all the virtues in the proletarian class; as for ourselves we know that this class which carries in itself all the seeds of the future is still dull, ignorant, lacking in any clear consciousness of its duties, crammed and bloated with dogmas that remain roughhewn, however real they may be. The motivation for their struggle often comes from the base instincts of the belly or lower down; thirst for material enjoyment often pricks their flesh and drives them to fight. But these are inveiglements that the demon of every age loves to arrange in order to attain his ends: ends that always transcend the desires of the combatants. Unless something excited the base instincts of the masses, their fever for battle would cool and the ascent of humanity would slow down and become jeopardized.

118

While they surge toward the satisfaction of their instincts, the masses, without knowing it, are serving a higher purpose.

"It's all like the greedy insect that jostles the petals as he swoops down on the honey accumulated like bait in the very heart of the flower. The hungry insect has no idea of doing anything beyond appeasing his hunger; for him the honey has no other mission except to fill his belly. But while he gorges himself, his antennae and wings are being dusted with yellow seed; and the hungrier the insect gets and the more he digs and shoves, the more pollen he collects. And when he goes off and violates other flowers, he transports this mysterious dust, so that, without willing or knowing it, he fertilizes a whole garden. Such is the sacred destiny of material satisfactions. What is our duty? To participate in the work superior to ourselves but to do so consciously. To act as insects that eat and drink and know why. To discern the aspirations of the masses and not be disgusted by them.

"If we conceive the Idea in this way, and the higher mission of the base instincts, we are on the way, we think, to discovering the whole truth without any risk of debasing it. Aware of the universal selfishness and materialism of our age, we know that the newborn child is beginning to resemble its age: it asks to feed its hunger. Like every other organism that has recently become entangled in this world, it needs to eat and drink and to monopolize as large a share as it can of the earth's space. But before coming into the world no other organism ever had more thirst for the ideal than this newborn child; and none will have it tomorrow the way he will when he has become surfeited with bread.

"Like little Dionysus, he laughs, wails and dances out of a superabundance of energy; but his laughter is quickly smothered by the hostile powers watching eagerly on all sides for a chance to contrive his death. We have heard his laughter and his tears; and in anguish we hasten to his side. What we bring him for a present is neither incense

119

nor gold; but our troubled minds and questions full of love.

"So solemn is the moment we pass through now that any lie would be unpardonable. Everyone has an obligation to communicate the truth as he sees it, and to take his position in the great battle impending. If it were given to man to receive the whole truth—its luminous center and its vibrant nebulae—and if man could translate that truth into words, then our speech would become raw and visionary; it would blind. What is being done consciously in Russia today is pallid and ambiguous compared to what is exploding in the unconscious, without the leaders' knowing or willing it. Vaguely we divine that the seeds of gigantic happenings have been planted in this huge fat field of the muzhiks. But alas! We live a very little while, hardly long enough to divine the arc that shoots out on its soaring upward course from an evanescent point in our time. At best our intimations of it come to us too fleetingly.

"Anyone who wants to link himself with the spirit leaping ahead, destroying and creating, has to love Russia as a whole, in its totality, without the niggling reservations of metaphysical thinking or the petty calculations of arithmetic and science. Here in the U.S.S.R. you feel surrounded by blind forces that are creating the eye—the eye and the light.

"Beyond logic, beyond discussions and disputes, beyond economic needs and party programs, higher than the Soviets and the Commissars, the force at work in the U.S.S.R. and controlling it is the dark, intemperate, ruthless Spirit of our age. From the most bestial muzhik to the sacred face of Lenin, everybody, whether he wishes it or not, is an instrument and collaborator of this reeling Giant in Moscow.

"Pure ardent hearts of all countries, unite! Let us pull in our belts and start on our way! A cry has come from Moscow!"

120

Geranos slowly folded the sheets. His heart leapt and clamored in these lines hurriedly scribbled in a firm, impassioned hand. Geranos had poured his whole soul into it without any thought of Azad. They were in the coach and already getting close to Baku. Bent forward as if still listening to Geranos' voice, his eyes moist with tears, Azad pressed his friend's hands.

"I don't understand everything," Azad said, "but in the rhythm of your words I recognize my whole soul: suffering, hope, struggle."

Later on, Geranos recalled this moment with a torturing intensity. Steep cliffs, desolate villages, a voracious sun. An old woman stood watching at the door with a rooster under her arm and a big knife in her right hand; a few Moslems with fine, impassive, bovine eyes laughed. In the distance a heart-rending voice chanted in monotone a cantilena of death. A little white coffin emerged from a cabin, while the mother hurled herself upon it trying to hold it back. As she clung to it, she tore her hair and intoned the death chant:

"My little green parrot—who spoke so nicely like a human being—your sweet voice gave us joy, and here you are leaving us, burning and shivering with fever."

Two old Armenian rhapsodists came into the coach; in thin broken voices, with their ears fast to their instruments, the *tchoughi* and the *tchianouri*, they started to sing some old songs erotic in flavor. "My heart is red as the poppy but the heart of my heart is black. . . ."

A few months later when Geranos reread the manifesto, he smiled sadly. How pure man's intentions could be! How superhuman the first upsurge could be, as if cowardice, laziness, habit, as if matter in short, did not exist! All this emotion was irrevocably linked to these erotic songs and death chants of the Caucasus. And long months afterward Geranos felt on his lips the sharp tang of love and death.

121

II

Baku. It was raining. The dense rolling waves of the Caspian Sea were the color of mud. One wallowed through greenish-black ooze under a monstrous forest of scaffolding, with a nauseating smell of naphtha soaking into the brain. The infernal fluid gushed out of the slime; workers emerged from it reeking with oil to stir about in the poisoned air. A group of foreign writers had scattered themselves around this inferno, pencils in hand. The inspector of labor, Dmitrakof, a rough, ardent muzhik, who was high-handedly conducting the group, faced the Caspian Sea and exclaimed: *"Nashi!* (Ours!)" He pointed out the wells, the workers, the machines: *"Nashi! Nashi!"* Seeing Azad approaching, he called out to him as he presented the group: *"Nashi pisateli!* (Our writers!)"

"Let's go see the fire temple of the ancient pyrolaters!" suggested a stoutish German in gold spectacles. "It must be on this hill!"

Dmitrakof turned around in perplexity. "What?" he said. "Temple! Pyrolaters? *Chto eto takoye?* (What's that?)"

"Zoroaster!" the German writer explained.

"Some engineer," said Dmitrakof, racking his brains to remember.

"No!" cried the group with laughter. "A god!"

"Tovarishch," he said severely, "we have no time to waste."

Azad took hold of Dmitrakof's arm. He had just endured another cruel disappointment. That morning he had had an urge to visit his friend, the old hero of the

122

Cheka, Maxim Sergeyevich. How he had yearned to confess his anguish to him and ask him for help! Azad had felt stronger in his heart when he remembered this friend of his. The gaunt man, with eyes scorched from lack of sleep, hating no one and loving no one, staring out with the unseeing, penetrating gaze of a person obsessed. Maxim Sergeyevich loved nothing but one distrustful and bloodthirsty wild beast: the Revolution.

Azad had inquired after his friend from a passer-by.

"Yes, yes, I know him," came the answer. "He made the *Dollar Princess*. He works in the cinema."

The cinema! Azad's knees folded under him. Mechanically he followed the directions given him. They were shooting a new film: commotion, female shrieks, laughter, a sickening smell of mingled perfume and sweat; the blinding light of projectors. . . .

A man disengaged himself from the mass of naked flesh and workers' blouses. He was accompanied by a woman elegant in a dull and dubious way: vegetable silk stockings, peroxide blond hair, scarlet fingernails. Could the fellow with this heavy face, these listless eyes, this bulging belly really be Sergeyevich?

"My wife," said the man, as he introduced the silk stockings, peroxide hair and scarlet nails.

"Maxim Sergeyevich, you've put on weight, you've gone slack, I don't recognize you any more. Ah! flame of the Cheka!"

The man lowered his voice and whispered in Azad's ear: "Don't talk about the Cheka, you're mad! My wife gets nervous!"

"Ah! Your wife gets nervous!"

"What do you want of me?"

"I was looking for Maxim Sergeyevich, the Chekist. I find this potbellied cinema director. I don't want anything! I don't know you."

Now, as he hung on Dmitrakof's arm, Azad felt consoled.

"Do you know Karl Marx, *Tovarishch* Dmitrakof?"

"Yes, yes . . . we have his bust in the entrance to our offices."

"Have you read him?"

"Read him? Why? Lenin read him."

"That's a sublime remark you've made!" exclaimed Azad, and he gave Dmitrakof an embrace.

Dmitrakof turned round in astonishment, eyed Azad, and shrugged his shoulders.

"*Ya ne ponimayu!* (I don't understand!)" he said.

Geranos, who had mixed with the group in the early morning, now lingered behind. His tall body was vibrantly alive, and his voice had grown deep and warm. He was talking to Rahel. Amita followed a step behind, out of breath. He did not participate, he merely listened, and a bitter smile twisted his drooping mouth. Rahel's eyes were fixed with a greedy, devouring look upon the strange man risen from the bottom of the sea.

"Like Loyola," said Geranos, concluding, "I, too, have my spiritual exercises. First step: contemplate the whole circle, the waves of human beings undulating up and down. Second step: train every beam of light on the precise point marked by my own epoch. Third step: burn it up."

Rahel grabbed Geranos' arm, and Amita stood still for a moment, feeling as if the whole forest of scaffolding were shaking. But he quickly recovered his balance, and he heard distinctly what Rahel said:

"Comrade from Crete, you bring me a precious gift. I had the flame; you give me the light. I see clearly now. As I was listening to you, I could see the whole circle and on this circle I cut off the little arc of my own epoch and on this arc I located the little red point of my own existence. Now I see, I am happy!"

She clapped her hands in delight and turned around. With a surprised start she noticed Amita; she had forgotten him. He seemed to her all of a sudden small and stunted, and his long gray hair made him look to her like a gentle Protestant pastor or indeed, she thought with a burst of laughter, like a virtuous old lady. At that moment, Dmitrakof's shrill voice interrupted:

"Come on, comrades, hurry up. Step on it! The manager is waiting for us!"

Office of the manager. The Big-Jawed Man gathered up his notes, and remarked to him: "I like your brutal way of looking at reality. I like your exact knowledge of remedies; you know what needs to be done. But I don't like the smug optimism you show when you say that you will do it."

The manager, a blond giant with clear, steady eyes, smiled.

"I detest phrases," he said. "I've given you figures."

"I don't believe in figures. I know how to handle them myself and I know their value: it's nothing extraordinary."

Just then the group came tramping into the office. Tea was brought in; people warmed themselves up and got comfortable. An outburst of shouting and laughter and discussion ensued. The Big-Jawed Man leaned against the bronze bust of Lenin, scrutinizing the chattering men with a look of contemptuous hostility.

An expert in Esperanto, a man with a childish mouth, said: "The impression I get is a painful one, I have to admit. All these machines worry me. The new culture ought to be free from the blemishes of our Western civilization."

Several people could not keep from laughing, and the Esperantist lost his temper.

"Why do you laugh, comrades?" he asked. "I know what I'm talking about. Man has ceased to be the master and has become the slave of this ferocious beast, the machine, that he himself brought into the world. He has gotten caught in its iron cogwheels. The spirit gave birth to matter and now the spirit has grown dull, become mechanized, turned into matter. What are we to do? What are we to do?"

125

"Learn Esperanto," said a Norwegian dramatist, with a mournful air.

"Be serious!" said a French critic. "Our Esperantist comrade is right. The problem he poses is so insoluble it has ceased to be a problem and become a necessity. Our own diabolical creation—the machine—has enslaved us. In the West our soul has already sunk into this slavery; our civilization is cracking up. What was the duty of this new culture which has just sprung into being here in the U.S.S.R.? To continue on the dizzy incline down which the West is plunging? Or to retrace the way instead and return to the simplicity and independence of patriarchal times? Lenin or Gandhi? That's how the problem should have been posed to the Communist leaders in the decisive first days of the great revolutions."

"No dilemma," interrupted the manager in his firm, soft voice. "Lenin or Gandhi? Not at all! Only Lenin! Our enemy, the capitalistic world, is armed to the teeth; unless we want to be snuffed out, there's only one way: industrialization to the limit! We've all strained every nerve in a desperate drive toward this one avenue of salvation. We've attained our pre-war production and in certain points surpassed it. That's not enough. Now we must compete with world industry."

"Who will win?"

Everyone turned abruptly. Who had uttered this war cry? The voice had a deep and ominous ring.

Amita and Geranos came in. Rahel halted at the threshold, her body rigid: the mysterious man with the cold fire in his eyes stood before her, a powerful, thickset figure who was sizing up the whole assemblage like a bull in a ring. For a moment, seized by a new attack of panic, Rahel had a mad desire to flee. But she controlled herself, and with a resolute smile stepped across the threshold. The Big-Jawed Man moved away from the bust of Lenin, advanced a pace, and in a vibrant voice repeated his challenge:

"Who will win?"

"The system that can achieve a higher economic level," answered the manager quietly.

"Exactly!" exclaimed the stranger. "But that's a terrible admission, Mr. Manager! You have admitted your inevitable defeat. Why? I'm going to tell you: in order to vanquish the capitalistic world, you must surpass its industry. Outdo them in quality and quantity and in cheapness of price. But you have exhausted your productive capacities by using up your reserves. Your equipment is threadbare. It's absolutely necessary to bring in new resources. How? No money! No money!"

He said this in a tone of savage joy. Azad restrained his rage with an effort. Geranos tried to decipher the cruel mask.

"If you increase the price of industrial products," the Big-Jawed Man continued in his trenchant way, without making a single gesture, "the peasant, who is almost your only consumer, will cease to buy. And as you well know, he can scrape along for centuries; you can't for a year. If you continue to upset the balance between city and village, you are lost!"

Silence. Rahel felt a chill in her heart. "I hate this man! I hate this man!" she cried in despair from the depths of her being. She turned toward Geranos:

"Comrade from Crete, answer him! Demolish him!"

But Geranos bit his lips and murmured between his teeth: "He's right."

A sense of tragedy spread over them all. Only the manager smiled calmly.

"We need time," he declared after a few minutes. "Time is on our side. Yes, the enemy knows it and he's getting ready; but he doesn't dare to declare war. He trembles, for the social war lurks in the offing; the world proletariat is getting organized; and oppressed peoples are waking up. Shall we have the time we need? If war is declared right now, shall we be able to hold with our inferior technology? Will the world proletariat, the oppressed peoples, be ripe? Comrade, the moment is solemn."

"Only one man could save you at this moment," said the stranger, laying his heavy hand on the bronze bust: "Lenin! He had the pliancy, and he had the inflexibility as well; he had the clear head and the ready hand. He forced reality with tricks. More than that: he was reality. But Lenin is dead!"

He uttered this dictum with such an air of triumph that everyone there felt a tremor of discomfort. In a low voice the Norwegian dramatist muttered to the Frenchman, who stood near him: "Not even Lenin. He was very clever: he died at the right time."

Rahel saw Amita beside her, ghastly pale. She looked away from him and tried to catch Geranos' attention. But her glance encountered Azad instead. She was startled to find Azad devouring her with his eyes. When he met her gaze, a cry of fright escaped from him. He parted the writers in his way, took a step and stopped. As he bent forward, Rahel felt a feverish breath on her face.

"Jewess?"

"Jewess."

"Loevenstein?"

"Loevenstein."

"From Lodz?"

"From Lodz."

Azad constricted his hand and clutched his throat. Then he went back to his place. For an instant the whole room spun around, men and ideas engulfed in the blackness of vertigo. But Azad quickly came to himself and stared with an expression of hatred at the stranger. Rahel had understood. She raised her eyes and fixed them on Azad. Emaciated, back bent, face ravaged by the hunger of former days, eyes sorrowful, frightened and tender: Rahel felt a thrill of horror and admiration. She kept watching Azad's right hand and saw it clutch his frail, wrinkled throat again.

128

"This is the hand that killed her," she breathed. "This is the hand that killed her. . . ."

The big jaws snapped open once more, and a sarcastic smile appeared on the thin lips.

"Now you have Trotsky, the Flame," the stranger said. "Just at the moment when only the Light could show you the way!"

Silence again. In the corner a cry was emitted, harsh but smothered. A Dutch writer turned around and had a moment of fear as he saw a spare man with a lofty forehead craning his neck and staring at the whole assemblage out of piercing eyes, like a bird of prey. But the Dutchman quickly repressed his anxiety and began to study his pipe. The Esperantist wanted to speak but didn't know what to say. The German writer meticulously wiped his spectacles. And an English poet selected an apple and began disposing of it with his beautiful teeth.

Then Azad got up with shaking knees. So the danger was more terrible than he had imagined! He could feel the whole edifice creaking. His choking voice reverberated through the room.

"Comrades, you have heard," he said. "The moment is grave. Let us stretch out our hands to our Mother Russia! She is in danger; let us run to her aid! Let us take our pilgrims' staffs, comrades, and scatter over the earth like apostles. Let us preach love among nations, let us preach justice, let us preach war against war!"

"Yes . . . yes," answered several voices evasively.

"Who is this fellow?" asked the Englishman of the person next him.

"An Armenian or a Greek, I don't know. He looks like a Jew."

"Well," Azad went on," we're going to draw up a manifesto and sign it!"

The Dutchman lit his pipe and said to Azad: "With your permission I'm going to smoke."

"We're all going to swear to sacrifice our lives to this humanitarian mission!" exclaimed Azad.

"Yes . . . yes," repeated the evasive voices.

"But why the devil are you in such a hurry, comrade?" asked a jolly-faced Bavarian. "We've got time."

"Yes . . . yes, we've got time!" they all shouted in chorus and got up.

Just then Dmitrakof came in, beaming. He had photos and pamphlets and diagrams. He distributed them all round and gave everyone's hand a squeeze.

"*Nashi pisateli*," he said with feeling, "don't forget your Russian brothers. Tell them abroad that we are not bandits, that we love men who toil and that we believe in justice."

The Big-Jawed Man did not wish to leave with the rest. Leaning on the bust of Lenin, he watched these men go off, knocking each other over: the lean ones and the hulking ones; with spectacles and without spectacles; with pipes or with cigarettes; sloshing through the mud with galoshes or without galoshes.

"Pff!" he grunted. "The intellectuals! These old trousers, these pumpkin-heads!"

Geranos went up to him; he felt attracted to this brutal man, and at the same time irresistibly repelled by him. Rahel, beside Geranos, opened her eyes and ears.

"There was a strange hatred in your words, for all the cold logic in them," said Geranos. "You must have a fiery temperament in the service of an abstract Idea."

The stranger subjected Geranos to a severe scrutiny. "Abstract Idea," he sneered. "You must have chewed and chewed and chewed the books!"

After this remark he turned his back on Geranos and went out alone, with his heavy rhythmical step. He went on with his own thoughts, summing things up as follows:

"A powerful political framework. A weak economic framework. My great hope: the muzhik. My great fear: the Americanized Russian. He sees clearly, he acts clearly, he must be something formidable. Let's make haste."

Rahel stamped her foot in anger.

"Why didn't you answer?" she cried to Geranos. "Were you afraid?"

"I wasn't afraid," answered Geranos, looking the Jewess straight in the eye. "But he's right. . . ."

"I shall go with him!" said Rahel in her sibilant voice, and her eyes played like a flame about Geranos' eyes, lips, forehead, about the whole of Geranos' intense, insatiable face. "I shall go with him!"

"Go, Comrade Rahel! Go, Comrade Rahel! I like solitude."

Rahel smiled scornfully and went away.

"The other one is stronger!" she thought with a thrill. "The other one is stronger!"

Geranos returned to the streets of Baku in confusion. He could feel his cheeks burning with shame, as if someone had struck him with a riding-whip.

"I like this man," he thought. "If I had more courage, I should be like him, intransigent, blunt, possessed. I'm ashamed! I've wasted my life playing with ideas and words. My son is right. My epitaph: 'Here lies a man who danced on a tightrope over the abyss.' I haven't loved anything except the curves and colors of objects against a background of shadows. Chewed, chewed, chewed. Yes, this monster is right; my soul is a goat."

At the hotel a surprise awaited him. Fiodor Touganof, the great poet of the muzhik earth. He had come down the Volga and traveled around the Caucasus; he had a desire to become acquainted with a distant brother hailing from that East he had so often sung about and yearned for:

> Joy is a caravan coming from the East with
> saffron, perfume and silk.
> The pads of the camels on the sand echo in
> our hearts.
> And the sweetness of the white night will be
> soaked in Arab tar.

About fifty and bald, Fiodor Touganof had a little snub nose, a faint, musical voice and the gentle, humble and sly look of a monk. High muzhik's boots and a white blouse sprinkled with little red and blue flowers (like those often worn by the young saints of old Novgorod) against the milky background of ivory.

Thus did Geranos encounter the mystical and sensual poet of Holy Russia, of Our Lady of Hell, in whom the Devil became one with the Angel of Sorrow.

An excited conversation started immediately.

"I'm not one of the Russians who occupy themselves with politics and canons," declared Fiodor as he introduced himself. "I hail from the golden thread that runs through legends and icons."

"What is your conception of life, Master Touganof?"

"We've come upon the earth," breathed the poet very softly, "sent by God to fulfil a duty."

"This duty changes its face in every age. A new demon is the master of every age. Who is the demon of our own time?"

"A demon and an archangel are always fighting in every age. Both of them carry a sword. We mustn't mistake one for the other."

"What are the distinguishing marks of the demon and the archangel? For me the archangel is the one that drives upward, the one who helps me overcome my laziness, my cowardice and my selfishness; the one that enlarges my heart and brain."

Geranos paused; then, in order to shake the poet out of his deliberate torpor and cautiousness, he slowly added:

"For me today the inspiration that drives me upward is Communism. That's my archangel."

Fiodor Touganof delayed answering, and Geranos realized the painful effort he was making to repress his indignation. Then, while his sensuous fingers crept caressingly along the embroidered border of the tablecloth, he murmured in his dulcet voice:

"This is the first time I've heard such a definition of Communism. Perhaps you're not talking about Russian Communism. The people here—that is, three-quarters of the Russian people along with myself—picture Communism to ourselves as Satan arming men to fly at each other's throats."

"I speak only from my own personal experience. If what ennobles me is Communism, is it my duty to follow it? I'm addressing you as a spiritual father."

Perplexed, Touganof lapsed once more into silence.

"Is there only one way to salvation?" Geranos went on. "Or does everyone have his own way that leads him to his own deliverance?"

"Everyone has his own way of salvation. For myself I've found mine. I've recovered my tranquillity. The Orthodox faith awakens a complete response in my heart."

"Well, I'm still looking for my own way of salvation. I'm struggling, groping, suffering still. Communism I regard as nothing more than a harbinger of salvation. A John-the-Precursor. It doesn't awaken a complete response in my heart."

"I pity you, my brother," said Touganof.

"A rabbi once said," Geranos answered, " 'Man is higher than the angel. For man has not yet attained perfection, so that he can still advance; while the angel, having arrived at perfection, is incapable of advancing.' "

Fiodor Touganof relapsed anew into silence. His bald skull reddened and his full lips worked. For a moment he leveled his periwinkle blue eyes at Geranos with an expression of uneasy circumspection.

"My brother," he said slyly. "I'm just a poor muzhik, I don't understand."

The great representative of three-quarters of the Russian earth, the man with the deep, mystical, prudent soul, scented an enemy in front of him and said no more. The vodka came; he savored a few drops of it with relish.

"God is great," he said. "Russia is great. I'm not afraid."

133

In the evening, in the artists' club of Azerbaijan, a formal reception in honor of the foreign writers. A young boy got up on the stage; he was very handsome, his eyes were made up with courma, his body swayed from right to left. He began to sing a passionate Oriental air, while an old blind man in the corner swayed his head in ecstasy and, holding his long santouri on his lap, accompanied the sweet, monotonous song. A little girl appeared: with her heavy golden cope one saw nothing of her except her serene face, her hands with their red fingernails and her little bare feet. She danced a still, liturgical dance, her white pointed teeth sparkling like some little rodent's. Geranos felt thrilled. This world had only two spectacles that filled him with a sense of mystery and awe: the starry heavens and the dancing woman. Once when he had seen Sent M'ahesa in some African religious dances, he had understood in a flash of intuition how man of clay can abruptly pass beyond the frontiers of life and death. But this young Moslem dancer in Baku, with her motionless dance, revealed the supreme ecstasy to him, the essence of the dance, the fixed vertex of the flame. Turning, he found Azad at his side in tears; the Europeans had ironical, bored smiles on their faces. Never before had Geranos been so intensely aware of the chasm separating the Oriental soul from the Occidental. Two men who vibrate to the same dance and weep for it are brothers; all the rest are infidels and enemies.

Then Geranos realized how much he loved Azad. He gently rested his hand on his friend's shoulder. It startled Azad and he turned around; for an instant their weeping eyes met and at that instant both of them experienced an ineffable happiness. They felt so happy they wanted to be alone. They left and roamed about the streets, contentedly inhaling the damp, cold air. At the entrance of a big hotel, the bezprizornyïs were hugging the radiators; they laughed and frisked about, picking up cigarette butts. Some young streetwalkers, frightfully made up, passed up and down on the quay of the harbor, in front of the cinemas and at the streetcar stations. Two tipsy workers came staggering along.

"Is this a Soviet night?" Azad remarked with a laugh. At that moment he felt too happy to get angry.

"I'm happy," he said, grasping Geranos' arms. "I'm not alone on this earth. When I talked to those Europeans, do you think I was entirely taken in? I saw it all; I saw the irony in their eyes; I saw them pursing up their mouths; and I heard the Englishman say, indicating me out of the corner of his eye, 'Who is this fellow?' But I myself was making fun of all those practical Europeans with their refined, skeptical ways, for I saw the sparks flashing from your round vulture's eyes."

Geranos felt Azad's feverish breath on his temples. He drew away. Ah! If his heart could only loosen up a little tonight! Geranos waited for an instant; but his heart remained tight-shut and hard.

"I could feel my own spirit gripping those Europeans' heads," he finally said, puckering up his lips. "Like a raven. And I heard your heart beating against their trunks, smiting them like a woodcutter. I was so hungry I didn't even want to smother my outcry."

"What outcry?"

"I don't exactly know now. Some inarticulate bird of prey's cry. A cry that would mean something like this: 'Corpses! Corpses!' Or perhaps, 'Azad, strike!' Or perhaps, 'War! War!'"

12

THE CASPIAN SEA. Stealthy, forbidding, smelling of nothing. A naked sun; a few clumsy sea gulls stuffed with fish. As he stood on the bridge of the boat taking him to his native city of Astrakhan, Azad talked in a troubled, emotional way about Dzerzhinski. The Big-Jawed Man listened to him eagerly. He liked Azad, this simple, impulsive man who had no logic in his make-up. A lump of earth. An undraped animal.

Rahel sat on a bench listening absent-mindedly to Amita. Her prying eyes shifted back and forth between Geranos and the brutal man. She wavered, unable to settle on either one. She was intrigued by Geranos' clear and interesting mind; the strength of the other one drew her by main force. For four days she had been spying on every word they uttered, peering at every movement. In a report she had drawn up for the Cheka, she had gone into great detail without coming to any conclusions.

One of them, she reported, seemed to be a great enemy, a ruthless, self-confident power. Why had he come to the U.S.S.R.? What did he seek? "I seek," he had told her, "the heart and the heel of Russia." "Why?" she had asked. "That's my affair," was all he had answered.

The other one, Geranos, was a complicated soul. He went to the heart of everything with a blinding clarity. He observed fairly and defended Communism with ardor, but at the same time despised it; he thought it too narrow to satisfy his soul. What, then, did his soul want? Would it exhaust itself in its impotent and sterile quest? What did this Cretan seek in the U.S.S.R.? "I seek the red line," Geranos had once said to her, with a light tap on her

136

shoulder, in reply to her question. "What red line?" Rahel could not understand.

Rahel's glance flitted toward Azad. There was someone who rested her mind! They never spoke to each other, they avoided each other. But how she appreciated having him around! Simple, ingenuous, noble, unjust and good, buffeted by every wind, garrulous, superficial and appealing—a man! Rahel pricked up her ears: with his sweeping gestures and Oriental ejaculations, Azad was resurrecting the sober, taciturn, ascetic face of the Reds' Grand Inquisitor. Azad had worked under his orders in the Ukraine.

"He had gone there in person," Azad was saying, "and traveled about among the villages to collect the wheat hidden in corn lofts or underground caches by the kulaks. Russia was starving to death. Exhausted with fatigue, Dzerzhinski fell gravely ill. Lenin telegraphed to him: 'Come back immediately, take care of your health!' 'I cannot leave my work,' Dzerzhinski replied. 'Every grain of wheat will have its effect on the destiny of the world.' Often he would say to us: 'We Chekists have to have good hearts and stout ones; for the life of man is in our hands.' Later on, a comrade wrote me: 'We had gathered around his deathbed, all of his fellow-workers; we saw him die. No one dared to interfere with his death.' "

Geranos got up.

"Comrade Rahel," he said, "haven't you made up your mind yet?"

Rahel met his gaze defiantly. "No!" she said.

Geranos shrugged his shoulders. Ah! How far removed he felt from all these silly love stories! And yet, jealousy gnawed at his heart.

"In your eyes," hissed Geranos in a venomous voice, "in your eyes, Comrade Rahel, I see a little child."

Rahel drew herself up angrily, but Geranos had already departed, hardly able to hold back his tears. He went below and shut himself up in his cabin.

He felt a restlessness of the soul. He was passing

through a painful interval. As had so often happened to him at critical moments in his growth, all his agony had found concentrated expression one night in the plastic imagery of a dream. A military review, the general passing among the soldiers and staring point-blank at each of them individually. He was sorting them out, eliminating the cowards. "You are a coward," he would say to one of them, throw him out of the ranks, and pass on. All the soldiers were trembling. Geranos' turn came. The general stood before him and stared; for hours and hours he scrutinized him, his gaze piercing through Geranos' heart. "As for you," he finally said, "you can't fight on the left, because you keep looking also to the right. You can't fight on the right, because you keep looking also to the left. I don't know what to do with you. . . . You irritate me!" He grabbed him by the shoulders and shook him. Geranos had awakened with a start.

From that moment on Geranos had gone through dreadful suffering. Harrowing bursts of pride and wails of despair welled up from the depths of his being. . . . And then that Azad, with his sentimental impetuosity, and Rahel, with her long eyes searching for the strongest male, and that monstrous man who had fired the terrible taunt at him . . . Amita, too, exasperated him with that martyred Buddha's sweetness of his and the deferential, tragic smile. Geranos watched the sea through the porthole, following with half-closed lids the gentle, rhythmic motion of the big waves. He became a bit more tranquil. In order to get complete control over his troubles, he directed his thoughts toward the marvelous country his eyes had just feasted upon. He felt the giant mountains of the Caucasus rearing themselves inside his head—between his two temples. Framed in that vast landscape he saw a figure arising: the deep, obstinate being with the pebbles in his brain—the peasant. Geranos had often gone up to the peasants during his travels in the Caucasus; questions and answers, lamentations and outcries crowded into his memory. He had an urge to set them in order. Once again he talked to his son.

"A peasant saw Amiran in chains on the edge of a steep precipice," Geranos wrote to Panteli. "Amiran gasped and moaned and kept tugging with all his might to reach the sword lying beside him. He called out to the peasant, summoning him to come to his aid. When the peasant drew near, Amiran said to him: 'Free me and all humanity will be freed; for I love the poor and oppressed.' He grabbed the bread from the peasant's sack and squeezed it in his enormous hand. Blood and sweat immediately flowed out of the bread.

" 'Unhappy man,' Amiran exclaimed, 'how can you eat such bread?'

" 'What could we eat then?' asked the peasant.

" 'Come, look!' Amiran replied.

"He squeezed another piece of bread with his hand, and milk flowed from it.

" 'If you free me,' he said, 'you will no longer eat bread made of blood and sweat.'

"I heard this legend one afternoon from a Georgian peasant in the village of Telav in the beautiful Kakhetie. We were seated on a rock at the foot of the fortress that belonged to the last king of Georgia, that fine unlucky fellow Heracles. Some wan, silent old village women sat on the ground beside us, with their scanty merchandise on display in front of them: a few half-rotten quinces, some big red gourds, a little maize; on a handkerchief some eggs and radishes. They knitted sadly and patiently. Far away, under the gentle sun, shone the wide, dried-up river bed of Alazan. The beautiful Caucasus peaks, which separate Europe from Asia, soared toward heaven, mighty and snow-covered. Gleaming in their serene inaccessibility, they looked as hard and pure as diamonds. But the peasant's melancholy words had brought affliction to my heart. It was there at Telav that I found myself confronted

139

for the first time by the terrible problem of the Russian peasant.

"A few days later I entered the impressive gorge of Daryal. Hanging like an eagle's aerie from the sparkling, snow-covered sides of Mount Kazbek is a village. My heart leapt at the prospect of seeing strong-souled mountain folk. Once back home in Crete I stood on Mount Ida in the company of an old Cretan shepherd, and we had a view of the distant plain of Messara buried in the dust far below. My companion turned to me with the query: 'Do you think that the people who live on the plain have a soul too?'

"To this Cretan's way of thinking, the soul couldn't live and breathe except in the mountains. Well, I sat down happily on a stool in front of a kulak's house; I ate a piece of bread, a little cheese and a few apples sold to me by the proprietor. Crouching before me like an aged monkey, he followed my slightest movements with curiosity. Primitive peoples see in every stranger a mysterious, semi-sacred being. Stealing furtive glances at him, I could detect that kind of intense primitive anguish in the old man's eyes.

"When I turned around suddenly, he hunched up his shoulders in terror and waited. I put a question to him.

" 'You have lived much, little father!' I said. 'You have seen many things. You have known Czarism, and now you see man freed: at last the earth belongs to those who cultivate it. Are you content?'

"The old man stretched his long wrinkled neck and swallowed his saliva. He made no reply.

" 'Surely you have cried out for liberty or death, along with the other enslaved workers and peasants,' I insisted. 'And now?'

" 'And now, God be praised, we have both of them, both liberty and death!' sighed the old man.

" 'I don't understand! Speak to me, tell me the truth!'

"The old man smiled.

140

" 'Anyone who tells the truth,' he said, 'has to have a horse saddled. I don't have any horse. Even if I had one, where could I flee?' He looked about him in dread. The U.S.S.R. struck him as one huge trap.

"But the real muzhik I encountered one evening half buried in the furrows between the two buffaloes hitched to his plow. His feet were dug like roots into the freshly plowed soil. As I approached him, he made a movement of fear and hostility.

" 'Little father,' I said to him, 'the earth is good. God is good. No one hears us, speak to me.'

"He drew back, blinking his eyes.

" 'I don't know your heart,' he said.

" 'I'm a man come from the other side of the world to see you, little father, and to hear you. You are the mouth of this land, speak!'

" 'I have nothing to say,' he answered. 'I haven't got children any more, I haven't got land any more, I haven't got God any more.' Crossing his arms over his breast, he added: 'I've got patience.'

" 'And your sons?'

" 'They're riding Red horses.'

" 'And your daughters?'

" 'They've got red kerchiefs on their heads.'

" 'And the land?'

" 'I don't recognize it any more. I plant it and a militia man harvests it.' Then, taking a frightened glance at the plain around him, he said in a whisper: 'Antichrist has come.'

" 'Antichrist has come, little father. Christ and Antichrist say the same thing: "All men are brothers," "The earth belongs to all," "He who does not work does not eat." '

"The old man scoffed. 'Christ is white as the lily,' he said. 'Antichrist is red as blood. He doesn't weep, not he; he doesn't get crucified; he lives in cities and carries a gun.'

" 'What are we to do?' I asked.

141

" 'Wait! Antichrist passes. He is the fire. We are the earth.'

"I shuddered. Sviatogor, in the famous Russian legend, was also the fire. He uprooted trees and rolled rocks along as if they were pebbles; he burned the villages. One day he noticed on the plain a slightly built and extremely ugly peasant who was carrying a sack on his shoulder. Sviatogor started in pursuit of him but his valiant steed charged across mountain and dale without catching up with him. The peasant for his part did not hurry at all; he merely transferred his sack at intervals from one shoulder to the other. Sviatogor scorched the ground under him, but in vain.

" 'Stop, *batyushka*, stop!' Sviatogor called out from a distance to the man who was apparently fleeing from him.

"The peasant threw his sack on the ground and waited for Sviatogor to arrive.

" 'What have you got in your sack, *batyushka*?'

" 'Pick it up yourself and you'll see,' answered the peasant.

"Sviatogor bent down and poked the sack with the tip of his whip. But it didn't budge. He made an effort to lift it with his little finger. He couldn't. He grabbed it with his hand: the sack seemed rooted in the soil.

" 'That's a miracle!' cried Sviatogor, panting for breath. 'I, the great hero, can't budge this tiny thing!'

"He dismounted, seized the sack with both hands, and pulled with all his might. He succeeded in raising it an inch, but at the same time he sank into the soil up to his waist. His face was covered with bloody sweat.

" 'So what have you got in that sack?' he exclaimed in terror.

" 'Do you want the truth?' answered the peasant. 'Well, the load I'm carrying in this sack is the land!'

"This Slavic legend sent a shudder down my spine. Could Sviatogor be Communism grappling with the muzhik?

"In my restlessness I climbed the lofty peak of Abbas Tuman. Ruined castles; poverty-stricken villages; women setting out tomatoes and onions on the roofs; old women at the doors spinning; and naked children rolling in piles of maize. As the road wound higher and higher, the air was filled with an intoxicating perfume. Apple orchards stretched to right and left, the trees laden with red and yellow apples bearing melodious names like *pashalma, makhara, soudalma, safran.* Heaps of apples were underneath the trees, and the Moslem women sitting cross-legged arranged them in little cases with their painted fingers.

"I sat under one of the apple trees with the Communist friend who was my companion. Max Ivanovich was very upset and he could not sleep at night. Far away at Rostov, on the banks of the Don, the State was preparing to throw seven hundred tractors into an area of fifty thousand hectares, and in ten days to plant this huge field with wheat. My friend was in a fever of impatience. Would this gigantic effort by the State turn out a success? If so, the Idea would take a step forward; if not, the Idea would retreat a step. The venture had ceased to be a matter of an agricultural enterprise. It had become a matter of the progress of the Spirit over the earth.

"I recounted my conversations with the peasants to him. Max nervously cracked the joints of his fingers and remained silent for a moment.

" 'The problem of the peasant,' he said finally, 'is complex; it can't find any definite solution as yet. It still remains impossible to reconcile its two principal aspects with each other: the economic aspect and the political aspect. The more freedom we give the peasant, the more production increases; consequently, from the economic point of view, we have to leave the peasant absolutely free. But the richer the peasant gets, the more reactionary and dangerous he becomes; consequently, from the political point of view, we absolutely have to restrict the peasant's freedom. Those of our leaders who dwell on the economic aspect declare themselves in favor of freedom for the peasant, while those who dwell on the political aspect favor oppression of the peasant. Where does the truth lie? Nowhere. The truth is still being made; it is fluid; it undergoes transformation as the problem is transformed, and that keeps developing and changing every moment. The truth depends in great part on our own strategy and acts.'

"It was then I noticed that my companion was a Jew; the way he expressed his thought warned me. For in Jewish mysticism this is how the Messiah comes, moving a step forward every time we perform a good and courageous act, and retreating a step with each of our wicked and craven acts. The Messiah depends on us; our acts determine whether the world will be saved or will collapse. We have a tremendous responsibility. At that moment I came face to face with the Jewish leaven which is today raising this enormous loaf, the Earth.

"On the lofty summit of Abbas Tuman, in the luxurious sanatorium where two hundred workers stricken with tuberculosis are being cured without any expense to themselves, I finally got far away from the peasant's gloomy soul. I found rest and in the end I discovered the worker who feels in harmony with everything and can sacrifice his petty individuality to the whole. By the collective nature of his work his spirit has become enlarged and his activity more interdependent. He can see and understand a general idea, and collaborate in a goal that transcends his immediate interests.

"An old worker on a garden bench underneath a fragrant pine tree serenely expounded to me the peasant's problem. Although this worker had played a cruel role in the October Revolution, his large blue eyes had become able at last to view the social struggle with tranquillity; the weakening of his body enabled him to rise above the battle.

144

" 'What is to be done?' he began. 'To strike at the kulak is to strike a death blow at production. So let's spare the kulak, while putting checks on his appetites. Let's attract the middling and poor peasants to ourselves; let's organize them into collectives. The collective is the Communist organism that must replace the kulak. We always come back to Lenin's point of view: the peasant will not become a Communist until he is surrounded by electric wires. The industrialization of our agriculture is the only definitive answer to the peasant question. The transformation of the peasant into an agricultural worker.'

" 'And until that day arrives?'

" 'We'll have to be patient, prudent, firm. We'll have to fight and suffer. Our generation must learn at last this simple lesson: whether it likes it or not, whether it knows it or not, it will be sacrificed to the new generation. We're still only the ones who sow; others will reap. And that's all right.'

"I pressed the tubercular old worker's feverish hand. Once again, so that I would never forget them, I stared into his sad, heroic clear blue eyes. Such eyes the Idea had when I imagined it to myself advancing on its bloody course over our hard earth. Between this old worker's temples I detected what I sought: the red line.

"Panteli, something has changed in me. Perhaps my heart is beginning to be involved. I can no longer watch this boundless struggle on the soil of Russia without emotion. But let's not talk any more. I'm passing through a crisis. Perhaps I shall never see you again."

13

NARROW-EYED KALMUCKS; Jews and Greeks
with the wily look of foxes sniffing the air; proud, bony
Kirghiz and Cossacks; wasp-waisted Georgians; exotic,
reticent delegates from Asia who had come for the
Oriental Congress . . . Then mountains of cantaloupes
and watermelons piled up around the foul, slimy waters
of Koutum; gourds, tomatoes, red pimientos, sickening
masses of fish; belugas, with the grease oozing out of them,
stretched out like slain wild boars on the black sand . . .
Then forests of masts and oars rising on the three hundred
malaria-infested arms that the Volga flings over the land
before vanishing into the Caspian Sea: forty thousand
boats and ships, with prows curved like the prow of a
gondola, or pointed like a sword, or flat like a tortoise.
And towering above all these races of human beings, above
these fruits and fishes and masts, a cathedral with rows
of high cupolas, pink as a sow's udders under the morning
sun. Astrakhan.

Rahel and Amita picked their way through the zigzags
of this feverish port. A madman with the wind whipping
his tatters passed along striking the prows with his stick
like a shaman exorcising an evil spirit and pronouncing a
curse. He spat and ran, while jolly-faced boatmen scuttled
up and laughingly threw him big pieces of watermelon.
Dark-haired women, with their hands over their mouths,
lolled in front of baskets filled with fruits, smoked fish and
scarlet pimientos. They looked on motionlessly, their eyes
brimming with the innocent lust of animals. Wide tables
were set up in the middle of the market; big bronze

samovars steamed, and the workers and fisherman all around poured their tea into their saucers, then put a piece of sugar, the *prikuska*, into the corner of their mouths and drank. Others gorged themselves on eggs and tomatoes.

Rahel and Amita walked in silence. Amita's heart overflowed with tenderness.

"Rahel," he said abruptly, "you don't love me any more."

Rahel faced him. "Comrade Amita," she said cruelly, "have we come here to the U.S.S.R. to indulge in idylls? To act like cooing doves? Aren't you ashamed?"

"Yes, I'm ashamed," Amita murmured. "I'm ashamed. . . ."

"Yes, I've ceased to love you, Comrade Amita," Rahel said with a laugh.

Amita felt for a moment that he was going to faint.

"I'm very tired, Rahel," he said in a low voice. "Let's sit down on this bench."

"Aren't you going to recite poetry, Comrade Amita?"

"No . . . no . . . I'm going to keep quiet."

They sat down. But Rahel felt restless.

"I'm going!" she said suddenly.

Amita followed her with swollen eyes. Her beautiful cherry-colored blouse flashed in the sun, the wind tossed her blue hair. Would she turn her head around? No . . . no . . . A cloud of black smoke and everything vanished. Astrakhan whirled around. Amita wiped drops of bitterness from his mouth.

Rahel hurried through the alleyways and along the stagnant waters. Her full lips were tightly compressed. Disturbing voices floated up from the depths of her vitals. Ancestral lust, flames, shrieks of pain.

"O lovely body, O marvelous play of light, O Comrade Rahel!"

Rahel turned in alarm. With the beggar's basin in his hand an old monk on the shore of the slimy waters of Koutum bowed to her in greeting.

147

"I saw you once in a dream," she cried in amazement. "Who are you?"

Silence. The old monk fastened his sad gaze on Rahel, devouring her face, her hair, her hands, her whole little body. Stricken with panic, Rahel paused for a moment to collect her thoughts. She relived the dream. A lofty tree, without leaves, blossoms or fruit. An old *bhikku* sitting motionless at the foot of a tree trunk, his hands and feet crossed, was smiling like a child. Catching sight of her as she passed, he whispered in a sweet voice that echoed in the dream like a clap of thunder:

"O lovely body, O marvelous play of light and shadow, O Comrade Rahel! Rush out into the streets and dance!"

"And I rushed into the streets and danced, danced wildly, shouting, 'It isn't I, Rahel, dancing! It isn't I, Rahel, dancing! Someone else is dancing in me.' "

"Yes," murmured the old monk with his childlike smile. "It was I."

"What do you want of me? Are you a messenger of joy? Are you a messenger of grief?"

"I have come to give you thanks, Comrade Rahel! You have danced well on this earth!"

When Rahel came out of the clouds, she saw the Big-Jawed Man in front of her, holding her up.

"You nearly fell, Comrade Rahel," he said. "You saw me from a distance, made a sign of greeting, and then I saw you totter."

"I've got the Astrakhan fever," said Rahel with a smile. "But I feel all right already. Let's walk a little way together."

"I'm going to a Kalmuck village."

"Kalmitzkii Bazaar? I too!" said Rahel. "Let's go."

Wretched hovels built on sand; not one green leaf. Clouds of blinding dust raised by the wind. One realized that one stood on the frontiers of the desert; the dry breath of the desert blew in gasps about the yellow heads of the Kalmucks, licking them like a tiger's tongue. A door opened, and a young Kalmuck girl came running out. Behind her, leaping like dolphins, dashed two superb white greyhounds, elegant in shape, beautiful of eye, their heads as long and delicate as a serpent's. A very fat Kalmuck woman at the doorway turned around and went on patiently munching something with the expression of a contented beast, of a cow watching apathetically as it ruminated.

On a low sand hill above the Volga, three temples side by side: a church, a mosque and a Buddhist pagoda.

"A sudden encounter of three sisters . . ." commented Rahel.

"I don't like sentimentality," her companion responded.

"I don't either!" exclaimed Rahel with pique.

"Then let's not talk, Comrade Rahel!"

Rahel became exasperated.

"You're playing a role," she finally declared in a dry, firm tone. "You're wearing a mask. You're harsh and strong and you know that I love you."

"Yes, I know, but I've overcome all my weaknesses. . . . You've come too late, Comade Rahel."

"Who are you?"

"A tower with neither doors nor windows. You prowl around me in vain and you break your nails in vain, Comrade Rahel."

Azad had been running around Astrakhan all day. A scandal had just broken in the city: the Cheka had discovered a house of ill fame frequented exclusively by Communist men and women. Wishing to express his indignation and grief to him, Azad hastened to visit one of his friends who worked for the Cheka. He would make one last appeal to the honest men. If they failed to listen, if they laughed in his face, then . . . then . . . Azad clenched his fists; crazy projects spurted from his unsettled brain.

When Azad got to his friend's house, he found him still

asleep. He was ushered into the living room. He looked about him in horror: in the corner, a big green parrot in a gilded cage; a Pekingese waddled up, dragging his fat belly on the floor, sniffed Azad for a moment and returned to his downy cushion. A few books . . . a soft sofa . . . Suddenly the clock began to play a piece of jazz; Azad looked up in rage; but he drew back with a cry when he saw, hanging beside the clock, a portrait of the pale, ascetic countenance of Dzerzhinski. Oh, he had to get out of there in a hurry! Now he saw, now he understood. Ah! Comfort! Ah! Red mire! Feverishly he scribbled a little note to his friend: "Listen, Ivan Andreyevich. Parrot or Dzerzhinski! Pekingese or Dzerzhinski! Jazz or Dzerzhinski! You've got to choose. Don't you feel any shame?"

He pinned the note on his friend's kepi, which lay on the sofa, and departed, banging the doors after him.

Geranos at the moment was sitting at the common table in the market, relishing the colorful scene while he enjoyed his tea. An Asiatic was using his fingers to eat the pilaf, molding it with leisurely movements. Fat traders, come from the distant reaches of the Volga, ate and drank with a young Armenian prostitute. A tall, stoop-shouldered, very dirty old priest, his beard stained yellow with tobacco, made the sign of the cross and drank. Khojas, sitting with their legs crossed, gazed intently at the masts in front of them until gradually their heads and shoulders fell in with the swaying of the ships.

All at once Geranos uttered a cry of terror. Azad, his face distorted, had silently emerged before him.

"Geranos," he said, "I'm ill. . . ."

He took a glass of tea, drank a few swallows, and felt a desire to sleep.

"Let's go," he mumbled. "I'm ill. . . ."

They rambled along the banks of the canals. Geranos watched Azad with anxiety. Azad halted before a little fisherman's cottage.

"This," he said, "is where I was born."

A little farther along, they stretched out on the sand. The bloody sunset dyed the stagnant waters a deep red. Azad watched the water flowing sluggishly along. His gaze turned into a fixed stare: horrible memories began to rise out of the waters, benumbing his brain. He was convulsed by a fit of arid laughter.

"Why?" he cried. "Why? As for you," he said, turning toward Geranos, "I hate you for smiling calmly there while I look at the water and remember. Once, during the famine . . ."

Geranos covered Azad's lips with his hand. "Don't talk," he murmured in dread; "don't tell me, Azad, let your memories go. . . ."

"Stop interrupting me! Stop interrupting me, or I'll scream! Let me talk! Let me ease my heart, I tell you!"

And he continued his story, blurting it out with breathless haste.

"I'd come here to crack down on the speculators who were hiding foodstuffs and leaving the city to die. I found my father starving in bed. My mother had already starved to death. . . . I found a bit of bread and a bit of meat; and my father revived. I got busy issuing orders and dispatching my men around the city. My father told me: 'This evening go to see your sister.'

" 'I don't have time this evening, father, I have work to do.'

" 'What kind of work? Accursed son! You kill men!'

" 'I don't kill men. I kill the wild beast that lies hidden inside some men. Father, I'm fighting for the deliverance of all humanity.'

"My father collapsed on his bed and cursed the day of my birth.

"That same night I boarded about a hundred speculators on a shallop; then I tied the shallop to a torpedo-boat, and we set our course for the Caspian Sea. A little before dawn I ordered my men to cut the cables tying the shallop to our ship and to uncover the cannons. When the specu-

151

lators understood, they shrieked with horror. I stood on the poop giving commands. The first cannon shot missed, and the second and the third as well. The fourth dropped into the middle of the shallop, and the speculators howled. As they raised their hands, I looked away; but gripping my heart with both hands, I turned back toward the shallop, which by now was beginning to sink.

" 'Shoot! Shoot!' I commanded. I saw the shallop awash and hands waving above the sea, and I heard the swash of the waters. . . . My eyes were red but dry."

As Azad finished his story, his left hand was trembling a little, and he hid it in his pocket.

"Why? Why?" he suddenly began to shout.

Night fell.

"Come on, Azad, let's go home," said Geranos, taking his friend by the arm. He helped him up and they walked a little way. Geranos could feel the quivering of Azad's worn-out body. A drunken sailor staggering along the harbor saw the two friends and stopped with a stumble. Abruptly he headed for them, pushed them apart and grabbed Azad's arm. Clinging to it to keep from crumpling to the ground, he started to talk. One moment he screamed, the next he stammered and came near whimpering.

"He was blond . . . spectacles . . . blue eyes. 'How old are you?' I asked him. 'Eighteen.' I led him into the courtyard; I had my revolver in my hand. The little one was trembling. 'Dyadya, give me a cigarette,' he said to me. I gave him a cigarette. He smoked it slowly to the end. Then he began to shiver. 'Dyadya, give me another cigarette!' he begged me. It was getting on my nerves. A cigarette? All right! And I emptied my revolver into his head."

Azad shuddered. He seized the sailor with both hands, shook him and shouted: "But why? Why?"

The sailor bent his head down, as if trying to remember. Then he shrugged his shoulders.

"How do I know?" he said.

All night Azad could not sleep. He had fever. He raved. His white lips writhed with the terrible question, Why? Why? The next day Azad was on his feet. His animal vitality had won out.

"I've got seven souls, like the cat," he said. "I've still got a few left."

Rahel had organized a boat trip to the Astrakhan desert. She wanted to show her companions the tremendous effort the Soviets were making to transform the desert into pasture-land. But Azad refused to go.

"I'm staying here," he said. "I have no more time to waste. I have work."

The rest sailed across the yellowish-blue waters on a stifling afternoon. Signs of the desert soon became visible: the trees got more and more scarce, the houses farther apart. Some buffaloes ranged sadly in search of one green leaf; a scrawny horse lifted its head in despair. The four friends had as companion a stern, attractive old man with paralyzed legs: Mitrofane Alexandrovich Orloff. He was commander-in-chief of the great expedition against the desert. For years he had fought against the sand. He had been severely wounded in this treacherous warfare: he had opened up a well, gone down into it, and stayed for several hours; when he came out, he was paralyzed in both legs.

Leaning on his crutches on the bridge of the little boat, Orloff sketched the plan of the campaign, and pinpointed the successes already achieved.

"Out of eight hundred and fifty thousand hectares, five hundred thousand are already covered with vigorous, hardy verdure. The sand is in retreat," said Orloff with a happy smile.

"Every strong soul has its own mission in the world," Amita thought as he watched the crippled man. "If it fulfils that, it is saved. The mission which this man has undertaken he fulfils fearlessly and patiently every day.

153

How can he fail to be happy? With every yard re-conquered from the desert he feels his soul liberated from a yard of desert. It isn't the Astrakhan steppe that he's reclaiming, but his own soul. . . . Ah! If I could only fight and move ahead like him!"

When they landed, evening was already beginning to fall. On the right side, the bare inhuman desert, on the left the struggling brushwood. The frontiers. As far as that green line the desert had yielded. The generalissimo hobbled along behind on his two crutches. One of these two marshal's staffs of his he dug into the gray desert, where it slipped, and the other one into the green earth, where it held firm among the roots. With a smile he turned his stern, kind eyes upon his guests.

"We'll bring cattle," he said; "we'll transform the desert into pasture-land; man will come. Our enemies are terrible: sand, wind, locusts. But we have patience and love."

Leaning on his crutches, Orloff gazed out at the still unvanquished sands on the right. To Geranos, in the darkness of the desert, his shaven, obstinate, inflexible head all at once looked like the gleaming, noble, marvelously poised head of Lenin. Rahel suddenly grasped Orloff's big hands and covered them with kisses.

14

THE BIG-JAWED MAN entered the hall where the Oriental Congress was being held. His eyes were momentarily dazzled by the scene: cloaks in every hue, red and green boots and sandals, slanting eyes full of fire, yellow, brown, black faces, a queer odor of sweating animals and arid plants. In the midst of this Oriental richness, Azad, Geranos and a few Europeans who were present had the mean, commonplace appearance of sparrows among a throng of peacocks with their tails unfurled.

At that moment, a white-robed old Hindu theosophist was speaking in a faint, ingratiating voice. He looked slowly over the whole gathering, his eyes lingering on each member with the insistence of a caressing hand. He raised his thin, tan arms, folded them over his breast, and with a solemn gesture took his leave. When the interpreter began to translate the speech, a scornful smile flickered over the face of the Big-Jawed Man.

"Brothers . . . sisters . . . do not seek Progress! Go backward . . . abandon the West! The abyss! A frightful war is about to explode . . . a prehistoric war of carnivorous animals . . . between nations . . . between classes. . . . Hatred! Why? Why? It will engulf all things . . . Return to the East, my brothers! Be simple and good! Love men, love animals and plants . . . Love matter; do it no violence! There are no nations. There are no classes. There are only human beings . . . shadows . . . for a moment, there is sun . . . for a moment the heart stirs . . ."

A young man got up and the President introduced him: "Hussein of Bokhara."

He mounted the rostrum, spread out his arms and burst into laughter, showing a set of brightly gleaming teeth.

"Go back to your ancestral spinning wheels," he cried. "When your face is slapped, turn the other cheek . . . be like dogs licking the hand of the master who beats them. Aha! Ahahaha!"

Again he burst into savage laughter. Then suddenly, his beardless face turned gloomy. He struck the rostrum with his clenched fist.

"The Orient is no vegetarian tigress!" he roared. "The Orient wants blood. War! War! We can endure no more—we people of India, China, Siam, Afghanistan, Persia, Arabia, Africa. All of us oppressed peoples! The machine is the weapon of the proletarian revolution, and hatred is our leader. Love will come afterward . . . we have time for that later. When our enemies—the English and Americans, the capitalists—have been hanged on our trees and eaten up by the flies and crows of Asia and Africa, we'll love them dearly then!"

A tremendous roar of laughter shook the hall. The delegates from central Asia pulled out their yataghans and brandished them in the air. Their eyes were bloodshot.

"Fraternity! Fraternity!" they chanted.

A young Hindu woman swathed in orange cashmere asked for the floor.

"Gandhara, delegate of the Hindu women workers!" the President announced.

Gandhara opened her mouth, but her voice was stifled with tears. Only a few incoherent words could be caught:

"English . . . hunger . . . wages . . . we are dying . . ."

A frail Chinese man with cold, cruel eyes and tight, drooping lips stepped forward:

"General Ti-o-lin, delegate from Shanghai!"

The general mounted the rostrum and dug his fingernails into it. Short, harsh shrieks. His macabre eyes stared at each of the delegates one by one. He gnashed his teeth, clamped them tight, snapped them open, putting an ominous stress on his syllables.

"Four hundred and fifty millions . . . souls of the Orient . . . Western technology . . . stored-up hatred . . . War! War without mercy! . . . Turn your other cheek? Aha! A jaw for a tooth!"

Rahel was in a state of exultation, but Amita was huddled up in a corner, listening in terror. Oh, where were the thirteen soldiers and the thirteen little children of his imagination? Where was that whole innocent mental game he had played for his own amusement? Millions of real soldiers were shooting off their guns, millions of real children being shot down all over the world!

"Can you see? War! All Asia is howling for it!" commented Geranos, as he turned toward Azad.

Azad had grown pale and tremulous.

"Does that make you happy, eh?" he growled furiously. "War!"

"I am neither for nor against earthquakes. War exists, and I simply affirm the fact."

"And are you glad?"

"Well, yes! Man will be able to progress more rapidly."

"And Russia?"

"Russia, too, will progress more rapidly."

"Toward catastrophe!"

"Toward her solution."

"You are a heartless man. To you, Russia represents no more than an interesting tragedy. Russia and the whole world too. You have your box-seat, you man of ice, and you sit there watching the play. If they play well, you applaud. If they play badly, you make a face. And why? Because you have no love in you. Anyone who loves doesn't watch things; he suffers. So I suffer! I suffer! Don't say anything, don't smile, I hate you!"

"Come on, let's go outside," urged Geranos. "I have to talk to you. I love clarity. I, too, am suffering. Let's go out!"

Once they were out on the street, Geranos was momentarily seized by a wild desire to throw himself into the arms of this good, but irritating, simple-minded man. Pardon everything, transcend all the agitation and pettiness of human nature, surrender himself completely, without reserve, in spite of everything, walk side by side with a man unto death! But this desire was quickly and angrily repressed by Geranos. No, walk alone, bereft of all the sentimental thrills enjoyed by common people. Alone and unsupported, never taking your eyes off the abyss.

Azad grabbed Geranos by the shoulders, and murmured in a moved voice: "I still love you in spite of everything."

Geranos heard a dreaded little voice inside his heart. He pulled away from Azad's embrace.

"I love you too, Azad," he said, "but I don't love your confused ideas. And when your ideas are not confused, I love them still less! You rant or say the most banal commonplaces!"

"I'm not a philosopher like you," Azad retorted angrily. "I'm no library rat like you. I'm a human being! Your soul is an elderly whore, painting herself up, simpering, flirting, giving herself, then pulling back, then calling— all without love. But my call comes from my own heart, and my heart never makes a mistake! It tells the truth!"

"The truth!" scoffed Geranos, his eyes clouded with indignation and sorrow. "Truth, Justice, Happiness! Have you no shame?"

"Then is everything in vain as far as you're concerned," shouted Azad, pounding his chest, "you defeatist, you? Love, friendship, the struggle of mankind?"

"It isn't moral problems that interest me," answered Geranos in a bantering tone. "These are the problems that vex your simple heart, but for the past three or four years, I've left these behind me. I'm aware of their importance for the individual and for society, but they don't torture me any more!"

158

"You mean it's only the metaphysical problem? That's all that's bursting your bladder, that big heart of yours! The egg before the chicken or the chicken before the egg?"

"Not even the metaphysical problem, Azad; only the throb on the edge of the abyss."

Geranos' voice reverberated like a sob.

"But then why did you come to us here, to Russia?"

"So that I could feel this throb more keenly. So that I could see the abyss at closer range. So that I could train my heart not to tremble. Don't you understand?"

"No, I can't understand," answered Azad, moved by his friend's sudden pallor.

"Today in the U.S.S.R., the human heart is beating more forcefully than anywhere else in the world. Once it was Athens or Benares or Mecca or Jerusalem. Today, it's Moscow. Here is where the human heart is fighting in the vanguard, shedding its blood into the abyss. And this is what gives me the great throb that is the aim of my life."

"I know, I've already told you the same thing," Azad exclaimed. "I understood it all from the first moment. You've come to us here as a spectator, to watch us starving and sinking in blood and agony."

"No! No!" cried Geranos, putting his hand over Azad's mouth. "I, too, am covered with blood. I, too, am struggling, here in the U.S.S.R. Understand me, Azad: tonight, I'm in an emotional state; I feel I'm going to be separated from you. My heart has opened a bit and longs to give itself. . . ."

"That's the kiss of Judas," Azad shouted. "Ah, you want to go away all alone! Well then, go, and forget your fine phrases!"

Geranos had no more to say. As he watched the starry night, he saw the abyss yawning between men, he saw himself in boundless solitude. He clutched at his heart and reflected to himself, with a smile:

159

"God is like a human heart standing on the edge of the abyss!"

The Oriental Congress was still in session. They had approved a forceful order of the day condemning Fascism.

Shame . . . violence . . . the Black Terror.

Then the Big-Jawed Man asked the President for the floor. He was very calm, and as he stood up there on the rostrum, he looked like a block of marble. He stared into those violent brown faces, those treacherous, cruel eyes, and he thought:

"This is Asia . . . we must talk to Asia!"

His voice, perfectly controlled, rang out with warm resonance. Amita, who reported the speech to Geranos the next day, was in the rear of the hall, so he missed many of the words.

" 'To dare to see reality . . . War is a reality . . . it is on its way. Two Ideas: the Black Idea and the Red Idea. Everyone has the right and the duty to kill his enemy. We must belong to our own time. Let's leave the pacifists, theosophists, vegetarians to their bleatings . . . We must be fighters. Red or Black, that's of secondary importance . . . To be a good fighter, that is our grand duty. Black Terror does exist and that is as it should be. Idea without Terror is an absurdity. Above all other Russian institutions, I love and venerate the Black Okhrana and the Red Cheka. And why? Because a soldier without weapons is an absurd soldier!' "

He had repeated this word "absurd" with terrifying disdain.

"As he talked," Amita added, "he glared at each of his listeners in turn, and wrestled with each one separately, for several seconds, before pouncing on the next one. By the end of the speech, they all felt overwhelmed. The Chinese general had gotten up and shouted out:

" 'The Red Terror!'

160

"The Big-Jawed Man, who had sat down, drew himself erect and answered the Chinese general:

" 'That's all right, comrade! If I were Mussolini, I would have yammered for the Black Terror. Who is right? The victor! We must wait, comrades.' "

At the end, after describing the whole scene to Geranos, Amita could not hold back his tears.

"Comrade Amita," exclaimed Geranos, bending toward the frail man from Japan, "are you weeping?"

Poor Amita hadn't dared tell the whole story. Rahel had rushed up to that barbarous man. From a distance, Amita had seen her talking with him elatedly, devouring him with her big, insatiable eyes. Some animal force flowed from him and crushed the lovable young woman.

"Comrade Geranos, I'm afraid," Amita confessed, bowhis head. "This Congress has confused everything for me. All of Asia is stirring menacingly: the Communist Idea is unleashing passions that used to be curbed by ignorance or fear. At Bokhara, I remember, I felt happy when I looked on these Asiatic races, for I thought I could see them surging up against the old Europe. I dreamed of the destruction and regeneration of the world. Now that I find the Idea being incarnated and advancing over the earth, I shrink back in alarm. Last night I saw people with bloodthirsty eyes. I heard them screaming for butchery. A terrible doubt has come over me: won't the Communist Idea be defiled when it treads on the earth? Comrade Geranos, help me! I am suffering!"

"What did you expect the Idea to do, Comrade Amita? Nestle inside your virgin brain, like an old maid? The Idea is a woman, with a belly made to digest and a womb to bear children. What would the Idea do inside the head of a poet and idealist like you? It would get bored and fade into childishness or madness."

"Yes, Comrade Geranos, but before the Idea can become a reality, everybody's soul must be ready to receive

161

it. Everyone must understand that the purpose of the struggle is not to feast the belly, but to transform the food and drink into Spirit. But the workers and these savage races dream only of juicy roasts and naked women. How can you expect such a mob to regenerate the world?"

"But, Comrade Amita, how do you think the world is ever regenerated?" came Geranos' answer. "What lure do you think is capable of exciting the masses? Are you disgusted when you see these masses responding only to the dictates of hunger and the flesh?

"This thought used to be a stumbling-block for me too. But one day on a Greek island—Siphnos—a fisherman revealed the truth to me in all its marvelous suppleness. I'd walked down to the shore from the Monastery of the Virgin of the Mount. I wanted to watch the potters molding their clay, throwing it onto their wheels as warm as flesh and giving it all shapes as the wheel rotated. A young worker, baked in the sun like a vase, offered me some figs, and we exchanged the quiet, timeless words men say to one another. Toward evening, I stretched out on a rock, near an old fisherman who had cast his line and was squatting there, waiting for the fish to bite. We chatted. About the sea, about wars, about the wretchedness of mankind, about figs . . . Suddenly he faced me and looked me up and down.

" 'You seem to me an educated man,' he said. 'Could you tell me how Christ gained his first disciple?'

"After I'd repeated what the Scriptures have to say on the subject, he shook his head with a smile.

" 'I'm the only one who really knows. What was his name?'

" 'Andrew.'

" 'That's right—Andrew,' he said. 'A storm had broken loose and the wind was raging; the fishermen were going home in despair, their nets empty. Suddenly a fire blazed up on the shore, and near the fire, loomed a man's shadow. "That man must be eating his dinner," thought one of the famished fishermen and he rushed toward the fire along the seashore.'

" 'It wasn't the sea, it was a lake,' I'd interrupted.

" 'Oh! What does that matter! That's what ruins you bookish people! The fisherman dashed toward the fire, found the smoldering cinders, and a few remains of fish. But the man had disappeared. He called. No one there!

" 'The next day the storm raged still more violently. Again the fishermen were returning home in despair, their nets empty. And again the fire appeared on the bank with the man's shadow! The same fisherman as the night before sprinted forward and this time, he reached the man, who was grilling fish that he'd strung together on a reed. The man was young, about thirty, and tanned by the sun like a fisherman. He had bare feet.

" ' "What are you doing there?" cried the fisherman.

" ' "You can see for yourself, I'm cooking my fish."

" ' "How did you manage with this wild sea? The rest of us haven't eaten for two days."

" ' "You don't know how to cast your nets. I will teach you."

" 'The fisherman, who was Andrew, as you've doubtless guessed, fell down at the man's feet, crying: "Master, I shall never leave you!"

" 'That evening Andrew said to his brother: "I've found a man who knows how to catch fish even in the worst kinds of weather."

" 'And the brother told his friends and that's how Christ, for it was He, recruited his disciples little by little. At first, He instructed them how to catch fish; then little by little, in time, from catch to catch, He made them His apostles!'

"Well! What d'you say, Comrade Amita? The most chimerical message that ever flowered on the earth! And see what solid ground it had to fall on before it could bear fruit: the belly! 'God's' infallible stratagem to gain man.

163

"In the course of the fisherman's monologue, I remembered a Descent of the Holy Ghost I'd seen on some old parchment: the Holy Ghost, swooping straight downward like a starving gull that has spied the Apostles from afar, and has seized hold of them by twelve red lines. The Apostles flounder about like fish, in their terrified efforts to loosen the hooks. But the hook has already sunk into their bellies and is yanking them up to heaven, never to let go of them again!

"The old fisherman was watching me with a sly smile:

" 'That's how God works, my friend,' he said to me. 'You educated people say that God's an idea, something imaginary, something rare, I don't know what. Other people even picture him as a bearded old fellow floating on the clouds!'

"The old fisherman burst out laughing.

" 'What are you laughing at?' I asked him.

" 'Well, He's a wheel, like the one you see over there. He's forever rotating; He rotates and makes whatever He wants to as He passes over the Earth: pitchers, vases, pots, kettles, lamps. You fill these with water or wine or honey or even dung; some of them you can use for cooking, others for giving light. And this is how we human beings come out of God's hands too. And if we get broken, it doesn't matter to Him very much. He just goes on forever turning and turning.'

" 'But why did He make me?' I asked him. 'And once He has created me, why does He break me? I don't want . . .'

" 'Eh, what do you think?' The old man laughed with a dry, sarcastic laugh. 'You think He asks our advice?'

"This is what that old man of Siphnos told me. And just now, Comrade Amita, when I heard you talking in such a sentimental vein, I recalled the heroic words of that good fisherman, with their tingle of wind and salt. You think that men have to see the Light before they can rise to revolt! But since when has Revolution ever begun with the majority? The masses are always organized by minorities which are driven by an Idea that has become a passion. Bloodshed and crime are the indispensable initiation rites. If it were in my hands to choose between bloodshed and peace to ensure the triumph of the New Idea, I would choose bloodshed. Not, of course, because I am bloodthirsty; but because I know that the more violent the reaction from evil and the more bloodstained the victory, the stronger will be the upward surge and the stabler the triumph.

"You see, God—let's give this name to our awe-inspiring Wheel—is no gentle paterfamilias. He is cruel; He has no concern for individuals; He kills, creates, kills again; He is beyond our own pattern of virtue. He's not to your liking? You would doubtless have preferred an affable God, with a human face, clean hands, white garments, a kind of theosophist or apothecary, with scales in his hands, distributing to all men equal shares of bread and brains? Ah, old man of Siphnos, how right you are! God does not ask our advice! He descends as He pleases, grasping anything he wants, the belly, the phallus, the human spirit. The first moment of His appearance is called Chaos. Gradually the fever subsides, passions are reduced, the forces become balanced. The new seed is sown in blood and tears. Eternal happiness? Peace? Justice? Heavens no! Not today or ever! There will always be injustice, hunger, misfortune. Justice and Happiness are soporifics for the sublime nature of life. New groans ascend. And for God, who is the general-in-chief of vagabonds and of the new downtrodden class, it's the New Year.

"With such inhuman clarity as this we must consider the present movement of the Proletariat and bow down in awe and terror before the new Russia. For in spite of hunger and bloodshed, she is forging the new road. In one of the apocryphal Gospels, a remarkable vision is described, that of John, the beloved disciple, as he stood in tears at the feet of the crucified Christ: here the cross was no longer of wood, but of light; and instead of a man's being nailed to it, there were thousands of women, men, children moaning and dying there. John was trembling and he couldn't distinguish the shapes or hold them steady: there were countless numbers of them and they kept spilling over like cataracts. Little by little they disappeared, and there was nothing left but a crucified Cry on the wood.

"Today this vision is alive, palpitating before us. The whole of Russia, millions of men, women, children are suffering on this cross. Every day some die; they perish of hunger or cold or hatred or love of the Idea. They are lost, they vanish, no face can be seen. But from these numberless dead, there will survive a Cry of freedom. And the world will be saved.

"This, Comrade Amita, is the way I see Russia, with patience, confidence and fear."

When he got back to the Hotel, Geranos was very pale. Azad lay stretched out on the bed, his eyes glazed, and didn't return the greeting. He seemed to be plunged in painful meditation. All night long he didn't close his eyes. Toward dawn he rose dejectedly and watched Geranos as he slept. Azad thought he could detect a smile of ironical disdain on Geranos' lips. Azad clenched his fists nervously. How wonderful it would be to run away, to walk out on this arrogant man, this puffed-up heart! His eyes filled with tears. How wonderful to go away, to go away, to follow the Volga, to lose his way among the villages, to live with simple-hearted muzhiks, and plunge himself in their flood of human concerns! To reach at last, by a long hard route, Moscow. To reach Moscow and preach the truth! Who was to blame? Why was everything going so badly in our Russia? The deep soul of the muzhiks would reveal the truth to him. And soon, Moscow would be hearing that truth, right in the middle of all her lovely celebrations! Azad wiped his tears nervously, then scrib-

bled a few words and threw them down on Geranos'
pillow:

"I'm leaving you," it read. "I'm walking out on you, I
am free! We'll meet again in Moscow. You'll be there with
your metaphysical bickerings: the egg or the chicken; the
chicken or the egg? And I'll be holding the truth in my
hands and I'll turn the world upside down. You'll see!
You'll see! I don't need you. I am free!"

15

ON A MELLOW, slightly subdued afternoon, Geranos reached the great artery, and silently began to penetrate into the huge body of Russia. He felt as if he were penetrating into a boundless, extraordinarily damp cathedral alive with forests and animals and teeming humanity.

The Volga—Mamochka—sprawling over her broad mud bed, has swarms of human beings riding on her fat thighs and swollen belly. They play there for a few moments in the sun, then slide back in masses into the mud of the Mamochka and stir no more. Geranos loved this Volga, so like some tremendous mother full of milk. Man approaches her in terror:

She is sitting down and her breasts reach to the ground and they are flowing. I went around her right knee and cried, "Mother, let me drink."

She lowered her right breast and I drank white milk. But I was dying, still dying of thirst. I went around her left knee and cried, "Mother, let me drink."

She lowered her left breast and I drank black milk. I ceased my entreaties. I ceased to move and my thirst was gone.

As Geranos penetrated silently into the huge body of Russia, his soul was troubled. Long hours on end he watched the flow of the mighty waters. What had been the fruit of his pilgrimage to the U.S.S.R.? When he had first come, his feeling toward man had been one of relentless scorn, and his spirit was depressed as he contemplated the rising red line. Little by little his heart had been moved in the U.S.S.R. He had felt the suffering and the tremendous human struggle. Profound pity first and then a sudden revelation of responsibility for the whole of existence . . . the decisive hour . . . the duty to become involved. Ah! To roll up one's sleeves and plunge one's hands into the dough, into this ponderous, resistant reality.

Wide black shallops glided slowly and noiselessly along, loaded with watermelons, cantaloupes, and red apples, their square sails gaily spread, like ancient Chinese shields as they advanced. Bearded men perched on the prows with their noses and moustaches and mouths buried in watermelons as fragrant as the sea. They passed Stalingrad, they reached Saratov. Throngs of people kept getting on and off the boat. Barbarous faces, blond beards, tiny blue eyes, women with big flowered shawls, swollen bellies and the smell of buffaloes. The left bank presented an idyllic scene, with its harmonious wooded hills and its beautiful isbas nestling among the birches; on the right bank, arid plains and delightful sandbanks. Wooden rafts floated silently along toward Astrakhan, following the full yet delicate breathing of the waters. A tiny isba on the rafts, the wife getting the kettle ready and the cock crowing on the rooftop . . . A young intellectual twenty years old, on his way to Nizhnii Novgorod, was chatting with Geranos:

"I feel tired," he said, "so tired. I have lived fifty years, a hundred years . . . I need to rest. A bit of comfort, a little house, a sweet wife, a canary, a geranium pot or two, a baby . . ."

At Saratov, a few days before, poor Amita had gotten a profound shock. Famine! Appalling stories. Children's corpses piled up in the streets. Parents exchanging the little corpses of their own children with other parents, lest they eat their own offspring. In the Museum, Amita had touched with his own hands the bread made of cow-

169

dung and straw that the Russians were eating. He shuddered with horror when he saw the photographs. Someone told him:

"People were dropping in the streets. I had a piece of sugar and a bit of salt carefully knotted in the end of my handkerchief way down in the bottom of my pocket. One day when I was eating a herring, I threw its head down on the ground and a peasant rushed over to grab it, licking it greedily. The Nansen Mission arrived and started distributing clothes sent us by good souls in the West. I managed to get hold of a frock-coat and a top hat. Decked out in this costume and starving to death, I rushed to a meeting, thinking I might be able to raise the spirits of the panic-stricken people by talking with them. We had long beards. We were thin, thin as specters. We couldn't even stand up. But as soon as they caught sight of me up on the platform, those poor starving people couldn't stop laughing! They held their insides with their hands—for when they moved, their innards hurt—and they went on laughing."

A worker told Amita:

"In the evening you couldn't walk near the houses or pass by the gates. You had to walk down the middle of the street. For there were starving men and women lying in ambush behind the doors. They flung lassos and caught careless passers-by by the neck and quickly dragged them into the courtyard to eat them. Once I was in a restaurant where there was nothing to eat, nothing but sausages. This restaurant was famous for its mouth-watering sausages and people used to queue up there every day. After waiting several hours, I managed to get in and, without sitting down, I had begun devouring some sausages. A woman was with me, a friend—she's dead now. Suddenly a militia man came in and shouted: 'Tovarishch, stop eating! Stop eating! Throw the sausages away! The police have just confirmed that all the sausages served in this restaurant are made of human flesh!'

"At once I threw away the little piece of sausage I had

left and nearly fainted from disgust. But the woman wouldn't let go of hers. She bolted it down, emitting little grunts as she did so."

Amita exclaimed: "Brothers, brothers, how you have suffered!"

When he found himself alone, Amita went down to the banks of the Volga. His knees were shaking. How insignificant his own suffering seemed to him, how shameful his life. Rahel! Oh, if only we could forget our own little sorrows and lose ourselves in the great grief of the world.

"Amita," he murmured, "no more of your miserable ego! Have you no shame? Idylls! Blabber! See how man suffers."

Amita gazed in fascination at the flow of the green waters. The Volga with her ample fecund hips and her numberless breasts. For myriads of centuries, generation upon generation, she'd been bearing and carefully licking and grinding and swallowing so many different kinds of people: savages, men bred of the Empire and by feudalism, the bourgeoisie and finally, the most recent stratum, the Communists! The muzhiks and the fishermen, men, women and little children, were lying on their bellies on the black sand, singing:

"Aïh, big wide Mother Volga—aïh, you lull us to sleep and rock us—and take all our strength away!"

Amita heard another story from an old man:

"We had nothing left to heat ourselves with. We had burned our furniture, we were shivering and starving. One morning at daybreak when I looked out the window, I saw a heavily loaded cart standing in front of the house. I ran to my wife and woke her up. 'At last they're bringing wood,' I said. 'We're going to get warm!' My wife jumped out of bed, with all the covers wrapped around her. We glued our faces to the window-panes. But slowly, slowly

171

as it got lighter, we could see better. These 'logs of wood' were just the arms and legs of corpses."

After telling this frightful tale, the old man laughed. Amita felt sick. "There must be something corporeal about the soul," he thought to himself. "After a few spurts upward, it gets worn out, dull and then quietly sinks back into matter."

The old man lit a cigarette, but threw it away at once with a nervous gesture.

"Near Samara, in a ruined isba," he went on, "we found the living carcass of a man one hundred and ten years old. He was hidden beneath his stinking rags, all dazed by age and hunger. His name was Serafim. 'Serafim,' I said to him, 'what is the thing that has made the greatest impression on you in your life?' '*Yest' khochetsya! Yest' khochetsya!*' he answered anxiously. 'The desire to eat!' "

Sailboats with their prows turned up in the shape of Tartar slippers were gliding back up the river. They were loaded with fruit. This was the bountiful and lovely season just before the sandy shores of the Volga get buried under the snow, when they are in a mad rush to blossom and bear fruit and nourishment for man and beast: watermelons, cantaloupes, onions, squashes, maize, wheat, *kasha* and huge expanses of sunflowers. Reeking of onions, and their beards dotted with little pieces of watermelon, the muzhiks felt happy.

Amita hurried on his way to Moscow, his heart in an uproar.

Heroic and solitary in its stark whiteness, a minaret loomed up among the autumn-wounded poplar trees. Kazan. Sturdy, ugly peasant women, their long poles across their shoulders, were carrying milk, apples, eggs to market. The clang of voices rose and fell on the street with a resonant, guttural sound such as little metallic birds might make. Slanting eyes, embroidered skull caps, turned-up slippers. A flock of pearl-gray pigeons darted from the white walls of the kremlin, landed on the sunlit round cupola of an old mosque, and spread their tails. All Kazan cooed with pigeons.

With his heavy, measured tread, the Big-Jawed Man crossed over Chernichevskaïa Ulitza on his way to the Congress of the *Komsomols*. Rahel hurried after him, out of breath. How thin her beautiful face had grown these past few days! And her long, gazelle-like eyes were ringed with shadows.

"I'm dragging toward the abyss," she thought to herself. "I've let myself down."

In her reports to the Cheka, she was already soft-pedaling her comments, cleverly toning down her expressions, showing an almost favorable attitude toward this monstrous man with the piercing, hostile eyes. She could not sleep at night. Lia, Lia, her sister's ghost obsessed her. How she must have loved! How she must have suffered! Whenever Rahel found herself alone, she burst into tears. In a numb, mute way she was beginning to be reconciled to death.

"Come on, Comrade Rahel, get along there more quickly. We're late!"

Rahel hurried on obediently.

"I've let myself down . . . I've let myself down," she thought.

They entered the huge crowded hall. Faces full of an expression of exaltation, young people, some of them pale and thin, some of them strong and barbaric-looking. The platform at the back was liberally decorated with long golden ears of corn and black silhouettes of factories. Right and left, the busts of the two patriarchs: Karl Marx, with his lofty, massive, visionary, prophetic head, and Lenin, with his smooth-shaven head bowed in concentration on the ground, fretted with the cares of working out all the difficult details.

Rahel's eyes regained their animation. She felt alive. She looked with hatred at her merciless companion. A Tartar workman was making a speech: the same key words, the same dogmas over and over again, the same rhythmic motions to beat the idea into the people's skulls.

"Exactly, that's it!" the morose man was thinking. "I love this motion the blacksmith makes as he strikes his anvil. That's the real way the man of action moves."

A ten-minute break. As she moved in and out among the Tartar *komsomols*, Rahel drank in their aura of youth and faith. She forgot her own petty miseries. She laughed and talked and felt free. A young Tartar poet, yellow and slender as a flame, told her:

"Our purpose is not pure beauty. Our purpose is to awaken consciousness and to contribute to the building of socialist Asia. We love and we hate, we are not aesthetes!"

Every muscle in the young Tartar's steel-hard frame was vibrating. His voice had become husky and broken. Rahel felt a thrill of joy. Wasn't this the impatient, troubled voice of Asia? She looked around at the Tartar countenances, their sleek hair and slanting eyes and powerful jaw-bones.

"Yes, yes, we are Scythians!" they seemed to be saying. "Yes, yes, we are Asiatics with hungry, slanting eyes! The centuries belong to you. But this hour here and now belongs to us! Ah! old Europe, batter your brains out and solve the puzzle! Russia is the Sphinx: tortured and blood-stained, she casts herself upon you full of love and full of hatred!"

Rahel raised her head. She could still hear the harsh voices of these young Tartars and feel their fiery breath on her thin face. Suddenly a terrifying decision rose in her heart.

"Ah, it's enough of that! I'm not going to let myself go any more. I'm free. I have salvation in my own hands!"

The Big-Jawed Man had pursued the President of the Congress into a corner. There he was plying him with clear cruel questions.

"Can sons do better than their fathers?" he asked. "That's what interests me."

The young *komsomol* concentrated a moment. His prominent eyebrows fluttered up and down. The young man seemed to be measuring and weighing his words. He answered with a sure voice:

"I know, we need new virtues, the virtues of the man who builds: order, stubborn tenacity, patience. New forms of violence and peace. New forms of work. Some of the ideas our fathers' generation held were dictated by the needs of their own destructive mission. These ideas must be repudiated by the sons. Have we done this? Are we, the sons, a bit more advanced? I don't know. I cannot know this. We are too intensely involved in living our own epoch to be able to see it and judge it. The answer you are asking me for, comrade, does not exist. Each and every moment, it is growing more and more ripe."

The Big-Jawed Man stopped asking questions. He went away with an anxious heart. How he loved this fanatical, disciplined young Tartar! Could this be the new type of human being Russia was forging? He felt terror.

"I admire and fear these Russians," he grunted. "Their aim is mystical, their means positive."

He left Rahel there and went off by himself. He wanted to be alone.

He walked out beyond the city-limits, wandering over the gentle, human, Russian countryside, quivering as the warm autumn rain fell on his hands and face. A muzhik buried in the furrows was scraping the earth up in heaps. An industrious beetle rolling a clod of earth along turned upside down, righted itself and fell over again, but still held onto the clod of earth as though it were holding a woman in its arms. Farther on, a Tartar village. Young girls on their way to the fountain held balanced poles with two big pails hanging from them across their arched shoulders. A downpour of rain drove the Big-Jawed Man under a tree which was giving its shelter to several rain-

175

soaked, laughing children. They stared at the strange man in fascination. When he started talking with them, the children gave him sharp, dogmatic answers, for these tiny creatures had no doubts about anything.

"What do you do every day when school is over? Do you play?"

"Oh, I don't have time," cried the child with the red tie. "I have many things to do. In the first place I'm on the editorial staff of our *Bulletin Board Gazette*. I have to write articles there to guide comrades who haven't reached the stage of Pioneers yet. Then there's our club: that's where we have our library and movie-house and the 'Red Corner of Lenin.' We have discussions and I make speeches. You see, I'm awfully busy."

The little chest heaved a sigh.

"And evenings at home?"

"First I have to study my lessons; then I've a very hard task to do. . . ."

"Very hard? What is it?"

"Teaching my parents. They're both very backward. I've taught them the alphabet. Oh! was that hard! Now they're beginning to read and write. I bring them books. Every day I read the newspapers to them and talk to them about Lenin. But they don't want to understand. . . ."

The child's face clouded, and he bit his lips.

"But they will understand!" he insisted.

The Big-Jawed Man gritted his teeth. For the second time today he felt afraid. He left the tree and headed for the village through the rain.

"Could this be the new type of man being forged in Russia?"

That agonizing question tortured him.

In a dung-strewn courtyard, an old kulak received him with a wary sort of curiosity. Huge dark rooms, women's voices. The stranger looked in vain for a portrait of Lenin. In the place of honor on his wall, the kulak had framed, not the piercing face of the Red Czar, but three lines of Arabic verse embroidered on black velvet:

O you who still enjoy the light of the day, behold! The world is nothing but an inn, we come in the evening and depart the next morning. . . .

The kulak kept his eyes lowered to avoid the stranger's gaze. But as he watched the stubborn, silent head, the stranger thought he could detect the tremor of a great hope. For this is how Lenin had come one evening and gone away the next morning. . . .

"Ah, ah!" the stranger murmured, patting the kulak's shoulders in a friendly way.

At that moment the young Pioneer came bounding in.

"My grandson," said the old man proudly.

As the Big-Jawed Man was leaving the kulak's house, a young soldier—a mere boy—was just passing by on horseback. The upper part of his body was rigid and he had a revolver in his belt. As he rode slowly through the village, his still gray eyes inspected and took stock of everything.

"Who is that?" asked the Big-Jawed Man.

The old kulak held his tongue, till the young rider had disappeared in the distance. Then he answered in a hushed voice:

"The Cheka!"

At Nizhnii Novgorod a horse ran across Plakhoutnii Most, the big wooden bridge over the Volga. Noble, lithe, head high, overflowing with vitality, streaming with sunlight. Whenever Geranos thought about Nizhnii Novgorod, this horse with the broad steel-blue breast all fuming at the nostrils sprang into his memory, covered in bronze and fully armored like the steed of some medieval knight, along with the rough, heavy *izvoshchik* astride him, wearing his enormous green velvet cap trimmed with

177

fur. The horse had passed by a church that was all decked out like some imperial coach on parade. For a brief flash, the horse was silhouetted against the pale morning sky, harnessed to the golden church.

The Fair, the famous Nizhnegorodskaïa Yarmarka, covered with big black and white stripes, was in its death-throes on its sandy bed between the Oka and the Volga. Silent, languorous-eyed Persians lay in ambush behind piles of dried foods—dates, figs, pistachios, onions, raisins, cinnamon and pepper. There was a puny, tubercular little monkey perched on an empty crate. An iron chain held it captive. Its sad eyes gazed at the men surrounding it, who just laughed and went on torturing it. Off to one side a pelican with heavy, dirty wings edged first one of its feet forward and then the other. It was bored. A merry-go-round creaked round and round while a sorrowful, appealing young peasant stood in the middle of it, head bent down, beating a drum. He was making an effort to breathe a bit of joy and life into these last moments of the poor Princess Yarmarka. All in vain: unawares, the young man, sad and exhausted as he was, was beating the drum too slowly, so that it sounded like a funeral march.

It was raining. Churches with their doors bolted, cupolas gleaming with gold, the great wooden bridge swaying gently like a gigantic wave every time a streetcar passed. Sensuously situated on the sandy banks of the Oka and the Volga, Nizhnii Novgorod sparkled with a melancholy tender light in the fine rain. The white kremlin in her midst soared serenely, harmless, toothless, with her gates open, languishing like a moribund lion among the surrounding grocery shops, cobblers' shops, milk shops and Soviet co-operatives.

Geranos visited the Museum. Catherines, Elizabeths, Generals plastered with decorations, and painted, powdered, flabby-lipped Princes. Boyars arrayed in red, great

178

ladies with fine *maquillage*, all forever vanished like the snows of yesteryear. The famous revolutionary, Pugachof, looked incongruous among all these refined, hothouse figures. This drew a malicious mutter from a bitter old nobleman who was there with Geranos.

"In Moscow you'll see this savage visionary painted over a badly scratched portrait of Catherine the Great. Between his muzhik shoulders, you can still see the two round greedy breasts of the great Empress."

After a moment's silence, he added in a whisper and with a glance around him:

"Almost like Lenin daubed in on top of the prolific body of Russia!"

The old nobleman invited Geranos to his home. He still had a collection of faïence cups and saucers. His palace had been confiscated. And he and his aged sister, both of them unmarried, had been crammed into a dark corridor. The rest of the palace was occupied by workmen's families swarming with children. When the old nobleman passed along the halls, the children tugged at his shabby jacket and called to him:

"Dyadya Mouseĭ! Dyadya Mouseĭ! (Uncle Mouseĭ! Uncle Mouseĭ!)"

As he scrutinized the old gentleman in the dimly lit room, Geranos noticed his silky flesh, his clean threadbare clothes, his velvety, sad, timorous voice. His beautiful faïence-ware sparkled on the shadowy surface of a glass stand.

"Write that it's hell here!" Geranos' host was saying. "Our houses have been taken from us. There is no freedom! Shout that at the top of your lungs! Reveal the truth to the world. We are ruled by porters, workmen, muzhiks, men who couldn't tell the difference between a Saxon vase and a Sèvres!"

"Why are you so unjust? You people have eaten and drunk your fill. Now it's time to let the hungry ones take their turn to come and sit at a dinner-table. Change the

179

guests, that's the great law! If I were you, I would just have picked up my hat without any idle complaining and gone out of the dining room, toothpick in hand."

The old nobleman looked at Geranos in terror. He made as though to get up from his seignorial throne, then sat down again, and fixed his shirt-collar, which was strangling him.

"I thought you were one of us!" he whispered.

"I am for man. I understand both those who rush to get to the table and those who turn away from it and walk off. I pity all mankind."

"Perhaps it's because you don't have a palace or ancestral traditions; you have nothing to be sorry for when you walk off."

Geranos laughed. "That's just it! Because I have no chains. If I had this splendid faïence you've shown me tonight, how could I have any feeling for any new idea?"

Toward evening, Geranos took a stroll along the beautiful drive over the Volga. The Radio Institute soared, stark with its straight lines and wide windows. On top of it, a web of ironwork radiated in every direction, picking up the mysterious currents. Opposite the Institute was a deserted church, where the grass had already begun creeping up to the doorways. God had abandoned this old tortoise-shell carapace of His and moved across the way to the Radio Institute. There he had sprouted antennae, breathed into the machines, turned steel-blue and started dancing inside big glass horns. He had descended on new priests and invested them with new virtues. Someday He would again, without mercy, abandon this new tortoise-shell too—for such has been His way of proceeding ever since time began—and He would move on.

For a few moments Geranos stared attentively at these two carapaces. He had often had the experience of discerning in a single flash the seed flowering, bearing fruit and then decaying, all at once. He took a fiendish delight in these flashes.

"The Communist Idea," his thoughts ran on as he went on walking up over the Volga, "the Communist Idea is a carapace too, a very new one. What can I do? Should I study its course from a long-range point of view, and enjoy its birth, its flowering and its decay in this transient moment that I am living here and now? Or must I obey and narrow my visual field, bury myself in a single detail and work? Yes, yes," Geranos murmured, "limit myself—this is the only way for ephemeral man to collaborate in anything eternal. Here, through this sacrifice, lies our duty and our salvation!"

His face became contorted with pain. He slumped down on a bench. Under the rays of the setting sun, the whole beautiful slope of Nizhnii Novgorod looked like soft, shadowy velvet. The interminable Volga flowed on silently below him, tinted with a deep red hue. The first lights lit up on the rafts.

"Yes, I know now," Geranos was thinking. "I have no more doubts: the first grand mission of Communism is a terrible and sacred one: to disintegrate Western civilization. To plough the land . . . to open its vitals . . . to prepare it for the new seed to be sown. This is why we can see our first duty with such utter clarity: 'To be Communist in spite of everything!' "

Geranos' eyes grew cloudy.

"Yes, yes, let us be Communists! Let us go on intensifying the cult of the Machine and of Matter. Let us tear through the stages faster and faster, like a truck-driver who is already too deep into the blazing forest, still faster and faster! The people who are genuinely adapted to modern life, the really productive people are the ones who fully accept necessity; or rather, the ones who drive necessity further and further on. What is the inexorable necessity of our time? The Machine. Let us drive the world to a furor of Americanization! There is no other way to liberate ourselves from the Machine."

Geranos got up and started pacing about with long strides. He felt relieved. He had found the answer to his

181

agonizing questions. Yes, yes, but his heart resisted. . . .

A sudden cry escaped Geranos. Way in the background, in the square with the mosque, a man whose legs were all wrapped in rags like a muzhik's was making wild gesticulations. It was Azad! Carrying a big, heavy bundle.

"Azad!" called Geranos, rushing on toward his friend.

"I've found it! I've found it!" Azad roared, dancing for joy. Let's go to Moscow! I shall climb up on the roof-tops and shout. I'll march the Truth stark naked through Red Square all day long every festival day! I'll lay the Truth in Lenin's arms!"

"What truth?" cried Geranos in fright.

"Here it is," said Azad, tapping his big bundle proudly. "Here it is."

Geranos stretched out his hand.

"No! No! Don't touch it!" cried Azad. "You'll see, you and the others too . . . Let's go now, I'm tired! Take me home. I haven't any more money left."

Geranos could hardly hold back his tears. Azad ate ravenously, mutely, like a starving animal. He drank his wine, clicking his tongue as he did so and staring with a smile at Geranos.

"Bless you, Geranos, I do still love you!"

He emptied his wine glass again and began to stammer. His right eye was lusterless and squinted a little. Geranos couldn't catch all his words:

"The village . . . muzhiks . . . *batyushka* . . . fireside . . . he was laughing . . . he'd closed the door . . . Chut! The Cheka! . . . worked all night . . . In the morning the Truth was there . . . stained . . . alive . . . You'll see . . . you'll see . . ."

Azad blinked his eyes, smiling with satisfaction.

"The very simple truth . . . in Moscow . . . Gift to Lenin . . ."

Suddenly his voice grew steady. Tormented questions streamed out one of top of another.

"Geranos, why were we born? Why do we kill? Why do we hate each other? Do you know, Geranos?"

182

"No, I don't know," Geranos answered. "I don't know . . ."

"Geranos, I've been thinking a lot these days. I want to take up my pilgrim's staff. I want to go find the people with large minds. I want to kneel down and cry, 'Save Russia!' "

Suddenly Azad began sobbing. Geranos took him gently by the arm, raised him up and led him over to his bed. Toward dawn, Azad woke up, shouting out Geranos' name.

Geranos was not asleep.

"What do you want, Azad?" he asked.

"I've had a horrible dream. A corpse was floating over the roofs of a big city, like a kite. It was all blue—eaten by the flies. It was floating very slowly. Its eyes were dripping. I cried: 'War! That's War!' and woke up with a start."

"Yes, that's war," murmured Geranos, and he shuddered.

16

Moscow. Dawn of the great day. Sou-ki could not sleep. He coughed and coughed. He sat up in bed and looked out the window. The streets all decked with red flags . . . electric lights strung in the shape of hammers and sickles . . . big red banners . . . white letters. Sou-ki's eyes blinked in their effort to read: "Proletarians . . . seven-hour day . . . Lenin . . . World Revolution . . ."

In the next room Amita was weeping softly. He was taking leave of everything he loved. Tomorrow he would be leaving, going back to his own country. To fight . . . to work . . . From now on he would feel Rahel inside him, in his breast, like a flame. He would be taking her with him. He smiled. In the stove he had lit, his manuscripts were crackling and crumbling into ashes. A few letters, a few half-charred words were still visible. As he bent down, Amita just managed to read the word "Rahel" before the flames devoured it.

As the great day dawned, the Big-Jawed Man leaned anxiously against the window. He was trying to delimit his anxiety in clear syllogisms:

"I love only that which is successful; and nothing is successful except what is conceived and executed according to the will of life. And where is the will of life? I ask my blood. My blood gives me a concise, clear answer and I follow it. Then someone else—Lenin—also asks his blood; his blood also gives him a concise, clear answer and he follows this. Now where is the will of life? Does this slut have many wills? Or basically, are all these wills, which seem opposed to each other, really collaborating? I'm utterly confused . . . Is this the only trophy I have won from my invasion of the U.S.S.R.? No, no! We must follow our own answers, even to the point of madness!"

He grabbed his notebook and hastily scribbled a few Spanish words in big letters: "*Hagamos un templo tal que nos tengan por locos!* (Let us build such a temple that they will take us for madmen!)"

In the adjacent room, Rahel was weeping too. The great day had already dawned, lead-colored, threatening, freezing cold. Rahel had taken a bath, washed her young body with care and arranged her heavy, blue-black hair. She had opened her shabby valise and chosen her daintiest underwear. "My underwear must be beautiful and sparkling clean when they find me," she thought to herself.

Already the first fanfares were resounding through Moscow. Horses' hooves, soldiers' cries, the rattle of drums in the distance. Rahel, freshly bathed and fragrant in her finest underwear, wept for shame. Oh, if only she could tear out her woman's heart, like a cancer. Yesterday she'd told that man: "Tonight I'm going to come to you."

He had frowned and answered gruffly: "I have no time to waste. I have only one goal. Women do not exist."

Lia, Lia! The bloodstained image of her sister sprang up inside her, making her tremble. Yes, yes, that was the way to shame, gaping open. Poor Lia. You had no strength —you had no time.

"I must act quickly," said Rahel in a calm, resolute voice. "I must act quickly!"

She began looking for a railway timetable. She found one and leafed through it. "9:10 P.M. . . . Poland . . ."

"That's fine," she said. With perfect equanimity she wrote a little note on a slip of paper and stuck it in her pocket:

"Itka, Itka, lioness' head, you must know . . ."

Geranos was writing a letter to his son:

"Panteli, the great day has dawned. I haven't closed my eyes all night. Now I am sure; I have made my

185

decision. My duty is to join the Communist Party and begin work. To limit myself, become a militant fanatic. To renounce all the delights of pure speculation and beauty. To plough my own furrow. There lies my sole duty. But I am incapable of doing it. I have chewed and rechewed too many books. I've lost the freshness of my heart, the simplicity of my mind. I see, I understand, I love the truth. But I cannot serve it. This, my son, is the ultimate stage of my own progress on earth. You, Comrade Panteli, must go beyond this point where I have stumbled. You must achieve what I have been unable to achieve. Leave me behind you and go on!"

As he walked down from the fifth floor of his hotel, Geranos felt relieved. After his lacerating vacillations, he had found the equilibrium of his own soul again. But he was worried about something else now: since yesterday, Azad had disappeared. Where was he? These last days Azad had done nothing but sob and howl continuously. A dreadful intimation of something violent flitted through Geranos' mind. In the corridors on the various floors, Geranos kept meeting official guests from every country: workers, intellectuals, peasants. They greeted each other in a fraternizing way. An Italian journalist whom Geranos had known before in Greece suddenly grabbed his arm.

"You here too?" exclaimed Geranos.

"I've been in Moscow for a long time. I couldn't live in Italy any more; I was suffocating under the Fascist yoke."

"And what are you looking for in Moscow?"

"Liberty!"

Geranos stared sadly at the Italian. The delicate, refined type, the intellectual with "noble ideas" and liberal traditions, crushed beneath the crudity of contemporary reality, whether Fascist or Bolshevik.

"Do you remember that famous comparison Manzoni made," Geranos asked him, "between clay pots and iron pots traveling in the same compartment? You're a clay pot!"

Geranos did not want to live this grand day of Moscow in the company of this refined, sheep-souled man, and so he left him abruptly.

The guests gathered at the entrance to the hotel. Sou-ki had already arrived, bundled up in his shabby sheepskin coat.

"Comrade Sou-ki," Geranos called to him solicitously, "dear Comrade Sou-ki, you are very pale. Haven't you slept?"

"I'm happy," answered Sou-ki gently.

Amita arrived, frail, smiling, his eyes all swollen.

"Comrade Amita," someone remarked, "you've been out of sight three days now! Were you sick?"

"I'm getting ready," Amita answered, "I'm getting ready . . ."

"For your own country?"

Amita felt a lump in his throat as he nodded his head "Yes." He was about to leave when Rahel made a sudden appearance. Her forehead shone and her extreme emaciation made her eyes appear larger than ever; they swallowed her face. Her whole body exuded an air of triumph and challenge. "Rahel, Rahel," thought Amita, casting his eyes down. Geranos darted a glance at the fragrant young lady as she walked by. He could guess the lethal suffering of this human being who moved along with her head so high.

"Rahel is very beautiful today," he thought. "Today Rahel is like that little flowering mandarin tree I saw once in Crete on the edge of a precipice."

Rahel walked on in a hurry. Amita stared at her; she was wearing her saffron-colored shawl, and her hair with its steely reflections glistened in the morning fog. The moment she felt she was no longer being watched by the men's eyes, her body slumped and her neck tensed. A squadron of cavalry passed by. Horses' flanks, black boots, spurs, drawn swords. The beautiful saffron color vanished behind the horses, far away in the fog.

The guests had a hard time pushing their way through the throngs of people who were already beginning to congest the streets. At last they reached Red Square and settled down in their reserved grandstand. The neighing of horses echoed on all sides, the Square was filled with cavalry. Lenin's tomb, dark and utterly balanced, like some strict, clear syllogism, was veiled in fog. And near the tomb, in the back of Red Square, stood that mad monstrosity, the beloved Cathedral of Ivan the Terrible, flaunting itself like a whole array of Asiatic emirs in big gaudy turbans.

Leaning on Geranos with his eyes closed, Sou-ki listened to the roar of Moscow. He sensed the vast commotion spreading over the entire U.S.S.R. as far away as Vladivostok and Mongolia. Rolling of drums. A rush of blood lashed his sweating temples. Sou-ki opened his eyes just in time to see the sailors of the Baltic and the Black Sea parading past, short, solid figures with rough, good-natured faces. Hurrah! The taciturn soldiers of the Cheka went by, their long gray cloaks trailing in the mud, their calm eyes sparkling in the damp air. Suddenly the whole tumultuous Square quaked. The cavalry streamed out! Kirghiz, Cossacks, Caucasians, Mongolians, Kalmucks. Their frenzied leader, out in front of them, let out a wild whoop and brandished his sword. Horses on their haunches, horses' legs and hooves—lances flying red, blue, violet banners—arched backs—stones flashing in the Square—russet-colored, black, white horses—white-bearded veterans marching by, their furrowed faces battered by the rain and sun.

Geranos stood still, his eyes wide open. "Open your eyes, you poor old carcass!" he told himself. "Look well! This is the finest day of your life!"

At the top of the reserved grandstand, two big jaws snapped open:

"Yes . . . yes . . ." they snarled, "yes . . . yes . . ."

Amita chafed and whinnied like a tethered horse. By his side, Sou-ki had closed his eyes; he felt dazed and a prolonged tremor gripped his frail body.

"Comrade Sou-ki," called Amita, "open your eyes; your favorite Pioneers are going by."

With a little birdlike cry, Sou-ki watched a river of red flow past, flooding the Square—numberless children—red ties. Little hands cleaving the air held still for a moment in front of Lenin's tomb, while the cry, "I swear," rang out as one clear, fresh, tremendous voice.

An old Norwegian workingman wept, others laughed. Two peasants in back of Sou-ki stared with the frozen gaze of buffaloes, their eyes reflecting the galloping horses and red ties.

A quick rhythmical tread—marching workers in leather shirts and dark caps, holding their guns on their shoulders; marching workingwomen with red kerchiefs on their heads and guns on their shoulders. In the little gaps between the solid masses, workmen in groups of four carried aloft replicas of their factories: the black building made of cardboard, the workers in silhouette, the smoke and the Red flag waving on the roof. . . .

Big vans . . . the war invalids crammed into them, triumphantly waving their crutches. Then on foot came immense throngs of jubilant mothers holding their little ones in their arms and around their necks. At that moment suddenly a cloud thinned and for a few seconds Red Square was gently flooded in sunlight. The whole human ant-heap glittered, eyes sparkled, foreheads and hands shone.

"That's a good omen, that's a good omen, comrades," exclaimed Sou-ki, hugging Geranos and Amita.

The muzhiks approached with a heavy tread, with their boots and sheepskin or cowhide *shubas* and their blond, black or red beards. Earthy faces, puckered brows, haunted eyes. Squeezed together in dense masses and shoving

189

against each other, they advanced ponderously and anxiously, like a herd of buffaloes. Geranos sprang up in amazement. There, trailing this motley throng of peasants from the Volga, whom should he see but Azad, dressed up in muzhiks' rags and swaying like a drunkard! Azad was towing a big wooden puppet. A current of angry surprise ran through the spectators. Who had the audacity to flaunt such a caricature of Communism right here in the midst of this triumphant celebration of the proletariat? Azad marched on slowly and solemnly as though at a religious procession, in melancholy silence, bowing to right and left and directing the spectators' attention to his puppet. A big wooden creature, daubed with red, a huge belly, gold teeth, and the hammer-and-sickle insignia in his buttonhole. He had a big cigar in his mouth and he was grinning; one of his feet was trampling on a weak muzhik and the other on a starving worker. Azad inched along, escorted by a few muzhiks and unemployed workers whom he'd collected. He kept bowing to both sides, and then in front of Lenin's tomb he halted. There he salaamed to the ground three times, raised his coarse Communist puppet up over his head, and then suddenly, with a gesture of rage, hurled it down on the ground, jumped on it furiously and began tearing it to bits, laughing idiotically as he did so. A flash of lightning! Then new throngs of muzhiks surged forward and Azad disappeared. Geranos sprang down from the grandstand in horror and elbowed his way through the crowd, looking for Azad, who had vanished behind the Vaslii Cathedral.

Amita felt a thrill of excitement. "Comrade Sou-ki," he cried, "Comrade Sou-ki."

Sou-ki was smiling. A long file of camels. Arabs, Afghans, Persians, dressed in brilliantly-colored cloaks, parading by in silence, their mouths opening but uttering no sound. In front of Lenin's tomb, they jerked their camels to a halt abruptly. They remained there mutely for a few moments, with their hands outstretched; then the file of camels resumed its rhythmic pace and marched off on its way to Arabia, Afghanistan, Persia. Their little bells tinkled gaily, then were gone.

Sou-ki jumped up and down; off at the far end of the Square, he caught sight of a procession of shrieking, capering Chinese men. An enormous green and yellow dragon, made of linen and resembling a fish, twisted and coiled over their heads, slowly opening and closing its huge, bloodstained mouth. The Chinese men rushed on, emitting shrill screeches that pierced the air like arrows. Their procession also paused abruptly in front of Lenin's tomb. The massive, billowing crowds of white people gazed with a tinge of anxiety at the swarming yellow throngs. A long silence. Then suddenly there rose up from all these weak Chinese chests, from all these human vitals throbbing with blood, a single terrifying chorus:

"Lenin! Lenin!" They summoned the dead man, then waited for a moment. Then once again the terrifying chorus:

"Lenin! Lenin!"

Sou-ki screeched like a wounded bird and fell backward against Amita. With another cry, he crumpled to the ground.

"Comrade Sou-ki," cried Amita in panic. "Comrade Sou-ki!"

Sou-ki opened his eyes and made a tiny movement of his lips in an effort to say something. But he could not. With a smile, he closed his eyes. Two militia men came rushing up and quickly carried off the corpse. The incident caused a brief flurry in the grandstand. A little space opened up in the solid mass, but soon filled again. Now they were all intent on the Hindu workingmen and women who were passing by just then. Lean people, with long sleek hair and wasted bodies. Gandhara, tall and long-limbed in her orange cashmere, was marching at their head. Nestling in her arms over her warm breasts, she held the mosaic of Lenin inlaid with rice and red pepper.

Suddenly a clear, strong voice rang out: "Down with Gandhi! Down with Tagore! Long live Lenin!"

Rahel was screaming desperately, with her head thrown back and her arms raised high.

Amita heard her voice and had an impulse to rush to her.

"Rahel! Rahel!" he called.

But now on the far side of Red Square, the Negroes loomed up. Seized with terror, Amita remained frozen where he stood. Two huge drums and two Negroes who kept raising and lowering their arms, while their heads swayed frenziedly. They crossed Red Square on the run. Between the two drummers, Toda Raba towered, an enormous figure. Above his fuzzy head he held the black mask of Lenin with its bloodstains and its necklace of human teeth. The crowd drew back. The three Negroes drew to a halt in front of Lenin's tomb. They stood there with their bodies vibrating. Cunningly veiling their rage, the drummers growled in muffled tones like two wild beasts warily creeping along. Toda Raba hung the black mask on his broad chest and raised his foot. At once the drummers shot into the air and their growl swelled into a roar that burst like thunder. Toda Raba broke into the dance, shrieking and laughing and showing his gleaming teeth.

"This is no dance of death!" Amita exclaimed in a panic-stricken voice. "And it is not the dance of love! It is War!"

Abruptly Toda Raba tore himself away from the dance. Fuming with passion, he raised his arms to call out upon Lenin, but instead, only a hoarse, inhuman howl escaped his throat. The people standing near him recoiled in terror. In the Moscow fog Toda Raba's eyes rolled white, yellow, black. And his teeth gleamed like a tiger's tusks.

Amita couldn't see anything now; a mist had come over

his eyes. How terrible life is, he was thinking, the way it whirls about and snatches up and scatters all the yellow, white, black leaves of the human races, blowing them all over the earth. Negroes, Chinese dragons, Hindu rice, all mobilized to serve the frightful image, and then suddenly that black mask with its necklace of human teeth!

Evening fell. Moscow echoed like a battlefield. Azad went around knocking at the doors of his Communist friends. He visited the Commissariats and ranted there till they chased him out. Then he entered a house. He stared piercingly at the people standing there in front of him:

"How did you get so fat? Why are you sleeping? Why? Why?" he yelled.

He grabbed one Commissar by the throat just as he reached home in a state of utter exhaustion:

"Why are you so fat? Aren't you ashamed?" he cried.

The Commissar tried to calm him down and invited him to come in. Azad surveyed the scene and tried to examine everything close up with his myopic eyes. He saw the Commissar's wife and his maid and started railing at him:

"Why do you have a maid? Why does your wife wear silk stockings?"

Azad got angrier and angrier:

"You filthy curs. Silk stockings, eh? Do you think the Revolution wears silk stockings? You'll see! You'll see! We're going to sweep away all your great ladies and your silk stockings and your fat bellies!"

They put him out. Azad pounced on the passers-by outside, shaking them by the shoulders:

"Why? Why?"

Then he collapsed on the ground and started weeping. After a moment, two militia men approached and led him away gently. He offered no resistance. He twined both his arms around the militia men and fell asleep. When he woke up in the nursing home, he looked around him with a smile.

Nine o'clock that evening. In front of Lenin, the Red river still flowed on, sonorous, inexhaustible. Hammers and sickles glittering like ominous constellations of stars. Illuminated letters thrusting themselves into the night and patterning themselves mysteriously into fiery slogans of love and hate.

About 9:10 P.M. the express left for Poland. A few minutes later, they found the delicate body of a woman sprawling on the rails, frightfully mutilated. Beside it lay a saffron shawl spattered with warm blood. When they unfolded the shawl, a letter dropped out:

"Itka, I am no longer worthy of serving the Idea. For one moment, I let myself down. I must die."

About ten o'clock, Geranos came back to his hotel, exhausted with grief and fatigue. He hadn't found Azad. At the entrance to the hotel, he met the Big-Jawed Man who was walking home with his heavy, even tread. Geranos went straight up to him. Tonight, he felt attached to this man by the bonds of an implacable hatred:

"Did you see, comrade?" he whispered to him in a hollow voice. "Did you hear? That was the great Cry!"

The Big-Jawed Man stopped a moment, frowned, then shot his cold, piercing glance through Geranos. Then, without a muscle's moving in his face, he went off on his way. Geranos reeled. That was the glance of the general he had seen in his dream! At the same instant, he had the horrible sensation of having been discharged from the ranks.

Midnight. An old bhikku, dressed in an earth-colored cassock and carrying an empty basin suspended from a chain around his neck, was crouching at one end of Red Square on the top step of the Vasilii Cathedral. All through the day, he had stayed there, without moving, his neck outstretched like a chimera. He opened his eyes, he opened his ears, he opened his mind. Then slowly he shrank back. He closed his eyes so that he could no longer see the waves of people breaking against the walls of the Kremlin; he closed his ears so that he could no longer hear the drums and the deafening uproar of men and horses; he closed his mind so that everything was swallowed up in the abyss.

At that moment, the Russian sky, out of its pitch-black depths, suddenly blazed with the same play of light and color, the same Oriental sparkle and magnificence as in that splendid, barbarous Cathedral of Ivan the Terrible. Mysterious symbols, crosses and triangles, flowers and letters, sinuous dragons and huge scorpions with poisonous tails rose and fell threateningly. Wild beasts were lurking in the shadows up there, but all you could see were their blue and red and yellowish eyes.

17

Red Square. The walls of the Kremlin. The sun a red cannon ball suspended over the West. Strange constellations rose on the horizon: fiery hammers and sickles and Lenins. Rain fell. Fell on the land. Toda Raba stood gritting, gritting his white teeth. Yellow, black and red gleamed in his rolling eyes. In the splashing evening rain he stared straight ahead at the iron-colored carapace of Lenin. He felt it stirring in the mud, like some nocturnal animal commencing to roam at the approach of evening. Toda Raba gritted his teeth; he was scared. Scared of being annihilated: the carapace was moving toward him. He dodged to the right out of its path, but the little Chinese man beside him barred his way. When Toda Raba looked back, his black pupils dilated in the darkness. He saw the tail of the carapace unwinding in a spiral and twisting and coiling over the wet stones. It had eyes, ears, nostrils and mouths scattered all over it. Growls and muffled roars issued from it; it laughed and wept and tinkled like a belled serpent. Toda Raba growled and roared; he laughed and wept and the big bronze chains around his ankles flashed. He addressed the Chinese man:

"Don't you want to dance, yourself? Don't you want to grab the stiletto and plunge it into your leg?"

But the Chinese man turned away, his face livid, his lips parched.

"Shut up!" he snarled.

Rain fell. Men shivered. Women were terror-stricken. Children implored with outstretched arms: "Open, little father Lenin! Open, little father Lenin!"

The mouth of the carapace opened. Those nearest it were the first to disappear. Then the others . . . and the others . . . In his shock Toda Raba dug his heels into the earth to resist. Someone underground, who held himself stock-still, grabbed him and pulled him. Toda Raba grasped the Chinese man by the nape of the neck, took a step or two, gritted his teeth and disappeared.

Toda Raba could see nothing. The splayed soles of his feet shuffled along the pavement, groping. . . . They encountered the step of a stairway and clung to it; they left it, venturing downward, found another step, and clung to it. The heat was suffocating. Who had cried out? Someone had cried out! Drums beat in Toda Raba's temples, his throat swelled up. He felt stifled. . . . He lifted his hand. He ripped open his big red-plaid shirt. Then he could breathe. He felt happy and laughed while the Chinese man to his right turned round in anger. Toda Raba raised his right foot, bent his big body, and curled up his toes, as he prepared to get a footing on the next step. All of a sudden a blinding light. Toda Raba reared up, his temples bursting. Lenin's skull! Lenin's skull! Toda Raba stumbled and his right foot with the curled-up toes remained hanging in the air.

Ahouou! The forest was on fire. Red stars floated by, streaming hair, pennants, flags! Toda Raba rushed on, head bent forward. His eyelashes, his eyebrows, his fuzzy hair got singed and crackled. Toda Raba had black wings, a yellow beak, scarlet spurs like a cock's and scarlet claws. He tried to shout "Brothers! Brothers!" But a raven's hoarse croak—"*Kra! Kra! Kra!*"—tore his gullet. Plunging his claws into the blaze, he grabbed a firebrand and escaped through the window. Escaped through the window and for a moment held fast to the crenelated walls of the Kremlin. He saw white men and white women and laughed. When Toda Raba laughed, all the Red army drums hanging on the barracks walls skipped about.

Toda Raba darted up. He strode across Moscow, bounded over the plains of the Ukraine, cleared the Dnieper in one leap, and arrived at the Black Sea. When he arrived at the Black Sea, he bathed his black legs in the waves and felt cooler. His burning thighs bathed, he charged ahead, set his red heel on Istanbul, hopped from island to island over the Aegean Sea, trod the soil of Crete, crossed the indigo sea, and planted his big flat foot on Africa. Lenin's black mask was bouncing up and down on his back. Toda Raba's shadow blotted out the sun. The Englishmen in Egypt lifted their heads, their jaws yawned open, and their bruised eyes got blinder.

Holding the burning log over his head, Toda Raba scanned the horizon. His gaze swooped like a vulture upon Libya, the Sudan, the Cameroons, the Congo, Tanganyika. Deserts, marshlands, forests . . . He pricked up his ears and heard the whip whistling. Men rose up in revolt . . . women wept. The whole Negro world wept. Toda Raba took a leap and alighted with a thrill. The sweet hillside of his own village! The tombs of his ancestors! Red and black masks, grinning skulls, tufts of female hair, necklaces made of teeth! "Fathers! Fathers!" he cried. "Open your mouths! I'm going to pour you some blood! Open your mouths! I'm going to stuff you with food! Fathers! Fathers! Open your ears! Lenin! Lenin!" He planted the burning log among the tombs. He fastened Lenin's mask to his breast and danced. Lenin bounced up and down on the broad black chest and danced. The tombs reverberated with roars like lions' dens. The clubs, axes and knives at the sides of the skeletons wheeled slowly to an erect position underground. Toda Raba scooped up a handful of earth from the tombs and sprinkled it over his head. That quieted him; quieted him a little bit. He squatted down on a tomb in the sun, his whole body fuming with passion. His legs were caked with mud, his back was black and blue and kept swaying and heaving up and down. He gazed at the distant plain beneath him, using his awkward

198

left hand to shade his eyes. Were they ants? He could not tell. Beetles rolling their lump of dirt? Men? "Brothers! Brothers!" Long ant-heaps of men and women and children in the marshlands up to the waist, up to the neck. Cotton, rice, linen, rubber . . . Famine, slavery, fear!

Toda Raba bowed his contorted face, squeezed it between his knees and wept, wept. As the teardrops fell on the tombs, the soil began to swell and bubble. A flash of lightning came and went, a century came and went. All at once a cry. The whole plain had cried out like a woman. Toda Raba drew back, his hair on end: a helmet; spurs. The spurs advanced, getting bigger and bigger, like suns, turned round with a grating sound and blinded Toda Raba. A woman ground to bits under the spurs! The spurs retreated into the distance, retreated with their bloodstains. Toda Raba stood up straight on the hill, spread his arms, and abandoned himself to wild lung-bursting bellowing. "*Aho! Aho! Aho!*" He felled trees, started bonfires and crushed the stones to clear the space. He passed to and fro over the tombs, summoning the great warriors among his ancestors by name, thumping the earth with his foot, crying, "Help! Help!" The sun turned and turned over his head; the earth turned and turned under his feet. Between heaven and earth the crows flew back and forth hungrily. Toda Raba stood up straight on the side of the ancestral hill and extended his arms in the direction of the plain. "*Aho! Aho! Aho!*" he bellowed.

A stooping woman raised her body with a groan: "A lion! I heard a lion on the tombs!" The men paused, openmouthed, and listened: the whip writhed and swished, twined round the bodies, stained them with blood and swished again. But one child escaped. "Toda Raba!" it screamed. "Toda Raba!"

Then the Negroes darted out of the marshlands, falling over each other as they gamboled and scaled the hill. About their hips the gleam of their sickles flashed on and off. "Brothers! Brothers!" Toda Raba laughed and wept, distributed embraces, buried his nose in the warm heads, inhaling, inhaling, breathing in his race. "I have come! I have come!" he told them. The women rubbed themselves with grease, lit fires around the men, and uttered piercing shrieks. The Negroes pulled up stalks of sugar cane and filled a calabash of wine. These they set at Toda Raba's feet; then they withdrew to the background and stretched out on their bellies on the tombs. "Toda Raba, speak!" they bade him.

Toda Raba bowed his head and sprang up. With his big gnarled heels he pounded on the tombs one by one: "Fathers! Fathers!" he called. "Come up to the sunlight! I am speaking!"

He pulled Lenin's black mask from his breast, rammed it over his face and tied it with pieces of strong cord. He stumbled. A terrible Spirit had latched on to his face and penetrated deep into his vitals. It exploded and broke his heart. No longer able to walk, he danced. Danced, but slowly and tremulously. He grazed the earth with the tip of his toes, drew back in fright, and quivered. He stooped down and whimpered. "Pity! Pity! Masters!" he entreated.

He extended his hand toward the North, toward the South, toward the East, toward the West. His face became an immense army of wailing, screaming children begging for bread. "Pity! Pity! Masters!" Toda Raba paused, opened his eyes and opened his ears and waited. . . . He gnashed his teeth and rolled his eyes. The big veins in his forehead swelled and grew hard until they branched out like horns. The women lacerated their cheeks and collapsed in front of the flames. With panting breath the men raised themselves to a kneeling position. Toda Raba sprang forward. His face became a tremendous army on the march. Uttering a cry like a starving vulture, he pulled his body erect, clenched his fist, and drew it back. The dance broke loose, beyond all restraint: the soles of the men's feet quaked, the women lifted their breasts and yelled, "Lenin! Lenin!" Toda Raba grabbed a sickle, flourished it right and left in the air, and mowed, mowed, mowed. He seized the stalks of sugar cane between his teeth, broke them into pieces and spat them out on the ground. Then he trampled them under his feet. He laughed. He overturned the calabash, and dancing over the spilt wine, kneaded it into the earth.

For one hour, for two hours, Toda Raba danced. He sprouted innumerable hands and feet. Like a wheel he rolled and scraped and sank into the earth. His entire body, from his heels up to his fuzzy mane, spoke, spoke, spoke to his race. Steam exuded from his armpits. His eyes moved up and down. Sparks flew from under his feet, lighting up all the Negro heads. The dead emerged silently on the surface of the earth and huddled in the sun.

Mouths agape, the panting, sweating Negroes watched Toda Raba dance. They saw him and they heard him say:

"Lenin weeps, Lenin calls for help, Lenin appeals to the North, the South, the East and the West. Ah! War! War! A high red tower, high as the sky. Lenin stands on its summit, brandishing a sickle. He grabs kings, shamans, prostitutes, masters, and mows, mows, mows."

Toda Raba laughed, and said:

"My fields are going to flourish. My wheat is going to grow. My children will have bread."

He laughed and gazed down at the crowd. Spying a fat man, he stooped over, seized him, and cracked his skull with his heel. He caught sight of some spurs, chewed them to bits, and coughed them out. . . .

"Brothers! Brothers!" he exclaimed. "Eat, drink, sleep, make children, toil! The earth belongs to you!"

The black dance erupted. Shoulder to shoulder the Negroes strode over the land, the women felling trees and surging toward Toda Raba's firebrand to light their own. An old woman in a trance took possession of the drum. The dead sharpened their rusty weapons on the stones and shot up all around, underneath, above and alongside the living. The air thickened and turned royal blue; the living dispersed it with their hands, using them as oars, and so broke a passage through it. Out in front the black Lenin marched fiercely along with his necklace of human teeth. As the Negroes swooped down, all the wild beasts set up a mad roar. Hurrah! Toda Raba lifted his arms and waved the burning log, his flag. In the remote regions beyond the seas, a yellow Lenin vaulted ahead while the yellow masses rolled on like a storm, and swooped down with the cry, "Brothers! Brothers!" A child riding piggy-back around his mother's neck clapped his little hands and shouted: "*Aho!* fathers! *Aho!* fathers! *Aho!* fathers! Look to the North!"

Hurrah! In the remote regions beyond the seas, a white Lenin vaulted ahead while the white masses rolled on like a storm and swooped down! Blond heads tossed in the wind, crying, "Brothers! Brothers!" The earth rocked. The fierce beasts in the forest cringed and howled and gathered close together. "Pity, pity, slaves!" they implored. Toda Raba halted, wavering. The black mask jerked its head and shook it "no." It had an urge to flee. It broke the cords and with a cry departed.

A firebird darted from branch to branch and hung on . . . darted from tree to tree and hung on . . . darted from head to head and hung on. *Frou! Frou! Frou!* It laid the flame, round and shiny like an egg, and went on its way. The firebird, perched on the crest of the forest, spread out its tail. Its tail was on fire; its eyes were red, its claws were red, its wings were two furnaces whipped by the wind. The wind blew. The wind from the East and the West, from the North and the South. All the winds blew. The yellow wind, the white wind, the black wind. The bird cried: "I am Lenin! I am Lenin!"

One tiger . . . two tigers . . . three tigers . . . They leapt and tumbled upside down, paws in the air, into the flames. Countless round yellow eyes. Fear! The monkeys screeched and whined and dropped roasted into the fire. A big serpent writhed convulsively and coiled itself around a baobab tree, where its scales exploded. The moles came up to the surface of the earth. The big worms unwound like spirals on the glowing embers and the grease poured out of them as they burst. Canaries, parrots and hummingbirds opened their beaks once or twice and flew off suffocated. Aha! Aha! A master's helmet! Aha! A master's hand! It rose imperiously, cracked the whip and dropped, consumed by the flames. Oh! Some gold teeth! The gold melted and ran and formed globules like big tears in the ashes. Oh! The sweet odor of the enemy's burning flesh!

When dawn broke, Toda Raba was sitting on the hill. He saw. Saw the green earth. Rain fell. A gentle rain that cooled Toda Raba's hands and his scorched back. It cooled the earth. An aura of tender tranquillity hovered over the sleeping tombs, soothed by the warm raindrops. The smell of the earth mounted and mounted until Toda Raba's wide nostrils quivered and dilated with it. Toda Raba's brain became a steaming mound of earth. Rain fell. The earth drank . . . the stones laughed. . . . He felt the grains of wheat vibrating under the earth in secret joy, entwining themselves together like brothers, gradually modeling under the earth's hard crust a huge, vigorous body with hands folded, eyes closed, and a forehead sparkling and stolid: Lenin!

Toda Raba suddenly burst into tears. He could no longer contain his joy. He sobbed.

The little Chinese man beside Toda Raba became impatient, and gave him a push.

"Come, come, comrade, move on! Let us see too!"

The Negro's stiff toes relaxed. The Negro's right foot lowered itself to the next step. Toda Raba moved on.

AN AFTERWORD

by HELEN KAZANTZAKIS

A MAN WHO PREACHED VIOLENCE though he had no violence in himself; who was indulgent toward others, but remorselessly severe with himself; who, without gun or bullets, hunted an invisible, ever elusive quarry, lost in visions of the future—this is how Nikos Kazantzakis impressed me. In that now remote time between the two wars, he had already become a legendary figure.

In 1924, he was forty-one years old and had just come back from Berlin. The mad scenes engendered by despair had left their marks on him: the mothers who hurled their children into the river and then followed them over the embankment; the long hunger marches; the cartloads of devalued banknotes; the Messiah-obsessed Jewish girls holding their clandestine political meetings . . .

In that delicate, slender, disciplined body of his, in those burning eyes, in that dialectical talent which could bring order out of chaos, these young people had put their trust, and it was from him, so they thought, that salvation was to come . . .

Certainly he thought so himself for a brief period of time. He would abandon art, turn his back on beauty, deny his most recent love, Buddha. He would learn a manual trade in order to be able to earn his living. He would begin to test his strength. Then he would expand his field of action and go to the U.S.S.R. He knew what he wanted; he had confidence in his own strength; he would find the words to express it. "First duty: to help destroy this unjust world, unfit for the human soul. Second duty: to create the new myth, to reconstruct the Universe."

In Crete he had the joy of meeting companions who listened to him with approval. He also spent a few weeks in prison. A prison far too comfortable for his own exalted frame of mind, because his friends came to keep him company and the guards brought him food prepared by his mother.

A single level of activity was not enough for him. Like the Orthodox saints whose various deeds and exploits are recounted on our icons on several superimposed planes, he conducted at one and the same time a literary offensive paralleling his political activity. His pencil raced over the page at a wild rate, hardly even indicating the words, until it was almost impossible to decipher them.

In Berlin, the previous year, he had set forth his "meta-Communist creed," The Saviors of God. In Crete, he isolated himself in an abandoned house near the fierce, violet-hued sea, and began to write the first version of his Odyssey. "I must take care of my body," he confessed, "otherwise this work will play havoc with me."

For him, The Odyssey meant something more than writing a work of poetry. It was precisely like modeling the new mask of God in rock. Ulysses was to be the new man, he who had journeyed over the continents in search of God.

Like a Picasso, sacred-demon-of-a-thousand facets, Kazantzakis made use of everything that touched his senses: rare words or common words with their everyday flavor kept intact; colors, exotic plumes and plants, sounds and fragrances, African legends and masks, Greek popular songs, mystical diminuendos and crescendos as old as time. . . . He would weigh them for a few seconds, pass them through the sieve, prune or enrich them, distort or embellish them as he saw fit, and then with a completely sure hand—without the slightest hesitation—he would incorporate them into that vast composition destined to give our literature its most sparkling—and I should say, its most daring—mosaic since the days of his venerable ancestors: Homer, Dante and the enlightened writers of sacred literature at Byzantium.

He did not mind the mockery of his enemies, who rejected him without having read him, or the disappointment of those who had hoped he would produce political philosophy. For fourteen years he cheerfully burned the candle—his own body—at both ends, in order to finish his manuscript. Seven times the monster was immersed in his blood. And invariably, between revisions, he took some long, stimulating journey to "air" his brain. There were also a number of "minor works" (the words in quotations are his): his twelve tragedies in verse (Prometheus, Christ, Buddha, etc.), his cantos in terza rima, and also, "a sure remedy against boredom," his verse translations of the Divine Comedy, the Iliad, Faust, Othello, the modern Spanish poets and Rabindranath Tagore. . . .

When the first cantos of the Odyssey were done, Kazantzakis lifted his head "to get a bit of air." Unable to treat himself to the sort of long trip that he loved, he went to the Cyclades with a young journalist friend. He was profoundly gripped by the "Greek miracle." Mykonos, island of the moon, threw him into ecstasy. Suddenly he was panic-stricken and found it necessary to exorcize the superabundance of beauty. He wrote to one of his traveling companions:

After returning from the islands of the Aegean Sea, I really understood for the first time these two things:
1. What we call the Greek Spirit.
2. How far removed from our present anguish and hopes that spirit is.

All these divine spectacles on the islands—light, color, form, tranquillity, balance, proportion, harmony—are, for the time in which we live, "luxury articles," ornaments, shiny plumage, a schoolmaster's brand of wisdom. If by the word "civilization," we mean "fertile response"—that is, a response adapted to the period, the landscape and the race (the eternal problems)—then it is only in a very limited sense that we can be interested in the answer given by the ancient Greeks. For of the three elements—period, landscape, race—only the landscape remains the same. So that if we understand the mountains, the trees, the waters, the Greek islands, this can help us find the contemporary answer. Greece will once again give a harmoniously balanced form to her incompatible physical and moral energies. But the ingredients of this new balance will be entirely different.

Here lies the danger and the price of the love we bear Greek civilization. It is difficult to distinguish which elements are still useful and which will remain forever a divine spectacle devoid of practical relevance.

And again:

In terms of our obligation toward our own immediate epoch, there is another reason why it is dangerous for us to understand the Greek harmony deriving from the landscape: it might break our momentum toward destruction and Chaos. I believe that our first duty at the present time is to break the equilibrium, to destroy. Only in this way will the soil be cleansed and the Earth be seared so that it can receive the new seed. Therefore if we allow ourselves to be too much enchanted by Greek harmony, we are in danger of missing the first step of Creation—destruction and Chaos—and we run the risk of moving on prematurely toward our second duty: the establishment of a balance, which is certainly not the mission of our generation on this earth. . . .

It is curious—no, quite natural—that the contemplation of so much beauty has brought me, now that I have witnessed all the miracles of the Aegean Isles, to conclusions so contrary to peace, tranquillity and harmony!

For art and beauty, I often have the same feeling of hatred that the primitive Christians used to have. The first adherents of a faith always have a similar hatred for the lovely balanced form of the universe they are called on to destroy. For in truth this beauty is the great temptation; it gives the mystical enchantment to the idols—those "false" manifestations of God—as every new faith says about its predecessors.

1925 brought him an unexpected recompense: a trip to the U.S.S.R. When he got back, he first presented his impressions in the form of articles for the newspaper that had sent him on the trip. Then he condensed them, cutting out the superfluities and the material of merely transient interest, and brought out a book entitled: What I Saw in Russia. It had an enormous success. From that time on, in his own country Kazantzakis was always considered less a poet, novelist and essayist than a traveler.

How lovingly he sang about Russia, and how faithful he remained to it! To help it; to succeed in making it understood and loved—these were his goals. For there in Russia, the new myth of God would assume flesh and bones. From there would come our salvation.

Once again he was caught in the nets of necessity. Despite his external calm, we all knew he was battering his head against the bars of a cage. One day they yielded, and the door opened for him to soar away once more.

"Let's keep our souls intact," he wrote me, "let's have patience, let's not get lost in insignificant details. Our terrible, relentless God will grant us what we ask of Him. I put my trust in Him."

He went to Egypt where Ulysses was to found his Utopian city. Out of this pilgrimage came another book of travels. Countless verses too, whole cantos, for his Odyssey. For gradually Kazantzakis was identifying himself with Ulysses; they were becoming indissolubly fused into a single person.

208

He had seen too much, experienced too much; he could stand no more, and he broke. Like a woman whose time has come, he was racked with pain. All he wanted now was a solitary corner, "some quiet pension in Neuilly perhaps," to settle down and write the second version of the Odyssey. "I'll work during the day, and in the evening we'll dine together and take long walks. . . . Paris at the present time is the capital of the world. I think you will make me rediscover it and love it. I beg you to look for some quiet spot with big trees, where it may be possible to take long walks. . . ."

This dream of long walks in Paris never materialized. Nikos Kazantzakis came to Paris once or twice and tried to find solitude. But lack of money and comfort drove him back to the mountains and lonely beaches.

1927 found him again at Athens. He was impatient when he saw that, one by one, all the promises of the newspaper publishers failed him. The Greeks were spending their energies on politics. The air of Athens became unfit to breathe. With bitterness on his lips and gloom in his eyes, Kazantzakis got ready to take refuge on some island. But once again his God, "the terrible, relentless one," came to his aid. Isolated in a little peasant-house on Aegina, this time not even on the seashore, he had just finished the second version of The Odyssey, when a letter arrived from Moscow. The Soviet government had chosen this fiery visionary to participate in the celebration of the tenth anniversary of the October Revolution.

There he met Panait Istrati.

It is difficult to describe these two with a few strokes of the pen. They were garbed like a pair of twins from the country, in identical, soft blue suits, too tight because they had been made by a ladies' tailor. Though they were equally impulsive and generous, they had differences in character that were to become more evident the closer they came in contact with the Soviet reality.

209

The Russians loved them; they had confidence in them, unlimited confidence, and did not keep them under surveillance. The ambitions of these two men were unlimited. Standing before the unfurled map, Kazantzakis traced a single figure to show the route they should follow: a tremendous cross extending from Turkestan to Murmansk and from Minsk to Vladivostok. Why not? And, if possible, a brief visit to Japan, since the Soviets had promised to supply the two little portfolios that would permit us to take any train in their country and any boat flying the Red flag.

The next thing was to find the necessary funds for the four of us to undertake the expedition. A plan of work was drawn up on the spot. They would write articles and books. They would give lectures. They would even write scenarios.

They did in fact draft countless articles, most of which remained in their desk-drawers. They wrote books, too. But what helped Kazantzakis the most were his experiments with the scenario.

By now their friendship had been tested. They were constantly together, chafing with impatience—1928 was to be the year of the great voyage.

First, they returned to Greece; at their first public lecture—an enormous popular success—Istrati was asked to leave the premises. The government instituted proceedings, promising to make the case a "resounding" one so that it might serve as a lesson to hotheaded people. Together with Glynos—the noblest theoretician the Left had at that time—Kazantzakis prepared his defense. But, alas, as so often happens in Greece, the case dissolved like a soap-bubble. Once more Kazantzakis was free to leave. Once more he set off for the U.S.S.R.

The U.S.S.R. . . . . Istrati . . . Bilili . . . and myself. . . . Two Don Quixotes and two Sancho Panza–Dulcineas; two young women in love, fearlessly protecting their heroes.

Panait, who had been thrown out of Egypt, failed to wait

for Nikos at Kiev, as he had promised to do. He left for Moscow and came back much sooner than his letters had indicated he would. Impossible to recount his constant comings-and-goings. He was restless, tortured, in the throes of such a severe crisis that he could barely write. He could not stay put. Diametrically opposite, both by natural disposition and also by virtue of long self-discipline, Kazantzakis harnessed himself to the task which they had both agreed on as the most fruitful. And so he remained alone at Kiev, where he found a Russian collaborator and worked on his first scenario

May 18, 1928.

KIEV. I'm very sad today and I'm talking to you to find a bit of relief. It's dusk and I haven't been out all day. I read an excellent book by Moussinac about the cinema. Certain parts of it open up great perspectives, and I keep telling myself that while I am in Russia, I must go more deeply into this modern medium for expressing the human soul. This power man has to create people, ideas and passions, out of light and shadow, and to annihilate them, is beginning to affect me. I've been gripped by the thought of Buddha, who, in the fresh rotations of his own brain, similarly created the world out of light and shadow. This training in the cinema will help me in two ways. Perhaps (a) it will aid me from the financial point of view, and (b) it will certainly be good for the visionary quality of my mind. To succeed in transforming the abstract ideas into simple, clear images is my great aspiration. The Odyssey is to be full of images, Ulysses' eye a photographer's equipment for creating the Universe in the dark room. . . ."

Though he did not yet know it, this training in the cinema, in the use of precise, terse language to present images, would stand him in good stead in the first book he was to write after returning from Russia. He wrote Toda Raba in short, jerky sentences, as if he were writing a script. Moreover, it was while he was musing about another scenario one day that he conceived the figure of the Negro, of the Toda Raba who gave his name to the book.

Time passed. Kazantzakis followed Panait's incessant fluctuations with tender solicitude. Later on he used Panait as the model for Azad in Toda Raba. For the moment he merely observed their natures in order to acquire a better understanding of himself.

May 26, 1928.

KIEV. I am not acquainted with Istrati's plans, but more and more, I think, he is inclined to join the Party and become a man of action. If his writer's vein were exhausted, that would be the best solution; anyhow, if he devoted himself entirely to action, that would mean that the vein was already exhausted. As for me, I've definitely decided to remain aloof from any ephemeral action, however valuable it might be, and not to betray my great guide, Ulysses-Buddha.

It is natural that Russia should have ceased to awaken the same raptures in me that I felt at the time of the virginal encounter (a) because it has passed beyond the heroic phase itself and moves more and more in the direction of a normal balance, an overwhelmingly significant one certainly but one which cannot produce any violent excitement in my soul; and (b) because I am not a man of action and cannot be unremittingly interested in the amelioration of a social order. I love the first descent of the Spirit, the violent event that brings the fire. The sequel, the way that the dread moment gets channeled into a good everyday routine, holds no inordinate interest for me. My deepest joy is to see how the mysterious force takes hold of man and shakes him like a lover, an epileptic or a creator. Because, as you know, I'm not interested in man but in the being that I so imperfectly designate as God.

I should like to stay here for another year, but traveling about and coming in contact with the vast body of Russia. For I truly love this land more than I do Greece, this land and these people and the mission which Russia has agreed to fulfil in our time. If this insatiable soul of mine could have a country, Russia would be my country. But the terrible demon that devours me cannot be contained anywhere. Death alone will be able to contain it.

About the cinema I've done a great deal of thinking; and I rejoice that I can have this experience too. As I wrote you, it helps me with *The Odyssey*, which is the goal of my existence until 1933 (a) because it obliges me to change every abstract idea into an image; (b) because only the cinema can grasp the unconscious, the dreams and the visions; (c) because I feel a very wry, Buddha-like emotion in creating passions and involvements with shadows, and then in a flash, while they remain as mute as phantoms, annihilating them. Isn't that the vast screen of the Universe? Now I'm beginning to work on a new scenario: Lenin. It's a vision in the head of a Negro who has gone to Lenin's tomb to pay his respects; and it lasts a second, from the moment when he has seen Lenin in the subterranean resting-place and lifted his foot to place it on the next step till the moment when he actually sets it down. What goes on in this brain—the whole life of Lenin, of Russia, of the World, cactus plants, masks, African landscapes, terrible hopes—an African vision, deep, implacable and quick as a flash of lightning. Ah, if only you knew the way I feel when I think of being able to express this flash in images, so that millions of eyes can see it. . . .

June 30, 1928.

KIEV. The trip is now almost certain: Volga-Japan. We shall send articles to the *N.R.F.* and to German and Russian newspapers. We shall have an enormous amount of work, but I have assumed all the responsibility for it, since I want to contribute as much as I can to the common life with Istrati. When this trip is over (I estimate that that will be about May, 1929) we shall have nothing more to do in the U.S.S.R. and we shall go back to the Paris neighborhood (right now that seems like the best thing). There we shall write the three or four volumes about our trip, and I shall go into absolute isolation in order to work over *The Odyssey* again.

Life here with Istrati goes well. Bilili, who makes a perfect companion for Istrati, gets into moods sometimes, and as she told me one day, she has a mortal hatred for me. I understand and explain to her the reason why. I hope that my influence will do Istrati good, and that is what consoles me.

Beloved Lenochka, our destiny is extraordinary. If our dream about the trip really comes true, this life gives more than we ask. Never did I expect when we met each other the fulfilment we have today. We gave life a big fillip, and she acquired a divine power. God grant that you will experience great joys and great griefs with me, and never mediocrity or boredom. . . .

The trip materialized partially for three of us, and almost in its totality for the strongest one of all, Nikos Kazantzakis. We went down the Volga from Nizhnii Novgorod to Astrakhan, while the cantaloupes and watermelons, spectacular, mountainous piles of them, were going back upstream in the opposite direction. We were in no hurry, we traveled at night and slipped away in the morning to cities and villages along the river. We visited peasants and collective farms, historical monuments, museums and churches topped with fig-shaped cupolas, we ate dubious caviar, we took part in fishing and in the struggle against sand and dust storms, and we followed benevolent guides to see the lotuses, the only lotuses that had ventured outside of Asia. It was all just at the time when Stalin had succeeded in sacking Trotsky and exiling him to Alma Ata. I can no longer say why we did not go to see Trotsky as we had planned, whether it was merely negligence on our part, or whether we felt that someone was putting spokes in our wheels. In that period of gestation—the most marvelous time of all—most of the great ones who had unchained the Revolution and directed its course were still alive. When we put the question "Who is Trotsky?" nine out of ten Russians selected at random would answer with just two words: "Eto Bog! He is God!" Only Pushkin was accorded such unreserved admiration as Trotsky.

Crossing the malevolent, ugly Caspian Sea, we traveled about the petroleum belt of Azerbaijan, and then continued into Georgia, that idyllic land which still had aspirations to be independent. Next came Armenia, where we went as far as the foot of Mount Ararat and the Turkish frontiers. Kazantzakis had journeyed to this point a few years before to rescue the Greeks, who were being shoed like horses by the Turks and Kurds, and hunted and persecuted by the Bolsheviks.

How the Russians loved Panait Istrati, how they welcomed us, and how they allowed us to touch their wounds we ought never to have forgotten. That's what Kazantzakis asked of us. He maintained his trust in them, and shied away from furnishing ammunition to their enemies. "Let's not get lost in details! If we can, let's do something to help them; the battle is an unequal one, theirs is an arid task . . . ."

In Georgia, in a dusk as delicate and mellow as their wine, a man whom Panait had embraced for a long time and called "his brother" led us to a huge uncultivated field. "Comrades," he said, and his voice trembled a little in spite of his effort to repress his emotion, "here, even yesterday, ten thousand vines were growing. The kulak proprietor pulled them up by the roots with the help of

215

his wife and sons before he entered the kolkhoz. What should we do to that kulak?"

"Do you know how to stop an earthquake? How? Do you really claim you don't know? Well, I'm going to tell you: you have only to issue a decree! And do you know how we put out the fire at home? But let's see now, comrades! But of course, by pouring saltpeter on the blaze. . . ." Explosions of laughter at the stupidity and ignorance of some of the People's Commissars.

We took the longest way back to Moscow. The wide beaches of the Black Sea, where the tide flung the pebbles about with a torrential uproar, the light, fragrant shade of the lemon trees, mandarin orange trees and cypresses, the deserted monasteries—all served as a pretext for joy and re-laxation. But once in the northern snows, the disharmony brewing between the two friends came to a head, and they separated.

Kazantzakis went on alone, first to Siberia, and then to Turkestan, to complete this extraordinary trip. I shall let him tell it in his own words.

February 4 (night).

PERM. . . . I'm at the gateway to the Urals, about to enter Siberia. I'm all alone in a compartment, so I see no one and talk to no one. The divine silence that does so much to purify and nourish man's soul is flooding me, as the Nile floods Egypt, bringing calm and fertility. Only one of all the coaches for Siberia is badly heated, and that's the one that has fallen to me. They suggested that I change, but in the other compartment there would be people. I had rather suffer than be with people. At night the cold is intense, in spite of the protection I get from the mamochka.* That doesn't matter. It's the price I pay for my solitude.

---

* This is what he called his fur-lined coat.

I read, write verses and meditate. Ah! How good this silence cure is! The landscape is always the same: snow, fir trees, hamlets, sleighs, *valinki, shubas.* . . . This monotony is a subtle form of silence and it rests me. . . .

February 7 (I think).

Since Krasnoyarsk the hilly terrain has been very beautiful. Great joy: the vast Yenisei River. Other beauties: sunset and sunrise in Siberia, soft, tender, virginal. Today I've talked for the first time. I sat down in the dining car with a French missionary who has lived in Manchuria for fifteen years. He talked to me about the way people live there, about their souls and their sufferings, and it made my heart pound. I don't know why people who are far away seem closer to me and more like brothers. Do you remember the film that we saw? As long as I live I shall never forget the indignation and emotion I felt about these people who drudge and live and die so far from us.

Something else too. I shall do my utmost to be with you at the beginning of April. The great miracle at Werder when the cherry trees are in blossom we must see together. That was one of the most beautiful days in my life, April 13, 1923.

February 11, 1929.

CHITA, MANCHURIA. Last night I had an unexpected joy. Here at Chita there are one hundred and fifty Greeks. When they found out that I had come, they congregated in a house and took me to it, and for long hours I had a most interesting and warmly affectionate discussion with them. Simple men, bakers, cobblers, bootblacks. They put endless questions to me in that lonely place, and, as they told me, they got together every evening but never succeeded in finding any answer.

What is Communism? Why was Greece defeated? Why did man come upon the earth? What does "honor" mean?

217

Were I a Christ, people like these would be my apostles. Love, human warmth, trust. It is the intellectuals who are sterile and dishonest: they're the ones who are damned. I had been sad and weary, and with these simple people I regained my confidence in man. Chita! A little city in Manchuria. A thing that yesterday did not exist. Ah, "Travel! Travel! Travel!" as Rilke said!*

February 14, 1929.

MANCHURIA. We're crossing the Manchurian frontier, following the course of the Amur River. Monotonous landscape, desert plains with little birch trees, and sometimes a hamlet. Everybody gets off and runs to the *kipitok* (hot water), fills his teapot and goes back to the coach. Yesterday it was minus 36 degrees, but the coaches are well heated, and a different kind of martyrdom is commencing: we suffocate. The windows are all weather-stripped and frozen fast. The only joy is that there aren't many travelers and I'm alone in the compartment. Yesterday I worked well on the book or rather on the two books about Russia. Under the well-known title *Following the Red Star*, the first volume will be *Homo Bolchevicus* and the second *Meta-Bolshevik Man*. I now have the complete outline, and innumerable details. Only I must stop somewhere finally and write it.

A few minutes ago I wrote some lines of verse to be recited by a pair of mountain-folk, companions of Ulysses. I send them to you:

God grant that I may set foot on the mountain and air my brain. . . .

After Russia, I should need five months to write the two volumes, from May to October. Then two years for *The Odyssey*. The five months can be passed anywhere,

---

* "Reisen! Reisen! Reisen!" *Kazantzakis deliberately changed the "t" to "s." Rilke had written: "Reiten! Reiten! Reiten!"*

but the time I'll devote to *The Odyssey* will have to be on a high mountain. Otherwise the body will not be able to stand it. . . .

. . . The train was twenty-four hours late; hence I'm staying here another day, a *bezprizornyǐ* (abandoned child). Last night I went to the cinema to see *Genghis-Khan*. The twilight was marvelous, all blue, the Amur River azure blue and very wide, and over it all a green star was shining.

I'm making an effort to get rid of my bad mood, and I find everything that is beautiful and cling to it in order to keep from falling. I slept very well in the corridor. Thank God, I've known greater misfortunes!

When he got to Berlin—in the spring of 1929—he gave only one lecture in German, before a large audience. This man who held his friends under the spell of his charm, by day and by night, was entirely unable to overcome his timidity and felt unable to give a lecture without reading it. His voice became high-pitched and failed to carry.

So that he could write his books on Russia we took refuge in Gottesgab, in the Erzgebirge, in Czechoslovakia. Instead of the two volumes of travel sketches he had planned, it was the visionary and prophetic novel, Toda Raba, that he produced during a single writing stretch.

May this Toda Raba, which he wrote with so much fervor and such perfect honesty, help other people to understand the sufferings human beings endure as a new world struggles to emerge from the darkness. At school they taught us that the human heart—that little ball of flesh and blood—is warm and tender and softens when it comes in contact with human anguish. But I think that it is made of granite, and that like a jagged mountain, its peaks have never been scaled. Buddha was fond of saying that if a bird would fly over a mountain, grazing it with its wings, it would one day succeed in wearing the mountain smooth.

Let us hope that in a few thousand years—in time a

219

flash of lightning—the great generous ideas, rubbing their shadowy wings against our little granite hearts, will have same result. Let us have patience; let us trust. The day will come sooner than we dare to hope.

H.N.K.

Hadeya, January, 1962